Darkness in Málaga

Paul S. Bradley

Editor: Gary Smailes; www.bubblecow.com
Cover & Rear Illustrations; Jill Carrott; www.virtue.es
Layout; Paul Bradley.
Darkness in Málaga is the first volume of the Andalusian Mystery Series.
Publisher; Paul Bradley, Nerja, Spain.
Second Edition; March 2020.
Contact: info@paulbradley.eu
www.paulbradley.eu

ISBN: 9798606507139

Available in print and eBook on Kindle and most other online bookstores.

The Andalusian Mystery Series

Andalucia is wrapped in sunlight, packed with history and shrouded in legend. Her stunning landscapes, rich cuisine, friendly people and vibrant lifestyle provide an idyllic setting for four mysteries linked by shared darkness. Whilst each book can be read on its own, the author strongly recommends reading them in numerical order.

1- *Darkness in Málaga.* (2nd Edition)
2- *Darkness in Ronda.*
3- *Darkness in Vélez-Málaga* (published 2020).
4- *Darkness in Granada* (published 2021).

Dedication

To the memory of Cecilia Natalia Coria Olivares,
murdered in Nerja on September 8, 2008.
Your stolen life inspired this author to write.

Acknowledgments

Sadly, my mentor for *Darkness in Málaga*, author, humorist and old friend Drew Launay, died before the first and second editions were published. I hope they are worthy of his exacting standards.
My heartfelt thanks go to him along with Simon Cole, Jill Carrott, Daisy Carrott, Michael Kellough, Elizabeth Francis, Fran Poelman, and Renate Bradley.

Paul S. Bradley

1

"Don't you dare touch me," screamed Angelika in Spanish as she barged through the gymnasium door. Her long, silky, blonde hair swirling as she ran down the school entrance steps.

"Then stop running away from me," said Mateo letting go of her shoulder. "I need to talk to you."

"I'll miss my bus."

"Then catch the next one; this is important."

Angelika stopped and glared at him, breathing hard, "what do you want?"

"I don't like the way you treat me."

"We're dancing partners, not lovers."

"So when you thrust your hips against my thigh, it means nothing to you."

"We were dancing asshole, we're supposed to move sensuously."

"Then I'm sorry, I must have misread your signals."

"Not for the first time. What else can I do to make you understand? We dance and that's it."

"I don't turn you on at all?"

"For dancing, yes," she said, her pretty face softening. "But nothing else."

"Don't you like boys or something?"

"Typical macho. I'm automatically a lesbian because I don't fancy you."

"That's not what I meant," said Mateo raising his voice.

"Then say what you want, damn it."

"Can't we be more than just dance partners?"

Angelika stood her ground, gazing into the light-brown eyes of the tall, handsome, dark-haired teenager but she refused to be another notch on his bedpost. Half of her was tempted, but all the girls were after him and he was constantly overheard bragging about his conquests to his mates.

She shook her head, stroked his muscular arm and said, "Look, Mateo, I love dancing with you. We're not bad together and stand a great chance of winning the school talent contest. So can we please continue as dance partners and just that?"

Mateo grasped her hand with his and gazed into her ice-blue eyes and said, "I want more than that."

Angelika looked at him thoughtfully and said, "if you stop behaving like a stud and learn some discretion, then maybe, but I'm not promising." She pecked him on the cheek, adjusted her backpack and skipped out of the school gate in the direction of the Málaga bus stop.

She made her way along the deserted citrus tree-lined pavement in the fading evening breeze. Tiny, delicately-scented white petals fluttered on the slabs in front of her. She glanced over her shoulder, but Mateo had disappeared.

Angelika checked her phone. It was just after eight and there was a message from her Mom.

Fish tonight. Let me know when you're on your way. I don't want to put it in the oven too early.

Angelika began to tap in her reply. Her loose skirt billowing upwards revealing long, shapely and deeply tanned legs. Preoccupied with the message, she failed to register that a plain white van had pulled up beside her, its sliding side door open, and the engine running.

Angelika continued to type; totally focused on the reply to her mother.

A man in black clothing, his face covered by a dark scarf, jumped out of the van with a large red patterned shawl held tightly between his outstretched arms. He threw himself at Angelika, wrapped her head and shoulders in the shawl, jammed his hand over her mouth, and then lifted her up as if she were a feather. Even though her legs were flailing madly, he bundled her easily into the back of the van, shut the door and banged on the partition between him and the driver. The vehicle sped off into the twilight.

Angelika's phone lay on the pavement, blocking the flight of several petals.

The screen had cracked with the impact.

2

"May the prophet favor us with a gentle surf tonight," said Karim in Moroccan Arabic speaking loudly over the battered Land Rover's powerful diesel engine, as he wrestled with the steering wheel. "It will be easier to launch this damned lump of a boat."

"A moderate swell would be safer," said Mohamed, hanging on tightly to the grab rail in front of him. "Then there'll be enough of a breeze to blow it and its contents toward Spain when the fuel runs out. The last thing we need is disgruntled passengers landing back here."

"Fair point. They'll be wanting a refund."

"And our heads on spikes."

"Life on the edge brother."

"Beats herding goats."

"Or picking fruit."

Both young men laughed.

The daylight was fading fast, as they bounced down the almost sheer bumpy track toward the beach, threading their way through a dense copse of pines. They dared not turn on the headlights. Police boats patrolling the north-west coast would spot them instantly. Thankfully, Karim knew the way intimately, it was one of their regular departure points. He glanced in the wing mirror and sighed with relief. The trailer had stayed in the center of the track.

They reached the steepest stretch, where the weight of the trailer shoved them along even faster, forcing them closer to the tree line. Even with the four-wheel-drive engaged, Karim dare not touch the brakes on the treacherous muddy surface. They smashed into several lower branches which slid along the side of the vehicle paintwork making a piercing, scratching sound that set their teeth on edge. Karim changed down to a lower gear. The Land Rover slowed, and he managed to hold it and the trailer out of the wood.

Finally, they rounded the last tight curve where the track leveled out and drove across the beach toward the shallows, forging deep ruts in the soft sand.

"How many liters of gas are we giving this lot?" said Mohamed.

"There were only a few drops in the tank, so I added another three," said Karim. "That should be enough to get them out of territorial waters. After that, who cares?"

"How many suckers are in this group?"

"Assuming they all made the three-kilometer walk from Ceuta, it should be thirty-seven, but one woman is heavily pregnant. There could be thirty-eight by the time they reach Spain."

"Have they all paid?"

"A thousand Euros each, but I didn't charge the mother extra."

"You're too soft with them, brother."

"Nonsense. One competitor now includes onboard meals. I had to do something to sustain our reputation."

"But the flow of migrants to Spain through Morocco is booming, why give stuff away?"

"If we want to increase our prices, we need to improve our customer experience."

"What next; cushions, caviar and cruise attendants?"

"I was going to suggest lifebelts," said Karim, smiling.

The Land Rover reached the shore, Karim drove into the water and turned the vehicle around. He stopped facing the track, applied the squeaky hand-brake and turned off the motor. They opened the doors, clambered out and looked around them.

Other than the waves kissing the sand, it was totally silent.

"Where are they?" said Karim.

"They must be here somewhere," said Mohamed. "Any sign of the beach guard?"

"We agreed," said Karim rubbing his thumb and forefinger together. "That he should stay clear for at least twenty minutes, so they better hurry."

Mohamed removed the boat's tiny motor and gas tank from the back seat and took off their covers, while Karim unstrapped the inflatable rubber dinghy.

Demand for large boats like this was so high that they had become difficult to acquire. The brothers were continually on the lookout for more to transport their weekly consignment of human misery across the channel. Some, they purchased from the police, who as fast as they confiscated them, sold them back to other smugglers.

The brothers had stolen this complete rig late the previous night. It was parked outside a café, where the owner was using the restroom. They'd stopped alongside, switched his trailer over to their Land Rover, and driven away without anyone noticing. Even if they had been seen, their vehicle number plates were covered in sand, and they were two faceless men dressed in long black robes, heads wrapped in Tuareg turbans.

They looked around for their passengers. One-by-one, they emerged out of the gloom from under the pines, plodding toward them in bare feet, wearing an assortment of dark clothing, including jeans, T-shirts, hijabs, turbans, robes, and baggy trousers. Most had thick jackets to ward off the night chill on their imminent but dangerous voyage. Some did not and were already shivering. As instructed, no one carried belongings.

Karim read their body language. Unsurprisingly, they appeared terrified, but expectant. It was the same with every group. They knew the risks of crossing one of the busiest shipping lanes in the world with no radar, had heard the death by drowning statistics and accepted that their boat would probably be intercepted by the coast guard. It mattered not, the prospect of a new life in Europe drove them onward.

Many had been traveling for years to arrive at this point. They were from all over Africa: Gabon, both the Congo Republics, Nigeria, Niger, Mali, Mauritania, Senegal, and Sierra Leone. All escaping the mess that was the Dark Continent, riddled with poverty, sickness, war, corruption, and starvation. They'd left their loved ones behind, struggled across deserts on foot, hitched rides on occasional trucks, been robbed, beaten; often by policemen, and some of them sexually abused. Doggedly, they picked themselves up, dusted themselves down, and continued heading toward Ceuta, the Spanish enclave east of Tangiers, their portal to paradise or at least an easier death than from the horrors back home.

Most had tried on several occasions to climb the razor-wire fences surrounding this tiny patch of Europe in Africa, but it was too well protected by armed guards, sensors, and guard dogs with vicious teeth. Occasionally, one of them would make it over the top. Only to be sent straight back through a gate built into the fence solely for that purpose. Hands kindly bandaged having been shredded by the wire.

Their long, desperate journey had been in vain. The last chance at freedom cruelly dashed. Then they'd met the unscrupulous Mohamed and Karim.

The brothers were extraordinary salesmen who hovered on the edges of the Ceuta border, promising an easy ride to Spain and an introduction to fantasy employers in exchange for anything of value. If interested passengers didn't have the cash for their ticket, they faced an undetermined future in the hills above Ceuta, risking imprisonment, slavery, or death.

Alternatively, they could steal the fare. In return for a small fee, Mohamed would demonstrate how to pick the pockets of unsuspecting tourists shopping in the Souk Al Had in the nearby frontier town of Fnideq. Most accepted the brothers' offer; what else was there? Even though none of them had any idea what they would do to earn a living in Spain, couldn't speak a word of Spanish, and carried no papers. To them it was irrelevant. Any kind of life in Europe had to be a vast improvement compared with that they had left behind. It's what they'd been told, and what they chose to believe. It was this false delusion that had kept them going when they were dehydrated, cold, hungry, bruised or depressed.

Karim opened the back of the Land Rover and extracted liter bottles of drinking water. He passed them around. Each bottle was taken eagerly.

"Hands up; who's missing?" Karim shouted in French while counting the heads.

Nervous laughter was the reply.

Most understood some French. They might not be literate, but were accustomed to trading with neighbors. Hunger is a hard taskmaster, and in order to have survived this far, they would have quickly picked up the necessary vocabulary for basic communication. So it would be on their arrival in Spain.

"Then let's make a start," announced Karim to the group, satisfied that all were accounted for. "We'll launch the dinghy now. I'm going to reverse the trailer into the water. I need six of you to stand in the shallows and hold the boat steady, while everyone climbs aboard. Nine rows of four abreast, so board four at a time from the front and sit still. The final row is adjacent to the motor where there is only room for two. Who will steer?"

"I will," said a tall young Nigerian, stepping forward, dressed in dirty jeans and T-shirt.

"Keep pointing toward the northern star," said Karim, waving his arm at the darkening sky.

"I know where it is," answered the Nigerian. "How do you think we crossed the desert, signposts?"

"Allah be praised, we have a navigator on board,"

said Karim. "Listen, my friend, the little island, Jazīrat Tūra or Parsley Island to the Spanish, is two hundred meters in front of you. It disputably belongs to Spain. It's uninhabited but there are lethal rocks in the shallows that could tear a hole in the dinghy. You need to give it a wide berth and leave it to your left, heading northwest. Keep pointing that way, and you'll spot the lights of Gibraltar. Try not to bump into it. Aim to the right where the beaches are flat.

"I should warn you that, roughly halfway there, you will cross the main shipping channel. You have no reflectors, so these huge tankers and the like cannot see you on their radar, but they are brightly illuminated, so not difficult to avoid. The bus station in La Linea de la Concepción opens at six o'clock in the morning. You should arrive with time to spare."

The brothers looked on as the migrants struggled through the water and clambered on board the seven-meter long dinghy. A handsome teenage boy and his attractive younger sister helped the heavily pregnant woman over the side where willing hands made her comfortable, she thanked them profusely in French.

Five minutes later, they were all crammed into the boat. It sat low in the water, but seemed stable enough. "OK," said Karim. "All that remains is to mount the engine and gas tank"

"Wait," shouted a breathless voice in French from the darkness behind them. "I will go with them." Everyone turned to regard this last-minute arrival. A young man appeared out of the gloom perspiring heavily, he had long hair, a full beard, and lighter skin than the Africans. He was dressed smartly in new jeans, a dark-colored short-sleeve shirt, and the latest Nike sports shoes. A canvas bag was draped over his shoulder.

"Who told you our location?" said Karim.

"Your brother Abdul; I met him at the Ceuta frontier. I ran all the way here."

"And who are you?" said Karim.

"Never mind, but I need to reach France urgently. Here, take this." The man reached into his bag, extracted a billfold, and handed over a wad of euros. Karim thumbed through them adeptly, nodded, and slipped the euros into a pocket inside his robe. The man clambered into the back of the dinghy and squeezed himself aggressively into the tiny space next to the Nigerian.

The brothers picked the motor from the sand, stepped into the water and clipped it to the wooden transom. Then Karim reached into the mass of bodies, placed the orange fuel tank in the bilges by the Nigerian's feet, and opened the fuel line. Mohamed wrapped a cord around the starter and pulled. The engine spluttered into life on the third attempt. The Nigerian grasped the tiller and twisted the accelerator. The boat moved chugged slowly forward, the motor laboring hard.

"Bon voyage," said the brothers as they stood and watched its barely visible shadow flickering against the water's phosphorescence. Gradually, it melted into the darkness, and they were gone. The brothers threw the straps in the back of the Land Rover, climbed in the front, roared off up the track and into the night.

3

Detective Inspector Leon Prado scrutinized the name plaque mounted on the wall next to the full-height oak-veneered door. It read 'Jefe Superior, Provincia de Málaga: Francisco Gonzalez Ruiz' in white plastic letters stuck onto a black rectangular background. He rapped on the door twice.

"Enter," said a stern voice in Spanish from within.

Prado turned the handle, pushed the heavy door firmly, and strode into the Málaga Police chief's spacious office. Usually, Prado would have made a pithy remark about how the other half lived, as he walked toward the chair by his boss's expansive mahogany desk. The views from the massive picture window of Plaza de la Merced and Málaga old town were spectacular. Today, though, he said nothing; it wasn't that type of meeting.

"Sit down," said the chief, while continuing to tap away on his laptop. Prado waited patiently and watched his boss finish off whatever vital task he was doing. He was in no hurry; he knew what was coming.

Physically, the appearances of the two men couldn't have been further apart. Prado was medium height, well built, and in his early fifties, with a thick head of silver hair and round friendly face. Gonzalez was short, slight, and in his early forties, with thin black hair swept straight back from his forehead. Chiseled features, a Roman nose, and cold obsidian eyes lent him a hard, imposing disposition.

Prado was familiar with his superior officer's body-language games to intimidate and gain the upper hand with his subordinates. Usually, they didn't worry him, but today his stomach churned with anticipation about what he might hear.

With a final flourish, the boss hit the Enter key, closed the screen, and looked directly into Prado's brown eyes. Prado didn't flinch, he was used to hiding his true feelings, especially from this man, and returned the piercing gaze with equanimity.

"Inspector Prado," said Gonzalez, picking up a beige folder and scanning its contents. "During the last six months, nine girls have been abducted off our streets and it's been over a fortnight since you fucked up that kidnapping case. Not one single girl has been found and the pathetic number of leads you've stumbled on has yielded nothing. Furthermore, since the kidnapping, you've been off sick for over sixty percent of the time, and when you do bother to turn up, you don't contribute anything worthwhile to our heavy workload. What do you have to say about that?"

"Actually, Sir, it has been thirteen days since Angelika was taken," said Prado in clipped tones. "And in all my years serving this department, I've never come across such an elusive perpetrator."

The boss continued to glare at Prado.

Prado was not at all surprised by his senior officer's rant. He'd expected it days ago. The long-awaited call, though, only came yesterday. The chief's administrative assistant had politely requested Prado to attend what she'd referred to as an 'appraisal'. However, Prado had already heard the rumors flying around the office. He was about to be sacked from his job, heading up the Málaga Serious Crime Squad. He even knew who his successor was to be and surprisingly approved.

"Have you learned anything?" said el jefe. "That might assist your colleagues in finding these girls?"

"It would have helped if I was allowed to publicize names and photos of the girls," said Prado. "But you, and the powers that be, seem more interested in protecting visitor numbers than solving crimes. Given that I have to work with the limited resources available to me, I feel confident that there has to be a connection between them, sir. Although of different nationalities, they are all well under twenty, beautiful and have an advanced knowledge of English."

"And what have you concluded from that?"

"These are not random acts of madness. Each girl was thoroughly researched, because the abductors knew precisely the best time and place to take them without leaving any trace. How else could they vanish into thin air?"

"Like a magic trick?"

"Despite all our cameras and amateur photographers, there isn't one single clue. That and the lack of resources has been driving me crazy. All I can tell you, is that I am convinced there is only one person or group responsible?"

"That sounds plausible, but why would they want so many?"

"Sex; Sir. What else?"

"Oh. I see," said el jefe, puzzled.

"They'll be for some kind of slavery ring or selling them to the wealthy. I don't think they are for the abductor's own use."

"And your reasoning is?"

"No dead bodies, sir. These girls have been taken for a purpose and have at least a short term shelf life. If they were for personal use, they would have been used and disposed of. We'd have found some of their remains by now."

"Very well, and is that all you have to say on the matter?" said el jefe glancing down at Prado's personnel file in front of him. "No groveling, or lame excuse for your time off work?"

"The doctor's report is also in the file, sir."

"Doctor's report, Prado? At this level, we don't take any notice of medical opinion. Depression, it says. We're all fucking depressed, but it doesn't stop us from getting up in the morning and doing our bit for the taxpayer. You're a senior policeman; you should be immune to illness. Next, you'll be expecting to enjoy the damn job."

"Something less demanding would improve my health and effectiveness, sir."

"Less demanding he says. Such as what, school-crossing controller?"

"Your job looks just about perfect, sir."

El jefe looked taken aback, then smiled, and chuckled, his grim face softening at his elder colleague's insolence. "Ha, you don't care, do you, Prado?"

"No, sir. I've been working here for thirty-two years; I've seen it all, heard all the bullshit, thrown away the T-shirt, and frankly, I've had enough. Now fire me, or give me something passably worthwhile to do. And yes, I would like to enjoy what I'm doing; otherwise what's the point, and don't tell me money."

"I could let you go now. It's within my power."

"That would hammer my pension payments."

"So it is money. Anyway, why would I care about the size of your pension? You could always apply for work as a private eye or security guard, and the reduced costs would look good on my statistics."

"You may be younger than me and have the support of the politicians, but you aren't insensitive. Your low-budgets might appeal to some, but I know that firing me would be difficult for you personally. You would find it hard to live with your conscience. Wouldn't you, sir?"

The chief looked long and hard at Prado, who returned his gaze, unflinching.

The chief shook his head. "I never thought that I would have to say these words to you, Inspector Prado. You were a rising star on my team. I had you earmarked for greater things, I can just about tolerate the lack of progress with the missing girls, but the way you handled that kidnap was a disaster, and your performance since can only be described as pathetic. Regretfully, it falls upon me to confirm that as of the last day of April, your employment as head of the Serious Crime Squad is terminated."

"Thank you, sir," Prado said, standing up.

"Sit down, Leon. I haven't finished with you yet."

Prado slumped back down in the chair, his worst nightmare playing out before him. El jefe picked up another file on the far corner of his desk and tossed it over to Prado.

Prado turned it around and looked at the words typed on the front label - 'New role—responsibility for crimes involving foreigners throughout the province of Málaga.' Prado opened the file and speed-read the single printed sheet inside but the title had described the job perfectly. He looked up and found the chief regarding him with a kindly expression. "It's tailor-made for you, Leon."

"Except for one minor thing, Fran."

"You don't speak any foreign languages."

"Correct."

"You also won't have any staff or budget, but you may liaise with appropriate departments as needed."

"So, it's a political appointment?"

"Yes, the marketing boys at the tourist office dreamed it up in response to the mayor's concerns about the increase in crime by foreigners against foreigners. They reckon it will enhance our focus on safer tourism. We're just a little ahead of ourselves for a change."

"About nineteen years, sir."

"Ha. We managerial types prefer to call it strategic planning. At the moment, there's not much to do, just the odd minor case here and there, so it certainly fits your criteria of not demanding. I can't quite see you signing up for any language courses, though, so I suggest you find yourself a volunteer translator, maybe two or three. English will be the most important, followed by German, French, Russian, and Moroccan Arabic. I wouldn't bother with Armenian or Swahili; they all speak English. You'll find plenty of volunteers to choose from at coastal medical centers, hospitals, or language schools. You'll report to me directly. Dismissed."

"Thank you, sir," said Prado, standing up. "When do I start?"

"First of May."

"But that was last week."

"I had every confidence."

"I won't disappoint you on this."

"I know, and by the way, I've moved your office up to this floor. It will look like a promotion to your colleagues."

"That wasn't necessary, but thank you again, Fran."

Prado picked up the file and headed for the door.

"One more thing," said the chief. "What with the illegal migrant traffic through Italy and Greece being curtailed by the European Union, they've started coming to Spain via Morocco. I'm informed that there is a growing network of crooks setting up to exploit them. Apparently, they offer a choice of career paths; selling fake goods on the street, forced labor or sexual slavery. See what you can do to close them down."

"But isn't that the responsibility of the Guardia Civil?"

"Yes, but they need help so I volunteered your services."

"Thank you, sir," said Prado opening the door. "I'll get on it."

Isabel, the chief's administrative assistant, a well-rounded but stylishly dressed woman in her late thirties with dyed blond-highlighted hair, was waiting for him outside. She had an uncanny knack of always being in the right place at the right time. She escorted him down to the far end of the corridor, opened the last door, and waved him in. "If I can help in any way, Leon, just call me," said Isabel, patting him on the shoulder as he walked through the door into his new domain. "It's good to have you back. We all missed your terrible jokes."

"Thanks, Isabel."

Prado looked around. It wasn't as big as his last office, but he couldn't spot any brooms, and the view could have been worse. At least the laundry fluttering from a line on the terrace opposite didn't have any holes in it.

A new phone and laptop sat on top of the reasonably spacious but cheap pinewood desk. He opened a drawer and checked the manufacturer's label. As he thought, Swedish; thankfully, somebody else had unraveled how to assemble it. He checked out his new toys. Latest models, even a protective case for the phone. Nice touch, thought Prado. He tended to throw phones at stupid people. Isabel had already loaded both with his customary password, files, contacts, and favorite websites. Málaga Football Club was in pole position. She's amazing, he thought.

Prado took his jacket off and tried out his new chair. It was surprisingly comfortable, so he decided to prepare himself for the first crucial task in his new career. He sat back in the chair, placed his feet up on the desk, and closed his eyes. He breathed a sigh of contentment and let his mind wander.

Why hadn't he settled for a less challenging career in the first place, what had made him push himself so hard, who had he been trying to impress with his success? His parents, wife, the pretty girl in reception, colleagues, the world at large? It certainly wasn't for money, or to compensate for lack of manly dimensions, so it must have been for that inner voice that nagged him onward and upward. Maybe, if he hadn't demanded so much of himself, perhaps he would still be happily married and could see more of his boys, he certainly regretted being on his own. On the other hand, was he deluding himself, maybe it was necessary for a man to strive for the top to gain a sense of fulfillment, a life worth living? But only a few make it right up there. Not everyone can be the boss, he reasoned. Most become stuck halfway up the ladder, becoming disillusioned and bitter. His eyes blinked open at this revelation.

"Am I bitter?" he said aloud.

4

The Vueling Airbus A320 banked and then leveled out onto the final stretch of its southerly approach to Málaga airport. From his window seat on the port side, Phillip Armitage admired the sparkling-blue Mediterranean some two hundred meters below. Blessed with miles of sandy beaches and a superb year-round climate, it was the magnet that attracted the annual invasion of millions of tourists to this southern stretch of Spain's Andalusian coastline; the Costa del Sol.

Phillip was forty-three years old, tall, medium build with shaggy blond hair, and steely-blue eyes. He was desperate to move his long, athletic limbs. Ninety minutes jammed into narrow seats was not his idea of fun, but it was quicker and cheaper than the train. He sighed in relief as the plane touched down on the western runway and then taxied toward the familiar gray steel-and-glass terminal-three building.

Phillip had boarded the plane at Santiago de

Compostela in northern Spain, where he'd just completed the longest walk of his life. The certificate to prove it was in his checked luggage. He'd managed all 780 kilometers, nearly 500 miles, of the ancient pilgrimage route of El Camino de Santiago, or in English, St. James's Way. The pilgrimage wasn't just another commercial video project for his and his business partner Richard's burgeoning Internet guide to Spain but a period of reflection. To call it a midlife crisis was a tad dramatic, but Phillip certainly had personal baggage begging attention.

The time alone had helped him battle against his inner demons, and yes, he had overcome them. And no, he hadn't decided to quit Spain, leave Richard to his own devices, switch soccer team allegiances, or bat with the other team.

His journey of self-examination had begun in St.-Jean-Pied-du-Port, near Biarritz in France. It was the most popular of all the routes to Santiago and referred to as El Camino Frances. It had taken him thirty-four days, despite the heavy backpack, terrible weather, soaking wet clothes, and a brief dose of food poisoning. As he walked, he'd filmed the route with his lightweight handheld video camera. Back home in Nerja, he would edit and upload the clips to their guide's section on Spanish travelogues. Viewers could then visualize what walking the Camino involved day-by-day and could make better-informed decisions before launching themselves on such an arduous journey.

Phillip could have gone in the summer. He would then have avoided the rain and, if so minded, slept under the stars, but that's when everyone goes. It's hot, the bugs are a nuisance, beds are hard to find, and there's little opportunity to think without interruption, which is the whole point of going. In April, when he'd flown up to Bordeaux and caught the bus to St.-Jean-Pied-du-Port, the weather was comfortable for walking, and his fellow travelers were thankfully serious pilgrims, meaning there were no idiots around to ruin it for everybody else.

Some days he walked alone. During others, if he caught up with someone and the person was inclined to be chatty, he would stay with them for a while. On one occasion, he was overtaken by a group of incredibly fit Finnish women celebrating their fortieth birthdays. They all came from the same town, went to the same school, and were happily married with families, but they had wanted to reexamine their paths through life in one another's company. They were taking bets as to who would be the first husband to call for advice, having been left in charge of domestic duties during their absence. They were fun.

Surprisingly, Phillip had discovered most of the pilgrims he'd met were not religious, but were using the experience to challenge themselves physically and to explore their spirituality. The long hours struggling up steep hills, through vast fields, vineyards, and olive groves, mostly in solitude, presented a unique opportunity to reflect on the values of life and resolve any mental turmoil.

Phillip was no wimp. Life had thrown much at him during his early years on an army base in Germany, then military boarding school in England, followed by service in the British Intelligence Corps including two bruising tours in Afghanistan. The experiences had toughened him mentally in most aspects of life, but had been particularly light on one key ingredient; women.

Most of his youthful exposure to the female gender had been in the form of half-naked pin-ups stuck on barrack walls. He liked what he saw, but had no idea how to communicate with them. Consequently, his first marriage ended acrimoniously in divorce, his gorgeous Russian wife Valentina having left him for one of her fellow countrymen.

To recover from the emotional devastation, he'd opted to sell out his share of his technology business in London and retire to Spain to lick his wounds and begin again.

His mental healing was going wonderfully.

Then he'd met a beautiful British waitress nearly half his age.

It was Juliet that had driven him to such solitary therapy.

The Jetway lumbered toward the fuselage. The captain turned off the seatbelt sign while the cabin crew fussed with the front door. Phillip couldn't wait any longer; he had to stand and move his legs. Thankfully, he was in the third row. The seats emptied quickly in front of him, he grabbed his hand baggage from the overhead bin, which contained his camera and laptop, and headed out to baggage reclaim. His backpack arrived promptly; he heaved it over his shoulders, wondering how the hell he'd managed to carry so much weight over such a long distance, and then went to search for Richard and his wife, Ingrid. He hoped they had made it; if not, he'd grab a cab.

Málaga arrival hall was packed with the usual throng of meeters and greeters waving an assortment of welcome placards, floral bouquets, and helium balloons. Blocking the way ahead of Phillip was a group of well-rounded women giggling and chatting away with broad Scottish accents. They were tottering slowly and unsteadily on high-heeled shoes, dressed in bridal headgear, pink hot pants, and skimpy tops, printed back and front with the message 'Last week of freedom; don't ask, just grope.' They were yet another of the thousands of stylish hen and stag parties that swarmed to the Costa del Sol for the fantastic climate, cheap booze, inexpensive accommodation, and determined to make the most of their final days as single persons.

Phillip smiled at Richard standing by the chrome exit gate.

Richard was American. A chunky, congenial man from Boston, Massachusetts, in his early sixties with a ruddy complexion, thinning gray hair, twinkling hazel eyes, and a deep throaty voice. He raised his eyebrows. Phillip nodded yes. Richard looked relieved and whispered something to his German wife, Ingrid; a petite, graceful, woman in her late fifties, oozing confidence, with fair curly hair, gray eyes, dressed in blue jeans, loose beige blouse, and color-coordinated spectacles.

Phillip went through the barrier and exchanged man hugs and cheek kisses before they moved off in the direction of the easily accessible car park.

"You're sure about this?" said Ingrid.

"Definitely," said Phillip.

"So when you go for coffee in the morning and see Juliet, you'll be able to handle it?"

"No problem."

"Forgive me for being skeptical," said Richard. "But before you left, I recall you were in a right fudge about her. How can a mere stroll through Northern Spain clear your head so clinically, or more importantly, your heart?"

"Have you ever spent over thirty days on your own, trudging forward step-by-step, kilometer-by-kilometer with only one thing on your mind?"

"Thankfully not," said Ingrid. "But I think I know what you mean. You chip a little bit away from the lump in your head every day until eventually it either kills you or you deal with it."

"Precisely," said Phillip, grabbing her hand and squeezing it as they crossed the road and waited for the car-park elevator.

Richard pressed the down button. They stood in silence and, when the doors opened, crushed in with a mass of others and their luggage. They descended to the floor where Richard had parked his Mercedes, plonked Phillip's gear in the trunk, clambered in, and headed off in the direction of Nerja some seventy kilometers east on the coastal motorway.

5

A shapely, olive-skinned, petite woman in her early thirties with her long raven hair tied back in a French plait, approached the Guardia Civil patrol-boat moored alongside the quay in Algeciras harbor. She wore trainers, tight blue jeans and a baggy red T-shirt. She carried a shoulder bag so large and heavy that it almost dragged along the ground, but the weight didn't seem to bother her. At the bottom of the rickety gangplank, she paused and looked up. Her pretty, pixie-like face and light-brown eyes appreciating the sleek lines of the powerful vessel.

A sailor on the bridge sounded two short, loud blasts on the ship's horn. Within seconds the starboard rail was lined with half a dozen crewmen smiling and waving to her.

At the top of the gangplank stood a muscular, balding man in his mid-fifties smoking a cheap cheroot. He beckoned to the woman.

"Señora Salisbury?" he said as she struggled up the

ramp hanging on tightly to the hand rope.

"Call me Amanda, please," she said in Spanish.

"Antonio Gutierrez," he said, indicating the grinning sailors and blowing foul-smelling smoke in her direction. "It's my misfortune to be the captain of that motley crew."

They jeered and gave him the finger.

She smiled warmly at the men who gave her the thumbs-up and went about their duties.

"Welcome aboard," he said, reaching out to grasp a hand and guide her over the threshold onto the spotless timber deck. "The office warned me that you'd be joining us on patrol today. Something about a documentary on illegal immigrants."

"Warned, makes me sound scary," said Amanda. "I don't want to be a nuisance."

"Nonsense," he said. "It will be a pleasure to have you along."

"Thank you, captain, and yes, I'm making a film for CNN."

"Then keep my ugly face off-camera, otherwise they'll be a mass switch off," he laughed, then said, "Follow me to the bridge, you can stow your gear then wait for me there while we finish our preparations to sail." He made no attempt to help her with her equipment.

"Are we likely to find any migrants today?" said Amanda.

"No guarantees."

"Then fingers crossed," said Amanda looking around her. "It's a fine-looking ship, captain."

"Thanks," he said, sticking out his chest. "Twenty meters long, five meters abeam and powered by the latest water jets. She can exceed twenty–five knots."

"Is that fast enough to catch migrants?"

"People smugglers, yes. Drug dealers no. We need space to accommodate up to a hundred passengers. Our drug patrol boats are smaller and twice as fast. Sorry, but you'll have to excuse me, I need to be about the ship's business."

The captain grabbed his cap from the shelf in front of the large wheel, jammed it on his head and went to check everything was ready.

Amanda placed her stuff in the tiny chart-room at the back of the bridge where she discovered a small restroom. She had just come out and was slipping into a black leather jacket when the captain returned.

He grabbed the ship's microphone and spoke into it.

"Prepare to cast off," echoed around the ship.

Three crew members dashed out from the galley on the lower deck. Two jumped ashore and lifted the bow and stern ropes over the mooring posts and dropped each into the water. His colleague turned on the ship's electric winches, and the ropes snaked upward and into storage units on the deck. The crewmen leaped back on board, the captain activated the side thruster, and the ship moved slowly away from the quay then out into the mainstream. The captain turned the wheel, deactivated the thruster, and then moved the water-jet control forward.

The ship eased away from the quay, accelerated under the road bridge and turned right into the bay of Algeciras.

To the left loomed the 426-meter high rock of Gibraltar, its physical dominance of the surrounding landscape. A constant reminder to the Spanish that this pimple on the bottom of the Iberian Peninsula was

British territory. Once past the rock, the captain accelerated, and the ship surged forward through the calm sea toward Morocco.

A crew member delivered mugs of coffee to the captain and Amanda. She sat down and sipped, while he steered and slurped, occasionally glancing at the radar screen in front of the wheel.

"I'd heard that small boats don't show up on the screen?" said Amanda.

"Timber, fiberglass, or rubber boats are tough to spot and are obliged to carry radar reflectors," said the captain. "It means they can be seen well in advance by large ships. However, smugglers don't use them so it's a matter of luck if the radar picks them out. Thankfully, when it's flat calm like today and there are twenty-odd people on board the migrant boats, we have a better chance."

"Is there a regular route they take?" said Amanda.

"Usually, the shortest possible, which is the fifteen-kilometer gap between Ceuta and La Linea de la Concepción, but the wind often blows them way off course. With a strong easterly, they end up in the Atlantic, a westerly can push them beyond Almeria. In perfect conditions such as today, we're likely to find them in the middle of the main shipping lane. That's where most collisions and the majority of drownings occur. It's where we're heading now."

"I've heard that the number of migrants is increasing. What's your take on that?"

"This year we've seen a threefold increase over last. During the five months since January, we've rescued just under two thousand."

"How many escape your patrols?"

"I estimate about ten thousand."

"So at that rate, there'll be over twenty-five thousand migrants this year."

"Possibly more."

"Where do they go?"

"They disperse inland as best they can. We find them at bus stations, others steal bicycles or hide in the backs of trucks, and some are abducted by local crooks. You see them everywhere selling fake or cheap junk. However, the majority disappear into the dark underworld of forced labor and sexual slavery."

"What happens to the ones you pick up?"

"We detain them in the Algeciras Centro de Internamiento de Extranjeros or Foreigner Internment Center, pending deportation or approval of their asylum application."

"How long do you hold them for?"

"We're supposed to process them within sixty days, but if a flight can't be arranged or paperwork completed, then longer."

"They used to cross via Italy and Greece; what made them switch to Spain?"

"The Spanish route isn't new. Twenty years ago, they used to arrive in droves, using little blue wooden boats. We stopped that by agreeing on a policy of collaboration with the Moroccans. Recently, the European Union has practically closed down the Libya-Italy route, so they've started coming this way again. They can either jump over the fence into Ceuta or Melilla, the two Spanish enclaves in Morocco, or buy passage on a smuggler's boat."

"Do you think the numbers coming to Spain will continue to increase next year?"

"In theory, no. In reality, probably. Our collaboration with the Moroccans included them patrolling their beaches to prevent boats from leaving. However, their guards work long hours and are paid a pittance, so they will happily look the other way in exchange for smugglers' cash."

"Why don't they arrest the smugglers?"

"There's a relentless tide of humanity heading this way needing transport to cross the water. As fast as they apprehend the main players, new ones replace them. After drugs, it's the second most lucrative earner in Morocco but the perpetrators are equally as ruthless. They happily take the migrants' money, promise them a safe journey and jobs at the other end, but then pack them into dangerously overloaded flimsy boats with just enough fuel to exit Moroccan waters. They don't give a shit if they survive or not, there's always another desperate batch waiting in the wings. It's terrible to see so many lives wasted on such a fruitless journey."

"You feel sorry for them, captain?"

"I despair of their dire circumstances. They all have parents worrying about them back home, hoping that their perilous journey leads to some improvement in their wretched lives. In some ways, I admire them, especially women and children. It takes huge amounts of determination and courage to leave everything they know behind without any idea what will happen, where they will end up, or that death is a strong possibility. Can you imagine what powerful forces drive them to do that?"

"They've lived with starvation, sickness, war, and corruption for centuries. What choice do they have when there's no chance for better prospects by staying?"

"They could try to improve their own country."

"And so they should, but with no education,

opportunity, or money, it's difficult to reject the smuggler's tempting sales pitch. Do you have kids?"

"Three sons, all with university degrees, but could they find work relevant to their studies in Spain? No, youth unemployment is so high that they've had to go to England and work in hotels. They detest the awful climate and being away from home, but what else can they do?"

"That's exactly what the Africans are thinking."

"You'd have thought that a civilized world would have learned better by now?"

"Old habits die hard, captain."

The two looked out of the small side-window, as the wake from a passing super-tanker rocked the boat gently.

"You speak Spanish almost like a native," said the captain after a while. "Unusual for the English?"

"I grew up in Spain," said Amanda. "Actually, I'm an American. I also speak fluent French and Moroccan Arabic. My father was stationed at the Rota naval base near Cadiz and my mother's family were from Morocco."

"Impressive, I barely manage schoolboy English," said the captain moving to check the radar. He tapped the screen, turned to her then said, "Amanda, you're in luck; I think we've found you some migrants. Prepare your camera; we'll be there directly."

"Can I chat with them?"

"Yes, but it's best to wear a protective suit. In case of illness on their part or yours. There's one in the chart-room; it should fit you."

Amanda withdrew into the chart-room and slipped into the white nylon suit she found hanging in a sealed plastic bag on the back of the door. It was way too big for her, but it would do. She heard the engines slow as she zipped up the face-mask and breathed in through the filter. It was decidedly uncomfortable. She picked up her video camera and went out onto the starboard deck.

Thirty meters ahead, an inflatable rubber dinghy, some seven meters long and just under a meter and a half wide, was drifting on the calm surface, with its small outboard motor silent. It was crammed full of mostly young African men dressed in a wide variety of grubby clothing and turbans. The few women wore headscarves, wraparound skirts, loose tops, and thick jackets. None carried belongings or wore a life jacket. They were sitting on any available boat surface or on one another. Some dangled their legs over the side. Amanda started counting them.

"How long have they been out there?" she said.

"They probably sailed at dusk last night, so nearly ten hours."

"I don't see any signs of food and water; they must be near the point of dehydration."

"They're used to it. Crossing a desert is a lot worse."

"Yes, but deserts don't have supertankers to run them down, or great white sharks swimming underneath on their way to the Malta breeding grounds."

"No, you're right; just scorpions, poisonous snakes, and deadly terrorists."

"So what you're telling me is that they are accustomed to danger and fear and that this little journey wouldn't have worried them."

"Oh no. They'd have been terrified all right, especially as most can't swim. What I'm saying is that migrants are accustomed to living on the edge. It's part of what sustains their efforts to complete their journeys."

"Then they have my respect."

Amanda resumed her counting. Thirty-eight, sitting silently with sullen expressions. Several men were openly glowering at their captors, their illegal passage to utopian Europe officially over and dreams of a new life shattered. Few of them would be eligible for a visa or had any work skills to offer. All the money they had stolen, borrowed, or saved for this long, dangerous journey had been wasted. The risks they had taken had been for nothing. Several wept quietly.

Amanda filmed the approach to the dinghy, which appeared to be floating well and in reasonable condition. The coast guard ship circled them a few times while the crew inspected the migrants through binoculars looking for signs of sickness, distress or potential troublemakers.

Amanda found it difficult to distinguish one person from the next in the mass of tightly-huddled humanity, especially through her small screen. She zoomed in to capture a few facial expressions and was struck by the beauty of a young female teenager. A young man had a protective arm around her shoulder.

In the background, loomed the Rock of Gibraltar; further away, steam wafted upward from the oil refinery in Algeciras. Then a pod of dolphins swam by only meters in front of them, leaving a V-shaped wake. The migrants paused to admire them, providing some brief respite from the pain of capture.

The captain pressed a button on the control panel in front of the steering wheel. A prerecorded message announced over the ship's loudspeakers in Spanish, English, French, and Arabic that the Spanish Guardia

Civil was impounding their boat. All passengers were to be taken to a detention center in Algeciras for an interview, and if accepted, they could apply for asylum. Any sick persons, pregnant women, or those with disabilities should raise their hands. They would transfer to the coast guard ship. The remainder would stay on their dinghy for a tow into the harbor.

One heavily pregnant woman had her hand up.

The crew on the patrol boat lowered a small rubber dinghy over the side and into the water. It was laden with yellow life jackets. Two officers, also in white suits and face masks, clambered on top of them, started the motor, and sped across the few meters to the migrants. They talked with the pregnant woman for a few minutes, and then one officer picked up a two-way radio and spoke with the captain.

"They've been on board since dusk last night," Amanda overheard the voice from the radio. "They left the Moroccan coast from a beach just outside Ceuta, but the motor packed up hours ago. Somehow, they made it through the shipping channel, untouched. Shall I bring the pregnant lady?"

"Go ahead, but watch for any idiots with weapons as you transfer them over," said the captain. "We don't want them taking over our boat."

Amanda filmed as the officers passed around the life jackets and then zoomed in on the pregnant woman as she prepared to transfer into the smaller dinghy. She was about to clamber across when there was a wailing cry from the back of the remaining migrants.

Amanda's stomach churned as she heard the dreaded, "Allahu Akbar," reverberate across the water.

6

Phillip drove his BMW Cabriolet down to the second floor of the parking garage under Nerja's central square; Plaza España. He found a spot in his usual area near the ramp, opened the door, and eased his long limbs out of the car. He grabbed his sports bag from the back seat and headed off in the direction of his favorite beach; Playa El Salon.

He tried to begin the majority of warmer days with a swim in the Mediterranean. It was one of those to-do items on his bucket list when he'd come to live in Spain. Nerja was blessed with an absence of long, straight, beaches lined by tower-block hotels. Instead, cliffs provided shelter for several small, award-winning pretty coves. He'd settled on the centrally located Playa El Salon as his regular exercise venue. The long, steep slope down and back deterred most tourists, leaving uncrowded waters.

Phillip walked under the town-hall archway and across the Balcón de Europa. The Balcón, as the locals had christened it, earned its name thanks to a visit by King Alfonso XII. In 1884, after a massive earthquake, he'd stood among the ruins and issued a decree that this central area of the town was to be rebuilt and referred to as El Balcón de Europa. More recently, the council had installed a life-size bronze statue of the monarch leaning against its railings as a memento of his regal creativity. Tourists loved taking selfies, standing next to him.

Phillip headed into the passageway between Unicaja Bank and Marissal Hostel and began his descent down to the beach. He passed the Irish pub and, as he turned the corner, paused with one foot on the low wall to absorb the striking scenery below.

El Salon is an enchanting cove several hundred meters long with limestone rocks at both ends and a stark cliff to the rear that protects against the occasional northerly breeze. Perched on top of the cliff are holiday apartments and the romantic terrace of Restaurant Marbella, a popular venue for wedding receptions. A squabble of seagulls swooped and hovered over the sands, their persistent cawing reverberated over the beach.

There was a short palm-tree-lined promenade at the bottom of the slope in front of a row of whitewashed fishermen's cottages. At the top of the beach lay half a dozen colorful fishing boats, in various states of readiness. In July, the largest one is adorned with flowers and rowed around to Playa Torrecilla to collect an effigy of the Virgin Mary for her annual trip around the bay to celebrate the Fiesta of Virgen del Carmen. The populace admires her flotillas' progress from the Balcón, enjoying beer and tapas as she's delivered to the beach on the other side of the Balcón; Playa

Calahonda.

Adjacent to the cottages stands a forlorn concrete sea horse decorated with white pebbles. It marks the former site of a vibrant beach bar run by a British family from Sheffield in Northern England. Phillip recalled many happy hours there as a young man enjoying a few beers and watching Formula One with the owner. His sister Glenda had worked in the kitchen for a while; her delicious paellas had been much appreciated. The bar's sad replacement was a temporary kiosk serving warm beer in plastic cups. Customers have to battle for the few rickety chairs, and wobbly tables huddled tightly together under a couple of weather-beaten parasols.

Out by the water's edge, Phillip spotted a slender, heavily tanned senior man with white hair and an immaculately trimmed Kaiser mustache. He was wearing ill-fitting bright-pink bathing shorts, bending over at the water's edge and dangling something in the surf. The man was Didi. One of Phillip's many German friends in Nerja.

They'd met a couple of years ago in Phillip's regular café on the Balcón when Phillip had helped him out with a discrepancy on the electricity bill for his villa. Didi's language skills were limited to German and basic English. Phillip watched him swing the mysterious object up toward his face, catch it in his other hand, and inspect it myopically. Didi shook his head in disappointment and then plunged whatever it was back into the surf.

Didi lived near Nerja with his husband for most of the year. He was a retired hairdresser from Bremen in Northern Germany, but locally had become renowned for dangling his thermometer in the surf on a rope to test the water temperature. He justified his eccentricity on the need to know precise information before answering his big question. To bathe or not to bathe his delicate frame? Apparently in Bremen, dipping a toe in the shallows was considered way too slapdash. Didi tried to swim on El Salon as often as weather would allow, but only if the temperature was at least twenty-three degrees centigrade or more. He would stand at the water's edge for hours, waiting for the sea to warm up, patiently testing away until the mercury attained his minimum entry-level. If it didn't, he went home, disappointed.

Phillip joined him at the water's edge.

"Good morning, Didi," Phillip said in German.

"Hello, Phillip."

Phillip removed his outer clothing, revealing blue swimming shorts. He remained oblivious to Didi's blatant admiration of his athletic physique, placed everything in his bag and dived straight in. The water was exhilarating, and he relished its cleansing saltiness as it washed away his morning cobwebs. He swam fast for three hundred meters to a yellow line of markers that delineated the exclusion zone for Jet-Skis and motorboats and clung onto one of the buoys. While he bobbed up and down, recovering his breath, he looked back toward Nerja.

Blinds were being raised and curtains drawn in some of the rooms of the Hotel Balcón de Europa. Guests were collecting towels from the balcony railings and folding them tidily in preparation for another hard day's roasting on the sun lounger. In the distance behind the hotel, the craggy peaks of the Sierra Tejeda and Almijara reflected a delicate shade of pink from the early-morning sun.

He swam back to the beach and then chatted with Didi while he paced around, waiting for the warm sunshine to dry him off. Meanwhile, Didi continued his water-testing activities and, after a few minutes, happily announced that the temperature was precisely twenty-three degrees. At that, Didi swung the thermometer rope round in the air and let it go. It landed bang in the middle of his neatly folded floral towel. He turned and tiptoed down into the water until it came up to his waist, then launched himself into three breaststrokes, turned around, swam three back, and struggled out of the water. He was breathing hard.

"Warm enough?" Phillip said in German.

"Perfect thanks," said Didi. "See you at the cafe later."

Didi retrieved his gear along with the treasured testing instrument and then strode off to the showers. Phillip did a few stretches and exercises and then sat down on his towel, faced the water, and crossed his legs to meditate for a few minutes.

He gazed out to sea and let his mind drift back a couple of years when Juliet used to join him for his morning swim. With her wearing the skimpiest of bikinis, they would race out to the buoy. Phillip hung onto the slimy plastic, and she clung to his shoulder while they bobbed up and down talking about silly stuff such as favorite musicians. She loved Playa El Salon but when pressed would never say why or explain anything about her former life.

While they were nattering, she often twirled his chest hair in her fingers and her barely covered breasts would rub against his arm. He lost count of the times he yearned to kiss her, but something in him always made him hold back.

Back at the shore, Didi used to hold her towel to protect her modesty as she changed into dry clothes. They both adored her and referred to her as their beautiful English rose. Then she fell in love with her first boyfriend, and that was the end of that.

Phillip let the warm sun wash over him as he composed himself. He closed his eyes and prepared himself for his imminent challenge. He was about to walk up the hill, take a seat at his regular café, and be served by Juliet. This time, however, he would not behave like a lovesick fool.

Phillip opened his eyes, took several deep breaths, and asked himself out loud, "Am I ready for this?"

A seagull flying overhead at the very moment cawed loudly. It didn't sound like laughter.

Phillip took it as a good omen, stood, picked up his bag, and went to the showers. He washed off the salt and sand, dressed, packed his damp things leisurely back into his bag, and then ambled up the hill for breakfast. The salty, sulfury, green smell of the sea wafted up after him.

As he reached the bend, he paused to admire the impressive panorama. A few fluffy white clouds speckled an azure sky, contrasting against the deep blue-turquoise of the calm Mediterranean. In the distant haze, a supertanker was heading west to the Straits of Gibraltar. A little nearer, a couple of trawlers circled a swirling shoal of sea bream while seabirds wheeled above. Two hundred kilometers further south was Africa, where, on the occasional haze-free day, the Rif Mountains of Northern Morocco were visible.

Phillip continued his uphill walk, turned onto the Balcón just as the clock on the tower of the imposing El Salvador, Nerja's seventeenth-century Baroque-

Mudejar church, struck nine o'clock. He headed for the café, his heart racing and not from the walk up the hill.

This was it. The moment of truth.

7

Amanda put her hand to her mouth as she watched a young bearded man thrust his way through and over his fellow passengers. He elbowed some in the face in his desperation to launch himself at the police dinghy. He had long hair, a full beard, and lighter skin. His face screwed up into a fanatical ugly expression as he screamed, "God is the Greatest." He reached the side of the dinghy and continued yelling at the officer while fumbling in his jeans pocket and extracting a small knife. He snapped it open then squatted and girded himself to leap across the narrow gap between the two dinghies.

He didn't get far.

Several Africans grabbed him before he could jump. Their violent movement unbalanced the dinghy, causing many passengers to fall into the water including the attacker. The dinghy hovered on the verge of no return for several seconds, but then fell back to its original position with a loud splash.

The few who could swim helped those who couldn't back to the side of their dinghy. Several migrants, enraged by the attacker, swam toward him, grabbed his head, and shoved it violently under the surface. The long-haired attacker wriggled like a lobster dangling over a boiling water pot, seawater foaming madly from his kicking legs. They held him under until he stopped moving. One man removed his shoulder bag, and then they let him go, watching in silence as he sank slowly into the depths. When he'd disappeared, they turned, paddled back to the dinghy, and clung onto the edge. One-by-one, they climbed back on board and sat where they could.

Amanda watched the man who'd taken the shoulder bag and kept her camera running as he searched inside. He removed money, a passport and then threw the bag in the water, watching until it was out of sight.

In the madness of the attack, the pregnant woman had fallen from the migrant's dinghy into that of the Guardia Civil. She'd landed heavily, her swollen abdomen banging hard against an officer's head. He sat half-dazed, rubbing his neck, the woman lay on his lap, unmoving. The other officer grabbed the tiller, twisted the accelerator, and headed back toward the patrol-boat. The crew winched up the dinghy from the water, lifted the woman out, and laid her on the deck. She coughed and tried to sit up.

"Can I help?" said Amanda in french.

"Thanks," she whispered as Amanda put her hand under her arms and heaved her up into a sitting position. Amanda was shocked by her appearance. From a distance, she'd looked like a mature woman, but from up close, she couldn't have been much more than fifteen or sixteen years old.

The girl screamed and held her stomach. Amanda looked down and saw blood hemorrhaging from between her legs. It stained the thin material of her shabby skirt and pooled out over the deck.

The captain stood beside Amanda, looking down at the poor woman with a sad expression.

"She's about to lose her baby," he said.

"Do you have any painkillers?" said Amanda, watching the mixture of blood and birth waters flow toward the edge of the bleached wooden deck.

"Only morphine, but I can't give her that," said the captain.

The woman groaned and through gritted teeth said in French, "lift me up." She was trying to move to a squatting position, but her skirt was too tight. Amanda loosened the thin material, shoved it up her thighs and held her as she spread her legs.

"My baby is coming," she said.

Amanda held her gently. She could feel the tension in the girl's shoulders as her contractions hit. Her face was in agony, tears streamed down her face as the baby moved slowly along the birth channel. Amanda was impressed with her determination. The woman screeched, then bore down, and then again, struggling to control her breathing as the contractions increased their tempo and intensity.

This is going too quickly, thought Amanda. The woman clenched her teeth, took one huge breath, and pushed as hard as she could. What seemed minutes later, she opened her eyes, looked directly at Amanda and grinned with relief.

"Take it in your hands," she said.

Amanda reached between the woman's legs and felt the baby's head fully exposed. "One more should do it," said Amanda.

The woman grimaced and pushed. The tiny baby plopped into Amanda's hands with a squelch, followed by a massive spray of blood. The woman screamed and then slumped onto the deck, unconscious. Blood and mucous stained Amanda's white protective suit.

"Knife, scissors, anything to cut the cord and quick," said Amanda, cradling the still child in her arms.

"It's OK. I have the ship's first-aid box here," said the captain.

The captain reached down and snipped as near to the baby's navel as he dared with a small pair of scissors. He passed Amanda a blanket. Instinctively, she checked the child. Ten fingers, ten toes, and everything in place. It was a little girl. But the baby lay unmoving. Amanda's first reaction was that it had been stillborn.

Her emotions ran wild. Her first birth ever and it had come to naught. She thought desperately not having a clue what to do next, but some inner voice told her to clear the mucus out of the child's mouth. She took off her protective gloves, gently probed her little finger into the child's mouth, and then pinched its nose. After a few seconds, the baby snorted, gulping in deep breaths. Her little face scrunched up, and then it came. She took a deep breath and cried with the volume and intensity that is uniquely reserved for the newborn.

What a beautiful moment, marveled Amanda relishing the screaming baby wrestling in her arms. She felt privileged to have played a small part in her delivery. Tears rolled down her cheeks.

The captain grasped the mother's wrist and checked

her pulse.

"It's faint but regular," he said. "Let's take you all to a cabin and try the baby on her breast."

The captain wrapped the mother in a blanket and then picked her up as if she was a feather and led the way to a cabin behind the bridge.

Amanda followed the captain into a large room fitted with rows of wooden benches. The captain laid the mother on one and stood back. Amanda exposed the woman's breast and put the child on her chest. The baby stopped crying and latched on.

"Can you bring me some hot water?" said Amanda. "We need to wash the baby and her mother."

"Of course," said the captain as he went out and closed the door behind him.

Amanda nodded and turned back to the baby, who seemed none the worse for wear after her traumatic and rapid arrival into this world. The captain returned with a bucket of hot water, some soap, and a selection of towels.

"Thanks," said Amanda.

"The mother needs urgent attention," said the captain. "We're going to speed into Algeciras as fast as we can. A small launch is on its way to tow in the remaining migrants."

"What happens to these two when we land?"

"They'll be taken to the hospital. When the mother recovers, she and the baby will be transferred to the detention center for processing."

"And if she doesn't?"

"Try and think positively."

"How long before we arrive in Algeciras?" said Amanda.

"Half an hour or so?"

"Does it mean that we are still in Spanish territorial waters?"

"Why?"

"If the mother doesn't survive, this baby will need a nationality. She has no papers, and we have no idea from where she originates. If this child is to have any future life, it's going to need a passport and some official to accept responsibility for her. If we are inside Spain's maritime borders, the government is obliged to grant her citizenship."

"I see. I'll check our precise position at the moment she was born and let you know."

"Thanks."

Several minutes later, the baby stopped sucking and fell asleep. Amanda removed the towel and gently washed off the remaining mucus. When finished, she removed the baby from her mother's chest, wrapped her in a fresh towel, and tucked her under one arm. She undressed the mother and washed her as best she could before covering her with a towel and checking her wrist. Her pulse was still weak, but now intermittent. She laid the baby on her mother's chest and secure her there with another towel.

Amanda sat and stroked the baby's back and worried about the afterbirth. Her vague recollection of biology classes at school nagged at her, saying that it should be expelled as soon as possible. She thought about easing it out with the remaining umbilical cord, but that concerned her. Perhaps the placenta was blocking any further loss of blood. She did nothing but rocked the baby.

Amanda heard the ship's engines speed up to full power, felt it turning, and then settle into a straight run back to port. The captain returned with a mug of hot coffee.

"An ambulance will be waiting on the quay," he said handing over the coffee.

"If the mother does recover, what will happen to her and the child?" said Amanda after taking a welcome sip.

"They'll be processed by the asylum panel."

"Can I do anything to facilitate their application?"

"Such as what?"

"Offer the mother a job?"

"Are you a Spanish citizen?"

"No. American, but I'm a tax resident."

"Then it's unlikely."

"Could I go to the hospital with them?"

"Sorry, Señora, no. We have a process to go through; it does not permit outside involvement and definitely not media."

"Could I give her some money?"

"No, once we land, she will be given new clothes and be fed properly until the panel decides what to do with them."

"Can I visit her?"

"No, no visitors."

"Can I write to her?"

"Yes, but she probably can't read."

"Well, I'm going to put my card with the mother and baby and a note on the back, offering my assistance."

"Fine, good luck, but you're wasting your time."

"You're sure I can do nothing?"

"Señora, believe me, my wife and I have tried with other children but without success."

"Very well, but I'm determined to do something. I'll speak to an immigration lawyer to find out if I can take them both in."

"As you wish. Give me one of your cards. I'll send you the GPS coordinates for her birth location and contact details for the asylum panel."

"I'm much obliged, Antonio," said Amanda, taking his hand and shaking it.

"It's the least I can do," said the captain. "Now excuse me, but I have to prepare for docking.

8

Café-Bar Don Comer stood next to Nerja's church. It was extremely popular, not just with tourists but also with locals and particularly the business people based in and around the Balcón. Manolo, the proprietor, and his wife Pepa both spoke excellent English and had provided an eight-seater table reserved exclusively for their regular customers. They guaranteed a place and quick service no matter how busy they were. Phillip and Richard had adopted it as their morning meeting place. The coffee was excellent; it was convenient to the parking garage, the bank and was a short walk from Richard's house. Phillip took his seat. He didn't need to order. The staff would see him sitting down and knew what he wanted.

Richard was already there, chatting with Didi and one of the other foreign regulars - Klik, a Danish chiropractor. They exchanged greetings. Richard finished his conversation with Klik, who stood up, waved at everyone in general, and left to resume his daily wrestling with out-of-kilter body frames at his clinic across the Balcón.

Richard turned to Phillip and said in German, "Didi wants to sell their villa."

"You didn't mention it on the beach," said Phillip.

"I don't like to mix pleasure and business," said Didi.

"Why do you want to sell?" said Richard.

"Gunter and I aren't getting any younger, and although our villa is lovely, it's remote, and we are worried about ambulances or taxis getting down the track to us. We want to downsize to an apartment in the town center," answered Didi.

"Do you want to sell directly or use an estate agent?" said Richard.

"We'll be leaving for Bremen the day after San Isidro, so best to use an agent. Can you suggest any good ones?"

"Of course," said Richard, opening his small shoulder bag. "I'll write down the best three and the person to talk to." Richard scribbled the information on a page of his notebook and tore it out. "Here," he said, passing the list to Didi. "Please mention our name when you contact them."

"Thanks, I will," said Didi, who folded the paper precisely in half and slipped the list into his shirt pocket.

"Are you entering the dressage competition at San Isidro again this year?" said Phillip.

"No, last year was my final effort, but Gunter and I will be watching avidly. For the first time, I'll be free to take loads of photos. Gunter can't tell one end of a camera from the other. Perhaps we'll see you there?"

"I'll try, but my nieces will be keeping me busy so

I'm unsure of my timings," said Phillip. "Either way, I hope you enjoy it."

"It'll be mixed emotions," said Didi. "Half of me still wants to be competing, the rest of me remembers the aches and pains from last year. He took a final sip of his coffee, left some coins on the table, and left.

"Hi, Phillip, nice to see you back," a familiar female voice said as a hand stroked his shoulder, just as it always did. The same hand, then started unloading his order from a tray. Double espresso coffee and traditional Spanish breakfast consisting of a toasted *mollete,* or soft roll, smeared with garlic, drizzled with extra virgin olive oil, and topped with grated tomatoes.

Phillip took a deep breath and turned toward Juliet. His heart skipped a beat. She was looking more beautiful than ever.

She smiled warmly, pleased to see him.

Juliet Harding was twenty-one and had worked at Don Comer for nearly three years. Her pretty face, long blond hair, and shapely figure along with a warm, friendly disposition toward customers was a great asset to Manolo's business. It proved popular with young Spaniards and catered to the many British tourists happy to speak with another compatriot. Many of the male customers were enamored of her and pestered her for a date. She ignored them all and the café business soared.

"You missed me then?" said Phillip.

"Place wasn't the same without you," said Juliet. "I had to listen to Richard's awful jokes, and to make matters worse, he always forgets the punch line. Thankfully, I'd heard most of them. Any plans for San Isidro this year?"

"I'll be on the oxcart with my sister and her tribe.

Are you going with Hassan again?"

"Not bloody likely," she said, eyes watering. "We've finished."

"I'm sorry. I didn't know."

"How could you?" she said, sniffing and wiping her eyes. "You'd deserted me in my hour of need."

He reached out and patted her arm and said. "What went wrong?"

"His father was ill and the family summoned him back to Nador to help run the family hotel. I was angry at first. How dare he leave me? That sort of thing. But I'm OK with it now."

"Does that mean you are alone for San Isidro?"

"Not exactly," she said brightening. "But I could fit you in later in the afternoon. I was hoping for another chance to dance the Sevillana with you."

"Have your feet recovered from last year."

"I've invested in steel toecaps."

"How could I refuse such a beguiling invitation, shall we confirm timings on the day?"

"Service," shouted someone.

Phillip and Juliet both turned to see a stocky man with a shaved head sporting a Real Madrid tattoo on the back of his neck, standing behind the bar and pointing at Juliet. It was Manolo. He gesticulated to Juliet to serve the two new customers in the process of sitting down at an adjoining table.

"No rest for the wicked," said Juliet, grinning, as she moved over to the new arrivals.

Phillip watched her move away, but only for a second. He turned back to Richard, took a long sip of his coffee, then picked up his *mollete* and took a bite. The combination of flavors was mouthwatering.

"I thought you handled that well," said Richard.

"Not your usual blubbering self."

"I thought I was going to lose it when she stroked my shoulder."

"But you resisted. Perhaps all that walking worked after all. Good. Now that I have you back and firing on all cylinders, we can do some serious work?"

9

An ambulance was waiting in Algeciras Harbor, its rear doors open and a stretcher lying on the quay. A nurse and medic dressed in green overalls stood nearby looking anxiously at the ship as it moored. Amanda sat in the cabin next to the mother, the baby sleeping peacefully in her arms but the mother's pulse was terribly weak.

As soon as the gangplank hit the quay, the medics picked up the stretcher and ran on board. Within minutes, they were on their way to the hospital, siren blaring. Amanda watched sadly as it headed out of the harbor and into the town.

When it was finally out of earshot, she went up to the cabin, changed out of the protective suit and gathered up her gear. She said farewell to the captain and headed toward her car parked at the end of the quay. Halfway there, her head reengaged itself with her documentary. She recalled that she hadn't talked to any of the migrants and really needed their input to produce an authentic, moving film. She turned back and went to talk again with the captain.

He'd been watching her from the bridge.

"I imagine that your emergency midwifery services distracted you from your real work?" he said as she climbed up the gangplank to stand beside him.

"Perceptive of you, Antonio," said Amanda. "I need to know more about the migrant's journeys and the man whom they drowned. Otherwise, my video won't be powerful enough."

"Difficult," said the captain. "Once migrants leave my ship, they are in the hands of the immigration services and out of police jurisdiction. On this occasion though, we may want to bring charges against the men who drowned the guy with the beard. If so, I may be able to lead the investigation and obtain access to the immigration center to identify those who drowned him. For that, we'll need your video as evidence. However, I will need to consult with my superiors first. Having said that, I'm not sure how I could justify taking you in with me, especially as you are a member of the press."

"I could translate for you."

"Mmm… Food for thought, but until they have landed, I can do nothing."

"I can wait."

"They will be hours yet; our small launches can't tow these dinghies faster than a snail's pace. Anyway, my boss will need a day or two to decide. I'll call you as soon as I know something."

"Thanks, Antonio, and please don't forget those GPS coordinates."

"Have a little faith in us civil servants, Amanda. We might be slow, but we get there in the end."

"In that case, I'll say my goodbyes and wait with bated breath to hear from you."

They shook hands, and Amanda crossed back over the gangplank and this time made it to her car.

She drove her silver Prius out of Algeciras harbor with a heavy heart. The emotional highs and lows of the day had drained her usual resilience to human tragedy.

As she queued in the heavy rush-hour traffic heading toward the motorway, she tried to remain focused on her film. What should be the central theme and title? Usually, she'd relish these creative tasks, but today she couldn't think straight. As soon as she was out on the open road, she let her mind wander over the day's events.

Her eyes watered. There had been two firsts. A man had been killed in front of her, but she decided that her film would not be about him. Viewers were already overexposed and desensitized to the mindless violence of terrorists; they wouldn't appreciate more of the same.

But the baby.

Seeing a baby being born had been a miracle in the circumstances. However, for her, it had been a bittersweet moment.

On the one hand, she'd marveled at the power of nature and the strength of the young African girl. On the other, she'd despaired at the hopelessness of their situation. Miles away from home, alone and vulnerable. Unclear citizenship status. Who was the father, was it a loving relationship, or had she been raped? What did she hope that emigration to Spain might bring to her life? Did she even know where she was?

Amanda was proud to have helped with the birth,

but in reality, the event reminded her of her own situation. Thirty-four years old, single, no children, and not a decent man in sight.

Holding the baby had penetrated deep into that particular cerebral recess. The one she used to bury her yearnings for a child by pretending her career was more important. Yes, she was successful, earned good money, and owned her apartment in Málaga center outright. But where was all this going, more money more success?

"Are material things all I need to be fulfilled?" she said to herself out loud. "If being such a smart woman is so fucking wonderful, why do I have this gaping hole in my soul?"

Once again, her eyes welled with tears.

"Come on, you stupid bitch. Stop this nonsense," Amanda shouted out loud, pulled over to the side of the road, and wept desperately, banging the steering wheel with a clenched fist. "Bugger it," she said eventually and rejoined the motorway. She switched on the car communications system, pulled up her playlist, raised the volume, and had an exclusive car Karaoke with Adele all the way back to Málaga. Her harmony reminded her of a wailing cat.

An hour later, Amanda's tears had dried up. The sun was setting behind her, illuminating the sky with a kaleidoscopic array of color as she turned into the garage under her apartment block opposite Málaga's historic Mercado Central Acarazanas. The impressive wrought-iron and glass marketplace had been built in 1879 and refurbished in 2008. Today it was a thriving food hall combined with superb tapas bars.

Amanda unloaded her camera gear from the trunk, walked over to the elevator, and went up to the seventh and uppermost floor. She inserted her key in the lock, turned it, went inside, kicked the door closed behind her, and went through to the kitchen where she dumped her stuff on the black-granite worktop of the island. She poured herself a glass of Verdejo white wine from the Rueda wine region in northern Spain, slid open the full-height glazed doors, and went out onto the terrace with her phone.

The views were spectacular as the fading sun reflected the last of its rays on the surrounding rooftops. She sat down at the terrace table and sipped her wine while checking her emails and social media. She brought herself up to date with everyone. It was just the usual trivia. She didn't know why she bothered with it, but didn't want to stand accused of being unsociable. She spent little enough time with real people as it was.

She went into the kitchen, made herself an avocado salad, with walnuts, garlic, and olive oil and carried it through to her study, where she kept her editing equipment. She munched on the salad while the camera transferred the days filming to her hard drive. She finished eating, put the plate to one side, and began by entering the video title.

'Stolen Lives'.

It was about the only thing that she'd been able to decide on in the car, but that was the extent of it. No matter how long Amanda tried to be creative, the ideas refused to materialize. Worrying about the baby was dominating her gray cells.

The nurse who had taken the baby and her mother off to hospital had given Amanda her card. She fumbled in her purse, took it out and called the number.

"Hola," answered a woman's voice after the third ring.

"Is that Nurse Mendez?" said Amanda.

"Amanda?"

"That's right."

"I'm sorry," said the nurse. "The mother died, she'd lost too much blood."

"Oh no, that's terrible, and er… the baby?" said Amanda, a sickening feeling growing in her stomach.

"Little Amanda is fine. She has a strong lungs."

"You called her Amanda," said Amanda, her eyes welling up.

"We couldn't keep calling her baby, so we named her after you."

"That's amazing. Where is she?"

"She's in the baby unit in the main Algeciras hospital, where she'll stay for a few days and then be offered up for adoption. We have a long waiting list of approved parents for these eventualities."

"That is good news. Just in case the new parents are interested, I have some film of her mother if they want a clip to show her when she's older."

"That will be up to her new parents. Most prefer a clean break from the past, so don't expect much."

"Oh, that is disappointing."

"I understand, you felt some bond with the child and don't want to let go."

"That's exactly right."

"Happens to me all the time, and I've been at it for twenty years. Listen, you were a great help out there today. Many couldn't have coped with the blood and everything."

"You guys are the real heroes facing this human agony every day. It reminded me of how ignorant I am about real life, and that's upsetting my usual thinking patterns. So much so that I've been sitting here all evening staring at my monitor, struggling to edit my work, but nothing is happening. Authors would call it writer's block, but talking to you has inspired me. Now I know what to do. Thanks again, Nurse. Adios."

Amanda worked until just before midnight, sketching out her concept.

I'm going to call the mother, Leila, she thought. I'll assume that she's from the Republic of Niger, ran away from her slave master, joined a caravan across the Sahara desert, and was abused by the men. Eventually, as she worked her way across Mali and Morocco, her young body matured, and she fell pregnant.

Her film was about Leila's incredibly painful and emotional journey, the delusions that drove her, and the people who exploited her. The final clip was of her lying still on the cabin bench morphing to her baby left alone but with a glimmer of hope to starting a new life in a civilized country. The point being that maybe, little Amanda made Leila's journey worthwhile.

She added an optional voice-over, and closed her machine for the night. She stood up, stretched, yawned, and headed for the bathroom. She showered, slipped into her striped sleep shirt, and collapsed into bed. As her head touched the pillow, she thought about her plans for tomorrow.

It was likely to be a mundane day.

She would complete the editing of the *Stolen Lives* video, but hold off on sending it to New York until she'd heard back from the captain about getting access to the detention center in Algeciras. The video would be so much more powerful with some quotes from the migrants in the captured dinghy. Other than that, she had to prepare for her documentary tomorrow.

Wednesday, May 15.

Nerja's San Isidro Festival.

10

The phone jolted Prado from his brief nap. He hadn't been sleeping well since the kidnapping and now that his future was once again secure, it hadn't taken him long to stop berating himself and nod off.

"Your first case," said el jefe.

"That was quick," said Prado, taking his feet off the desk and sitting to attention.

"It's a suspicious death in Nerja involving a Belgian and his French wife. Report to the Guardia Civil barracks. If my memory serves me well, you spent some time there a couple of years ago."

"You mean the Russian case?"

"I do, and that was you at your finest. See if you can repeat the outcome."

"I doubt it will be so profitable for the central bank."

"I don't care, just solve the case. Good luck."

"Thank you, Sir," but the line was already dead.

Prado slipped into his jacket, placed his Panama at

its usual jaunty angle and headed down to the basement to pick up a pool car.

As he threaded through the streets leading up to the coastal motorway, he thought back to his last sojourn in Nerja.

Nerja's history of any type of crime was insignificant. Mainly bag thefts, pickpockets, local youths baiting drunken, usually British tourists outside nightclubs, or the occasional tiff between minor drug gangs. A couple of years ago, local banks had reported the appearance of an unusual amount of €500 notes from their retail customers, particularly a women's clothing shop on Calle Pintada. Prado set up some surveillance, identified two attractive but gaudy women, and followed them to a large villa on the outskirts of town. They watched the luxury property for a while and monitored communications with the help of the Russian consulate. When the consulate identified the arrival of a Mr. Big wanted back in the motherland, Prado and his team raided and arrested everyone. They found several pistols and €4 million, mainly in denominations of the garish pink-colored €500 note. Prado had called the notes Bin Laden's; he knew they were out there, but had never seen one. Mainly because criminals had them stashed under mattresses or, in this case, in plastic trash bags.

The Russians denied any knowledge of ownership or the origins of the cash. Prado laughed in their face when Mr. Big said through an interpreter that they had found the money in the garage when renting the premises. Prado did them all a huge favor: he confiscated the pink bundles and presented them to the Bank of Spain as unwanted property. The bank, being on the verge of bankruptcy at the time, was most grateful. The Russians' expressions were epic.

Now he had an unexplained death in Nerja.

It took him just under an hour to drive to the Guardia Civil barracks on Calle San Miguel. The security gates slid open, admitting him into the congested car park. He blocked everyone in, left the car door open, and threw the keys at the desk sergeant on his way to the interview room.

Prado noticed a new sign on the interview-room door in three languages. He recognized the top one as being English, and read it to himself, "The official language of the Guardia Civil are Spanish. For them that necessitate it, a qualified interpretater might be instrumental." He understood the first sentence, but the remainder was beyond him. He opened the door and went inside. The only window was an opaque skylight; it was shut. A ceiling fan whirred noisily, but moved too slowly to generate any worthwhile ventilation.

It was hot, airless, and musty.

Sparse furnishings completed the dreary decor. In the middle of the room stood a battered wood-laminate desk. On its top lay a grubby laptop. In the corner was a shabby beige filing cabinet topped with a wilting spider plant in a cracked ceramic pot. A framed certificate was hanging on the rear wall. It was askew. On one side of the desk was a black plastic chair occupied by a senior Guardia Civil officer with whom he'd worked on the Russian case. They exchanged nods. On the opposite side of the desk were four unmatched chairs arranged tightly next to one another. One was occupied by a junior Guardia Civil officer, the other by the Belgian, a large bald man in his late sixties. He was dressed smartly in dark-blue trousers and a short-sleeved white shirt; he was perspiring heavily. He and the junior Guardia Civil officer were shouting at each other in a strange mixture of Spanish and English. It was quickly evident to Prado that Spanglish was not going to be the most effective communication method to solve this mysterious death.

Prado put his hat on the desk and sat down next to the Belgian.

"I'll take over now," said Prado.

The junior officer frowned at the inspector's intrusion, but he knew who Prado was and why he was here. He deferred to his superior and sat back in his chair, drumming his fingers lightly on the desk. Prado glared at him. He stopped.

Prado turned to the Belgian and asked in his limited English, "I am Inspector Prado, you have friend can Spanish speak?"

The Belgian replied, relieved, "Yes."

"You can mobile him to come?"

The Belgian nodded.

"Give him his phone," said Prado in Spanish.

The officer behind the desk, opened a drawer, extracted a phone and the passport, and slid them toward Prado. He inspected the passport. The man was Marcel Faucher from Brussels, aged sixty-eight and by his sweating and color was suffering from some sort of heart condition.

Prado gave the phone to the Belgian whose hand shook as he took it from him. He managed to find his contact and press the call button.

A man's voice answered in what sounded to Prado like German. They spoke briefly. The Belgian nodded and looked a tad happier.

"My friend is coming now," announced the Belgian

in English. "He will ask for you at the gate." He then put his head in his hands and wept quietly.

11

Phillip approached the robust steel security gate protecting Nerja's Guardia Civil barracks wearing a dark-blue polo shirt and beige jeans. He rang the bell.

"Si?" said a tinny voice through the small loudspeaker.

"Inspector Prado, por favor," said Phillip, staring directly into the lens of the video camera.

"Tiene cita?" said the voice.

"Por supuesto."

"Nombre?"

"Phillip Armitage."

"Vale. Momento."

Phillip waited on the busy narrow pavement while the inspector was located and could confirm their meeting. He knew that would take several minutes. Meanwhile, the typical Spanish street scene provided a wide range of entertainment.

The late spring weather created a glorious backdrop for this daily live theater. Tiny flecks of white marble clouds randomly decorating a ubiquitous blue sky, comfortable temperature, minimal humidity, and a gentle breeze that tugged at Phillip's hair. Competing aromas of ground coffee and toasted bread wafted from the café next door to the barracks but were immediately overwhelmed by the obnoxious exhaust fumes from the passing traffic. A disabled lottery-ticket vendor had parked his wheelchair outside the supermarket entrance opposite. He announced in a loud croaky voice that he had the winning number for that night's Loteria Nacional draw. A queue formed in front of him, waving bundles of cash and blocking the pavement, forcing pedestrians into the road. Car horns blared.

In Calle America, the street to the side of the Guardia Civil, a diminutive senior female, confident and comfortable with her ample proportions, was haphazardly wielding a mop in front of her townhouse. Her purple-dyed hair was set in curlers, and she wore the briefest of pink nightshirts, happy to display her spindly white legs gnarled with varicose veins as she twirled around in bright-orange sports shoes. She chatted with her neighbor while liberally squirting *aguafuerte,* or bleach, over her stretch of concrete. Her raucous cackles could be heard above the din. Occasionally, she dipped the mop into a water bucket and splashed the pungent cocktail liberally over another day's detritus from the inconsiderate: cigarette butts, chewing gum, and dog excrement.

Passersby kept well out of range.

On the corner nearest the barracks, a young scruffily dressed man of Eastern European appearance was thrusting clear plastic packs of cheap imported Chinese garlic under the noses of passersby. His stock stood behind him packed tightly into a canvas shopping cart.

"One euro," he said. He sold out in minutes.

Opposite the barracks, a sub-Saharan African man, elegantly dressed in a long, colorful robe, held up his merchandise and shouted, "Looky, looky," every time someone walked in front of him. He was touting imitation Rolex watches and could say, 'genuine' or 'very cheap' in at least nine languages.

A Guardia Civil officer in an ill-fitting uniform and cap patrolled indolently back and forth among the police vehicles parked tightly behind the high metal fence. His holstered pistol was fixed firmly to his black leather belt. He glanced at the street vendors disinterestedly. His responsibility was road traffic, minor crime, and to monitor Spain's borders, coastline, and highways. Unlicensed trading was the concern of the local police.

Beyond the patrol cars stood the barracks themselves, an aging three-story whitewashed stucco building with slatted green window shutters. The ground floor housed the interview rooms, cells, and offices. The upper levels were basic accommodation for the officers and their families.

A stone archway led to an inner courtyard. Carved into the curved upper stonework was the immortal words that appeared on every barrack throughout Spain - Everything for the Homeland.

"Come through," the tinny voice announced, and the gate slid open, squeaking intermittently as it rolled along its guide rail.

Phillip left the bustling scene behind him, went through the gate, and strode across the car park to the glazed entrance to the barracks. He stretched out his hand to open the door under the arch, but was beaten to it from the inside. A smartly dressed man stepped out through the door.

"Mr. Armitage?" said the man in Spanish holding out his hand.

"Yes," said Phillip shaking hands.

"Inspector Prado. Please follow me."

Prado led Phillip into the center of the inner courtyard. It was deserted.

Prado paused. Phillip stopped and looked at him curiously.

"Do you mind if I ask you a few questions before we go and talk to your friend?" said Prado.

"Please go ahead, Inspector."

"Did Señor Faucher explain that his wife was dead?"

"Yes, something about an accident with the car."

"How long have you known Señor Faucher?"

"About two years."

"Had he and his wife been married long?"

"They celebrated their fortieth wedding anniversary last year."

"Would you say that they were happy?"

"Sometimes, Inspector, you meet married couples who were made to be together. Marcel and Sophie were a charming, happy, and loving pair, with amazing children and grandchildren. They had plenty of money, a wonderful lifestyle, and treasured their time here in Nerja."

"Did he keep the car here permanently or drive it down?"

"He drove back and forth every year. They enjoyed meandering through your lovely country. Every trip they would try a different hotel. Marcel was proud that they had stayed in over forty Paradores."

"Impressive. Did he maintain the car?"

"Here, no, but in Brussels, regularly. He's a well-organized, conscientious man."

"Did he use the car much while here?"

"The occasional trip. They liked the market in Málaga. Sophie is, sorry was, a fantastic cook."

"Thank you, Señor Armitage. Your Spanish is excellent, but wasn't it German that you and Señor Faucher were speaking?"

"Yes, we met at a dinner party where the hostess was German. I guess we just carried on doing so."

"Do you speak any other languages?"

"My Russian is passable, but don't ask me to give a lecture on the Theory of Relativity."

"I couldn't even do that in Spanish. Shall we go and talk to your friend? He's distraught, so please be gentle with him."

Prado led Phillip over to the interview room. Prado noticed him chuckle at the sign.

"That bad?" said Prado.

"Terrible. If you give me your email, I'll send you the correct text in all three languages."

"You speak French too?"

"Some, but I have a French colleague who'll double-check."

Prado smiled and opened the door.

The Belgian still had his head in his hands, but looked up with tearful eyes on hearing the door open. On seeing Phillip, he struggled to his feet, and they hugged each other for several moments.

"Ask him for his full name and to relate what happened, please," said Prado in Spanish.

The Belgian sat up straight in his chair and did his best to compose himself. He spoke in German, and

Phillip translated simultaneously into Spanish.

"I am Marcel Faucher from Brussels," he said quietly and nervously. "My wife, Sophie and I, she is French from Strasbourg, were going to the market in Málaga. Sophie wanted some special fish. You remember her fish pâté, Phillip?"

"Divine, Marcel."

The door squeaked open to reveal a tiny, aging cleaning woman in high-visibility lime-green overalls, standing beside a well-equipped cart. She extracted a mop, entered, and when Marcel didn't raise his feet to allow her access to under his chair, prodded at his ankles.

"Is this necessary?" said Prado.

"We won't see her for another month, so yes," said the senior Guardia Civil officer.

Prado indicated that Marcel should move his feet and carry on with his explanation. Phillip wasn't sure if he should laugh or cry. Marcel soldiered on. The distraction helped him to continue with his explanation.

"I hadn't driven the car since we arrived just before Christmas, and it was immediately apparent that something was wrong with the engine. It wasn't firing correctly, some damp in the piston chambers I presumed. I persevered, and suddenly the engine caught.

"I had my foot down on the accelerator at the time, and I had already released the hand-brake. The car hurtled backward out of my garage like a wild animal and I had no possibility to control it. I turned off the motor and jammed on the foot brake. Somehow I managed to stop it before it hit the underground car-park wall behind me.

"Sophie was standing in her usual position on the driver's side toward the rear of the car, so I could see her facing me of the wing mirror. She warns me if I'm getting too close to the car-park wall. The car moved so fast that she stood no chance. Phillip…." Marcel stopped talking, overcome with emotion. Phillip rested his arm on his friend's shoulder and patted him gently. Marcel took a deep breath and said, "the wing mirror ripped out her liver. She bled to death in minutes. Her final words were, 'Sorry, my love. I was standing in the wrong place'. Phillip, I have to tell our children that I killed their mother. They will hate me."

"They will understand," said Phillip. "Try not to worry about it."

Phillip translated.

"Do you have photos of the scene?" said Prado to the two officers.

The one behind the desk rummaged in the drawer and passed them over. Prado flicked through them and nodded.

"This was obviously a terrible accident," said Prado, handing Marcel's passport to Phillip. "Señor Faucher has suffered more than enough. There will be no charges. After he's signed a written statement for the coroner, he may go."

Phillip translated for Marcel, who nodded and took a pen out of his shirt pocket.

The other officer went out to the next room, came back a few minutes later with a piece of printed paper, and gave it to Prado. He read through it, nodded, and added his signature. He passed the document over to Phillip, who checked the text, approved it, and handed it to Marcel. Marcel signed, returned the pen to his pocket, and then struggled out of the chair. Phillip helped him out of the tiny office.

"Do you want me to see you home?" said Phillip.

"Thanks, but I can manage," said Marcel.

Phillip stood with Prado and watched as Marcel walked slowly out of the barracks gate to begin his new life as a widower.

"A tragic moment in his long life," said Prado.

"All it takes is a blink of an eye, Inspector and everything can change."

"You've had your own experiences?"

"I served in Afghanistan," said Phillip.

"Then I understand. Here, take this," said Prado, proffering his card to Phillip. "Any problems, let me know and thanks for coming at such short notice."

"Glad I could help," said Phillip. "I'll email you those translations."

"Thanks," said Prado. "Next time you're in Málaga, give me a call; you may like to help me with other investigations."

"Really?" said Phillip.

"My department desperately needs people with languages."

"Well, that would be interesting, provided that it doesn't conflict with my business."

"It shouldn't be too demanding; Nerja isn't much of a crime hotspot."

"Then, yes, I'd be happy to help out."

"Then we should meet and talk it through. There's an excellent café near my office. In the meantime, I hope all goes well with your friend. I'd advise some counseling."

"Thank you, Inspector. Most kind of you," said Phillip.

12

The Nerja church clock struck ten o'clock as the official town firework igniter, dressed in his usual uniform of a battered straw hat, torn baggy trousers, and grubby T-shirt sent the first of a dozen rockets aloft into a clear blue sky. The explosions echoed around the countryside, summoning the surrounding populace to prepare for the San Isidro Romeria and head to the town center. While the bells tolled, the smoldering rocket sticks headed earthward with accelerating velocity. With luck to land harmlessly. One year the awning of the then Calahonda beach restaurant went up in flames. Another, the mayor's silk underwear drying on her terrace.

The word Romeria evolves from processions of pilgrims going to Rome. Sprigs of the aromatic herb Romero or rosemary were stuck in travelers' hats to ward off evil spirits and robbers. Romerias are famous all over Spain, none more so than the largest, held every May in Sevilla Province. Over a million pilgrims trail through the Doñana National Park to El Rocio, a village purposely built just for this one week. There are several hundred houses, a cathedral, and a couple of hotels. The roads are made of sand so that horses can be tethered right outside the property owners' doors.

From the edge of Doñana, it takes the pilgrims several days to reach the village. Campfire smoke, grilling meat, music, and song waft over the huge procession as it parks up for the night. It is a remarkable and spiritual occasion. The modest consumption of the favored fiesta beverage, chilled dry sherry, assists where it can.

Nerja's San Isidro Romeria procession is minuscule by comparison, but still attracts some ten thousand participants and onlookers. It starts at the church about midday and ends four kilometers away in the village of Maro in the gardens of the spectacular Nerja Caves.

Phillip walked up the ramp from Nerja's central underground car park and threaded his way through the boisterous crowds under the town-hall archway. He was dressed in his Romeria attire: a white linen shirt with a red bandana knotted around his neck, a gray cordoba hat tilted forward to shade the face, and black jeans held up by a black leather belt to which he'd attached his phone pack. A natty secure widget that contained his phone, keys, cash, and cards. Most men wore similar clothing, whether a participant or onlooker. Women wore brightly colored, tight fitting long Spanish dresses, which for San Isidro were traditionally patterned with polka dots. No matter what shape, age, or dimensions, these garments transformed the wearer into gorgeous, elegant women who carried themselves gracefully. They were a pleasure to behold. Most men were doing a lot of beholding.

Phillip turned right, out of the archway and threaded his way through the assembling masses, past the church into Plaza Cavana, one of Nerja's pretty tree-lined squares, where the oxcarts were lining up. On his way through the crowd, he chatted, shook hands, hugged, or embraced several friends, keeping an eye out for his brother-in-law, José. He eventually spotted him in deep conversation with his fellow herdsmen sitting at a table outside La Fragata café. They were enjoying a moment's respite from prodding their beasts of burden before the procession began in earnest. Most of them had already had quite a journey into town. It would have taken José well over an hour to lumber the four kilometers down the Frigiliana Road from their farm. José ordered a coffee for Phillip and more water for himself while explaining exactly where the cart was parked in Calle Diputación, in case they became separated in the crowd. They finished their drinks and headed off to join his sister and the girls.

They had just past the BBVA bank when a female voice shouted, "Phillip." He stopped, looked in the direction of the noise and spotted a woman coming out of an apartment-block entrance. It was Juliet.

"I'll catch you up," he said to José and crossed the packed street toward her. She looked stunning. The tightly fitting full-length black-and-red Spanish dress with white polka dots and frills hugged her shapely curves perfectly. Her glossy blond hair cascaded over her shoulders with a red rose pinned just above her right ear. However, Phillip immediately noticed that she seemed extremely miserable as if she'd been crying.

They exchanged cheek kisses.

"You scrub up quite well," he said.

"Not so bad yourself," said Juliet.

"You seem a bit down though?"

"Something on my mind."

"Want to talk about it?"

"Later, maybe. Are you still on the oxcart with your sister?"

"Yes. You?"

"I'm walking up ahead of the procession to meet my new friend in the gardens, but I'll be free later? Could we meet somewhere?"

"Cave Bar around four?"

"Good idea," said Juliet. "But, listen, Phillip, I'm not sure how long my friend might be staying, so don't worry if I'm not there."

"If you're there fine; if not, as you say, another time. But whether it's me or somebody else, you need to share whatever's troubling you sooner rather than later."

Juliet nodded. "Don't I know it? Sorry, but I have to go; hope to see you later, and," she reached out an arm, pulled him to her cheek, kissed him, and added, "thanks for being so supportive." Then with her eyes watering, she turned and melted into the crowd.

Phillip continued down Diputación, worrying about her.

"Tio, Phillip," screamed three young girls.

He peered through the masses and spotted José's cart. His three nieces were jumping up and down in the back waving at him. His sister Glenda was standing in between the two oxen as they took turns at lapping from the plastic water bowl she proffered up for them. She smiled at her elder brother.

He put an arm around her shoulder and kissed her on both cheeks.

She'd pinned up her long, blond curly hair and

clipped a bright-red rose above her right ear. She looked pretty, happy, and serene in a blue-and-white polka-dot dress.

"Are you sure you're up for this?" she said, as he followed her to the back of the cart where she hung the water bowl on a hook.

"I can't think of anything worse," he said, grinning at the three expectant faces gazing down at him.

He heaved himself up the short ladder and sat down on the bench opposite his nieces underneath a shady polka-dot awning. Anna, the eldest, at nine, Louisa at six, and the youngest, Tina, at four leaped on him simultaneously, kissing his cheeks and hugging him, all demanding that he play with them first.

The parade marshal blew a whistle.

"Right kids," said Phillip. "We're about to move off; sit down and hang on tight to the cart."

José returned from the shop opposite with a plastic bag full of chorizo, Serrano ham, and Manchego cheese. He handed it to Glenda who climbed up onto the cart and sat next to Phillip.

José wagged a precautionary finger at each of his daughters and moved forward to take his place by the oxen. Stick at the ready.

One-by-one the carts in front of them lumbered off. Then it was their turn.

Nerja Caves, here we come, thought Phillip. Would Juliet be there at four o'clock?

13

It had taken Amanda over an hour to reach Maro from Málaga. Her first appointment was with the director of the caves. They were rediscovered accidentally in 1959, by five local boys watching bats disappear into a crevice in the rocks. They decided to enlarge the entrance to see where the bats were going only to tumble into a hole. After their initial screams of horror had subsided, curiosity drove them to venture further where they discovered an enormous cavern littered with human skeletons and broken ceramics. They ran back home to inform their parents.

Further exploration by the experts revealed an enormous underground complex of impressive rock formations, columns, stalagmites, and stalactites. Nerja Caves rapidly became one of the most popular tourist attractions in Spain and today continues to draw hundreds of thousands of annual visitors.

Amanda parked her Prius opposite the Hotel Playamar at the east end of the village. It was outside a builder's yard identified by a large sign. The yard was protected by a high white wall with tall metal gates and secured by a sturdy padlock. A moped with a twisted mudguard leaned against the yard wall. She squeezed in between a sleek black Porsche Cayenne and a white Renault Kangoo van. A swarthy man with unkempt black hair in Festival clothing was cutting out polka dots from different colored paper and randomly sticking them on the side of the van.

She checked her watch, climbed out, locked her car and went into the hotel cafeteria for a late breakfast. It was packed with more festival-goers chatting away noisily. There was only one seat free at a table occupied by three Spanish women. They indicated for her to join them. A young waiter took her order and they exchanged pleasantries until her coffee and food arrived.

As she smeared grated tomatoes onto her toasted roll, a quiet effeminate male voice said in accented Spanish. "Excuse me."

She turned to see a giant, obese man waiting to squeeze between her and the aisle. She stood and let him pass looking at his back as he left. He was enormous.

"Not quite your size," said one of the Spanish ladies when he'd gone.

"I'd need a step ladder," said Amanda.

They all cackled before returning to their family gossip.

Amanda sipped her coffee and pondered over the introduction to her video. She'd considered using shots of the San Isidro effigy being carried out of Nerja church and being loaded onto the oxcart. However, that would entail taking a ladder to see over the crowds, and that was way too complicated, logistically. To date, she hadn't done anything to learn about how camera drones could improve her filming, but she was at least thinking about them.

She'd researched San Isidro yesterday seeking inspiration for a theme for her film. San Isidro was born Isidro de Merlo y Quintana sometime in the twelfth century. Apparently, he'd performed miracles with never-ending sacks of corn and bottomless pots of stew. He was beatified nearly five hundred years later in May 1619 for his piety in sharing food with the poor, hence the loaves of bread on his processional oxcart. Amanda suspected that only a few seasoned festival-goers would be celebrating the day for religious reasons and be aware of the saint's achievements. Religion throughout Spain and most of Europe was fading rapidly out of most people's lives, yet Spanish religious festivals were more popular than ever. Why was this, she wondered?

She'd decided that this would be the theme of her video - piety or party?

Amanda settled her check, returned to the Prius, opened the rear door, and surveyed her camera equipment. A specially made organizer held her expensive gear in place while she traveled. She extracted what she needed and placed everything carefully into her large backpack. A handheld, lightweight video camera with a built-in microphone, plus a loose mike for interviews. Spare batteries, memory chips, and lens cloths. A retractable tripod, supplementary lighting, laptop, cables, two bottles of frozen iced tea, and several nutrition bars. She added a dash of lipstick, struggled into her backpack then headed off in the direction of the footbridge which crossed the autovia to a path that led up to the caves.

However, on the way, she couldn't help but notice how pretty the Maro High Street was, so dug the camera out of the bag, and filmed for a few seconds before crossing the bridge. She checked her watch. Eleven o'clock. She didn't intend an in-depth documentary about the caves. There were plenty of those around. What she wanted were clips of the key features and permission to use extracts from last summer's concert.

A young dark-haired girl, wearing jeans and a Nerja Caves T-shirt with a red cave-art goat logo on the front showed her into the director's office. She shrugged off her backpack, placed it next to the visitor's chair and then shook hands with the director. Angel Blanco was a tall, gray-haired, stooped, middle-aged man, reeking of tobacco smoke. Amanda noticed a pipe smoldering in an ashtray by the window. They exchanged pleasantries before Angel showed Amanda over to an easel covered by a large map of the caves.

"Since our boys fell down the hole," said Angel. "A huge amount of research by the finest minds in anthropology, geology, and archeology have been undertaken. So far we have discovered three separate sections. What we are about to visit is the tourist sector, here."

He pointed at the first section.

"The other two penetrate over five kilometers under the mountain, here and here. We suspect there's more, but to fund a professional team to explore that possibility would cost far more than the money we raise through our entrance fees."

"That's fascinating."

"To be frank, we're constantly trying to find ways

to raise more funds. Where did you say your film will be shown?"

"I work with CNN and other American broadcasters. I'm also expanding to other English-speaking countries. They use my videos to illustrate elements of Spanish culture and history."

"Excellent. Do you want to film everything?"

"As much as I can, yes. Why?"

"Because we have superb footage of last year's concert, which we've blended in with a short history of our findings so far. I'll be happy to let you use all, or some of it provided you credit the foundation. I have it all on my computer. Would you like to watch it?"

"Yes, please."

The director turned his laptop toward her and set the film running. He picked up his pipe and went outside while she watched.

It was an impressive film and included 3D animations of what life underground might have been like during Neanderthal times. She couldn't wait to see the actual caves themselves. Half an hour later, the film came to an end, and the director returned.

"Well?" he said.

"Amazing. I'd like to use some elements of it if I could."

"OK. Then I'll leave this film to burn onto a DVD, while we tour the site."

"Thank you. You obviously went to a lot of expense to make the film. The lighting is so much better than I could do alone. However, as we go round, I'm sure I'll see something that I want to shoot. Will that be OK?"

"Of course."

She collected her backpack as they left his office and walked the few hundred meters up to the entrance of the cave. The security guard waved them through to the stairs, where they descended into the damp, cool air.

At the bottom of the stairs was a narrow passage into the caves themselves, after which it opened out onto a massive gallery. Angel paused and began to talk passionately about the history of the caves.

"After the rediscovery, it took a while for the experts in Madrid to realize the significance of what we had here. Eventually, some bright spark in Franco's regime, who had guts enough to speak up, recognized it could be a potential gold mine. Only then did things start to happen and the caves opened to its first visitors in 1960. It's been an outstanding success and has dramatically changed Nerja, but it is so much more than a tourist attraction.

"While the caves were formed millions of years ago, they are a continual work in progress, as water continues to drip through the limestone, adding further deposits to the stalagmites and stalactites. Analysis of the artifacts and cave art has proved a mixed history: Neolithic burial ground, hyena hideaway, fridge for farm produce, animal shelter, and home to humans. They were inhabited by various tribes between 25,000 and 3600 BC.

"Recent testing of the seal sketches has proven that they were drawn with reddish pigments, indicating that they are forty-three thousand years old. This has generated much speculation that Homo sapiens and Neanderthal man may have cohabited here which would give a completely new slant on our evolution."

"I'll take your word for it," said Amanda. "I never knew that there were seals in the Mediterranean."

"It was much colder and wetter in those days. The

water levels of the Mediterranean were substantially higher and the varieties of flora and fauna completely different."

"So no tourists."

"Exactly, but there would have been many nomads traveling to and from Africa looking for a better life."

"So the planet has changed, but people are still up to the same shit."

"Except there were no borders to deter them in those days, just pirates, thieves and sickness."

"I repeat, people are still up to the same shit."

"Er, yes," said Angel.

"Sorry," said Amanda. "One of my pet peeves."

"Shall we concentrate on the caves, or have you had enough?"

"How much more is there?"

"Nearly, done. For example, that column at the back of the gallery is noted in the *Guinness Book of Records* as being the widest in the world."

"Incredible."

"As are the acoustics. Placido Domingo, Dame Kiri Te Kanawa, and Yehudi Menuhin adored appearing here."

"I'm sure they did, but aren't you worried about the long term effects that all these human visitors might have on the cave's ecosystem?"

"It's true," said Angel looking uncomfortable. "That each visitor raises the ambient temperature and CO2 levels which can damage the plant life and deter the animals that feed on that. We've installed sensors to monitor the levels and during the busiest months, we do control the numbers entering at any one time more rigorously than off-season."

"And you're happy with that?"

"Some Scientists would prefer we reduced visitors, others not."

Amanda prepared her camera then filmed as they wandered along a roped-off footpath that guides tourists around a circuit of the caves. Half an hour later, they returned to Angel's office where he extracted the DVD from his computer and presented it to her.

"Thank you, Angel, this is perfect."

"Anytime, Amanda. Please send me the link to your finished product. Who knows, if we like it, we might ask you to do more work."

"Cool. Will do," said Amanda but she had the feeling that Angel wasn't too enamored with her outspoken views.

14

The San Isidro effigy passed through the massive entrance doors of Nerja church mounted on a portable throne carried on the sturdy shoulders of six Costaleros. The men, representing local religious brotherhoods, swayed in unison as they shuffled down the church steps and over to the lead oxcart elegantly decorated with palm fronds and dangling loaves of bread. The effigy was a wooden statue, a meter and a half tall, with a golden halo mounted over his head, wearing a long brown cloak, green clothing, and beige boots. A wooden carving of a pair of oxen yoked together, pulling a plow, were at his feet. The throne was placed onto the cart while colorfully dressed women danced, swirled, and twirled in front of the church, to shouts from the crowd of, "long live, San Isidro."

Once the effigy was secured, a single uniformed horseman carrying San Isidro's intricately woven green-and-purple banner led the procession off along the Balcón, up Calle Pintada, and along the coastal road in the direction of the caves. After the oxcarts came finely groomed horses of every color, then mules, donkeys, and a tiny Shetland pony. Some of the exquisitely dressed riders were accompanied by beautifully dressed girlfriends perched on the horse's hindquarters behind the saddle. They looked most decorous and were keenly photographed by onlookers as the procession crawled by them.

Following the riders were an array of stylish carriages. They varied from four-seaters drawn by three elegant matching pairs of horses to single-seaters pulled by Dobbin the bedraggled mule, a stubborn gray beast that needed constant prodding with a whip. The crowd laughed as the poor creature regularly stopped to nibble the grass at the side of the road, much to the annoyance of its owner.

Up next were sleek tractors towing decorated trailers that displayed shields representing their particular club or association. Many were equipped with generators to power fridges and the latest audio systems blaring with popular Latin music. On one rig stood a chef dressed in kitchen whites, flamboyantly carving a leg of Serrano ham. Each piece cut was added ceremoniously to a nearby platter accompanied by raucous shouts of "Ole."

People typically drank beer, vino fino; a crisp, dry sherry from Jerez de la Frontera; or a summer punch of red wine, ice, and lemonade known as Tinto Verano. The alcohol flowed pleasantly, but not excessively; this was a family occasion. Dancers, mainly women, followed the trailers and when the procession paused to give the oxen a rest, which was often in the searing midday heat, the women would dance together, receiving much appreciation from the spectators.

Finally the charabancs, a mixed array of new, old, and wrecked vehicles clad with an occasional palm frond, the odd polka dot painted on cardboard, and masses of soccer club scarves. Here were the town's youngsters enjoying themselves. Their music, if it could be called that, was so loud that the speakers were vibrating, but they were having fun, and their behavior, although boisterous, was inoffensive.

Cute children ran about everywhere wearing mini versions of whatever festival clothing their parents had on and endearing themselves to everyone by drenching them with water pistols. Few complained; they would soon dry off in the sun.

José led the oxen on foot while Glenda hopped on and off the cart to keep him well provided with water and a cloth to keep his shoes clean. The joys of processions with live animals. It was even worse further back, where over a hundred horses had added to the oxen's outpourings.

As they lumbered along the coastal road, Phillip chatted and joked with his three nieces. He was impressed with how they could switch from English to Spanish and back without effort.

As they approached the last stages of the procession, they had to cross Barranco de la Coladilla de Cazadores, a deep gorge with a historic aqueduct, which used to convey water to the old sugar mill whose ruins still dominated the area. At last, they reached the steep hill up to the cave where they all clambered off the cart to lighten the load for the oxen.

At the top, José maneuvered the cart into a parking zone to the left of the entrance. The girls all pointed to a woman sitting on top of a wall filming them and made rude faces at her before Glenda scolded them. The woman lowered her camera briefly, smiled, and waved before returning to her task. José and Phillip were busily tethering the beasts under shady pine trees. They left them with plenty of hay and water, unloaded the picnic stuff, and walked back down to the entrance of the garden. They were just in time to watch the statue of San Isidro lifted off his cart and carried once more by the Costaleros up to his tiny hermitage at the top of the gardens where he would repose for the remainder of the day. Some visitors would pay homage to him by picking a sprig of rosemary from nearby bushes and sticking it in their hat for another year's good-luck symbol.

To the north of the gardens is the enormous national park; Parque Natural Sierras de Tejeda, Almijara y Alhama. It extends to over forty thousand hectares of craggy mountains, dense woodland and was a hideout for anti-Franco guerillas during Spain's Civil War (1936-39). The enormous variety of flora and fauna, including golden eagles, wild boar, and mountain goats, has made it extremely popular with hikers and photographers.

One of the advantages of Phillip's family being among the first to arrive at the caves was to have the pick of prime tables. They found one that overlooked a raised platform on the lower terrace that would be perfect to watch the later exhibitions. Flamenco displays by all ages, music groups of varying styles, and traditional Spanish guitarists would entertain the crowds until the late-night hours. They opened their cool boxes and a bottle of chilled Fino and enjoyed their picnic as the terrace filled up around them.

Between the tables and the stage was an open area

for public dancing, where, when sufficiently refreshed, many would dance the Sevillana, a traditional folk dance learned by all Andalusian children almost before they can walk. No matter how hard foreigners practice it, they can rarely match the fluid, elegant movements of the Spanish.

After lunch, Phillip danced with each of his nieces, who were grateful for only one bruised foot each. They congratulated him on his modest improvement from the previous year. He then escorted them to the dressage display, where they said hello to Didi and Gunter, then around the side stalls, where he managed to escape with only minor purchases of gaudy hats and sickly pink candy floss.

Just before four o'clock, Phillip returned the girls to their parents and headed off to the cave bar to meet Juliet. It took him a good ten minutes to reach the restaurant through the dense crowd of festival revelers. He walked into the crowded bar and looked round.

There was no sign of Juliet.

He bought a glass of Cava, perched on the last remaining stool at the bar, and waited patiently. Fifteen minutes later, Juliet still hadn't shown up. He finished his drink and went to rejoin his family down on the lower terrace.

Although she had said she might not show. He couldn't stop himself from being concerned about her.

15

Amanda spotted a thick, high wall to the side of the entrance to the caves gardens. She judged that it was broad enough to sit on top. If she could find a way to climb up, it would be a perfect position to film. She looked around for a ladder.

There was a selection of market stalls just inside the entrance with colorful displays of hats, typical festival clothing, and other accessories. She took out her camera then tripod and started assembling them.

"Making a video, are we?" said one of the stallholders.

Amanda gave him her best smile. "Yes, for CNN."

"CNN? Impressive. You could film our stall if you like."

"Of course, if you could help me up on top of that wall and then down in an hour or so, I'll happily include you."

A few minutes later, he returned with a step ladder, smiled, and said. "My son will assist."

The wall turned out to be higher and broader than Amanda had envisaged. She had to stretch to place her equipment on its top, but there was no way that she could climb up herself. She turned and shrugged at the son who offered to give her a leg up.

It was a tight squeeze together on top of the ladder platform, but he cupped his hands, she placed her right knee on them, and he heaved her up. He gave her his telephone number to call when she needed to come down and then disappeared back to their stall with the ladder. She straddled the wall and started organizing what she needed.

The procession was running late. She sipped some iced tea, nibbled on a nutrition bar, and waited. Ten minutes later, police motorcycles with lights flashing appeared. They were crawling so slowly up the hill that their riders had to weave from side to side to stay upright.

Behind the police escort was the San Isidro horseman with banner, followed by the oxcart transporting the effigy. The animals were breathing hard after climbing the long hill. They stopped just below her, where six strong men unloaded the saint and swayed off toward the hermitage.

Amanda turned on her camera and started filming. It was twenty past two o'clock.

The procession seemed endless. At first, she filmed the oxcarts as they trundled by up to their parking places under the trees disgorging their festival attired passengers. Three beautiful little blond-curly-haired girls distracted her concentration by waving up to her and when she looked stuck their tongues out. She filmed them, waved and smiled as their mother scolded them. An hour later, the traffic ground to a halt. A local policeman re-directed the tail-end vehicles up past the tethered animals to find a place on the country track that led up to the national park. The remainder was told to find parking elsewhere. The caves were now full.

A few minutes later, a heavy dust cloud billowed through the trees and over the tethered animals. A loudspeaker announced that the dressage competition had begun. The dust came from the horses prancing through their routines in a dry sandy arena.

Amanda was impressed with the haunting effect that it created and pointed her lens in that direction. She couldn't see much through her viewfinder as the screen was too small but she did notice some people climb into a white van, reverse onto the rocky track, and drive toward her.

The van bumped slowly under the trees, dust swirling around it as it weaved to avoid the crowd. She zoomed in on the van, kept it focused as it approached, panned with it as it turned the corner, and then held the shot as it headed down the hill and out of sight. As far as she was concerned, that was it. If people were leaving already, then it was time to go and interview some of the visitors and film the various attractions.

She turned and waved at the son to return with the ladder, but he was busy selling hats and T-shirts. She shouted, but he didn't answer, so sent a text, then re-packed her kit. She stood up gingerly and stretched and was bombarded with lighthearted offers to help her down but then her hero arrived.

The son barged his way through with the ladder.

"Excuse me, gentlemen," he shouted. "My girlfriend wants to come down."

They good-humoredly let him through, and Amanda was able to return to earth. She thanked him, smiled to herself, and headed down to the lower terrace to find some likely candidates to interview.

Three hours later, she was done, headed back to her car and returned to Málaga.

Back home, she emptied her backpack in her studio and started the download from the camera to the hard drive on her desktop. She grabbed a quick snack from the kitchen, settled down in front of her computer and when the download had completed began clicking through the days filming.

She picked out the most exciting clips of the procession and saved them to her editing software for later. Eventually, she came to the shot with the dust billowing over the tethered animals. She recalled the white van leaving and took a closer look at the moments before it reversed out and drove off.

What she saw, puzzled her. She ran the film again in slow motion.

A beautiful blond girl with a red rose in her hair, wearing a black, red dress with white polka dots, appeared to be arguing with two men on the far side of the van. The men had their faces partially hidden by cordoba hats and bandanas wrapped over their noses.

The girl appeared to cower away from the men. Then one of the men moved in close to the girl, his head jerking in a threatening manner forcing her toward the van. She looked terrified as the man placed his hand on top of her head and shoved hard.

The girl disappeared into the van.

Amanda watched in horror. "What am I seeing here?" she said out loud, as the man scrambled in after the girl. The other guy came round the back, climbed in, reversed out, and drove off. Amanda froze the frame when the van was at its nearest point to her camera. She noticed that there was a partition between the driver's seats and the back of the van, so she couldn't see any sign of the blond girl. The driver was still wearing his bandana and cordoba hat, so she couldn't see much of his face. A few variable color polka dots had been stuck on the side of the van, but there was nothing to identify its owner. Except that she had a crystal-clear shot of the number plate and the make; a Renault Kangoo.

Something nagged her. The van seemed familiar somehow.

She wondered if she'd filmed as it arrived with the procession. She went back to the beginning and fast framed her way through again. She couldn't see it anywhere, but hadn't filmed every vehicle, and had stopped twice to change batteries.

Amanda went back to her editing, added some voice-over, and saved the movie. She'd look at it one more time with fresh eyes early in the morning.

She stood, stretched, went through to the kitchen and rewarded herself with a glass of chilled Verdejo, took it out onto her terrace, sat down on her lounger, and reflected on the day.

Overall, she was pleased with her film. She'd integrated all the caves and festival elements and illustrated her *piety* and *party* theme quite well. Tomorrow, she would make a trailer, send it to her contacts, and wait to see who would bite.

She finished her wine, cleaned her teeth, and went to bed.

But the girl disappearing into that van nagged at her. She hadn't appeared to struggle, or scream. Was it a couple having a disagreement? She turned over and over, struggling to drop off. All kinds of nightmare scenarios danced around her head about what might have happened to the poor girl.

Eventually, she gave up, clambered out of bed and padded barefoot through to her study and recorded the abduction part of the film onto a memory stick. After her morning appointment, she'd take it to the nearest comisaría de policía. Maybe they could make something of it.

She put the stick in her bag, went back to bed and fell straight asleep.

16

Phillip strode down the slope to El Salon beach for his morning swim and was astounded to see a small group of boys in bathing costumes gathered around Didi as he went through his morning water-testing routine. He looked decidedly exasperated. As Phillip approached, he heard the youngsters bombarding Didi with questions about his thermometer. Didi pointed at Phillip with a sense of relief. The boys turned and ran toward him. He recognized them; they lived in the fisherman's cottages at the top of the beach.

"Hey, Mister," the eldest boy said in Spanish. "What's he doing?"

"Testing the water temperature," said Phillip.

"What's that thing he keeps dipping in the water?" said another child.

"It's a thermometer," said Phillip. "It tells him how warm the water is."

"Can't he tell from his foot?"

"He prefers a machine."

Didi stroked his mustache as he looked anxiously back and forth between Phillip and the children.

"What are you telling them?" he said.

"Relax, Didi, I'm explaining about the thermometer."

"Cheeky buggers, tell them to leave me alone."

"I don't think they'll take any notice. They live in the cottages and this beach is their playground. Why don't you show it to them, they've probably never seen one?"

"I don't like anyone touching my things."

"Come on Didi, loosen up. You'll help teach them

something they will never forget."

"Really?"

"They'll be telling the story at family gatherings for years. You'll be immortal."

Didi nodded and reluctantly held out his thermometer.

"OK, niños, who wants to see how it works?" said Phillip.

The four kids ran over to Didi, who even allowed them to pass round his precious gadget. Phillip slipped off his outer clothing and joined them at the water's edge. Didi bent down and showed the little ones how it worked while Phillip explained.

They were fascinated, and each took a turn at testing it. Didi held his hand against it and showed them how much higher the mercury went up the scale. They tried it on each other to a chorus of giggles, then took it in turns to test the water and run up to Didi to show him the gauge.

After a while, Didi declared that the sun had done its work and water was now officially warm enough for his swim. Phillip laughed as the kids accompanied Didi on his three-stroke out and back routine and then ran off back up the beach, mimicking his mustache stroking as they went.

"Was it so bad?" said Phillip.

"Actually, no," said Didi. "But I think I'll buy them a thermometer of their own."

"Great idea. How was San Isidro," said Phillip.

"I really enjoyed it," said Didi. "It was good to take photos for a change instead of wrestling with obdurate horseflesh."

"When are you off to Bremen?"

"We're leaving for the airport later this morning, no

time for coffee, I'm afraid."

"Then have a great summer."

"Thanks, we'll be back in the autumn; sooner if a buyer materializes for our villa."

Didi went off to the showers, Phillip dived in and sped out to his usual buoy.

After his swim, Phillip took his seat at the Don Comer regulars' table. Richard was already there chatting to Bruce, a young Australian guy who was the editor of a local English magazine. He was tapping his fingers impatiently on the table.

"Hi, Richard. Morning, Bruce," said Phillip.

"Gudday," said Bruce, glaring toward the café. "Service is damn slow this morning." He looked at his watch. "I'll have to go soon."

"Seconds later Manolo appeared with their respective orders. He was sweating and looked extremely harassed. "Sorry, gents, short-staffed this morning. Juliet hasn't shown up and won't answer her phone. I've had to call in one of my part-timers, but she hasn't arrived yet."

"That's worrying," said Phillip. "Yesterday morning, Juliet was upset about something. In the afternoon, she failed to show for a drink, and now she's missing from work. Perhaps there's a problem. When I've finished this, I'll go and check her apartment."

"I'd come with you," said Manolo. "But I can't leave the café. Let me know if she's all right."

"Me too," said Richard.

Phillip gulped down his breakfast, left payment on the table, and headed anxiously toward Calle Diputación. On the way, he called Juliet's number. It diverted straight to voicemail.

Hearing her voice refreshed his confused emotions

about her.

He arrived outside her apartment block harassed and anxious; he rang the bell. No response. He pressed several buttons, mumbled 'Amazon delivery' when one answered, was buzzed into the lobby and jogged up the stairs.

He arrived at her landing and knocked on the door, breathing hard. There was no response. He phoned her again, but, it still forwarded to voice mail. He put his ear to the woodwork and listened intently. Everything was quiet. Where the hell is she? He thought and turned the door handle. It was unlocked so he opened it a fraction.

"Juliet," he called through the gap. Nothing. "Juliet," he said again, this time louder. Silence.

He pushed the door wide open, peered inside and gasped in horror.

17

The meeting had gone well at the cruise ship advertising agency, except they'd altered much of the content for the summer cultural program. Amanda had to retranslate several pages of text on the spot so it was after ten o'clock when she arrived at the comisaría having had to skip coffee and breakfast.

She was feeling ratty and her stomach rumbled as she stood in line at the reception desk.

It was impossible not to overhear what the people ahead of her were saying to the portly desk sergeant who was brusque and unsympathetic. Most inquiries were curtly dismissed with a 'that's a civil matter, consult a solicitor or we don't send out patrol cars to look for missing parrots'.

His surly attitude planted seeds of doubt as the line shuffled slowly forward. Am I wasting their time? She asked herself. At last, it was her turn.

"Yes, Señora," said the sergeant not even looking at her.

"I witnessed what I believe to be an abduction at San Isidro in Nerja yesterday," she said. "I filmed it and would like to share it with a detective, please."

The sergeant scrutinized her through bloodshot eyes, sighed then said. "Why has madam waited until today to make a report; the abducted person could be in Timbuktu by now?"

"I realize that, but I saw the incident through my camera. It wasn't until late last night when I ran the film through on a larger screen that I noticed what had occurred. Would you like to see it first? Or are you going to make me drive all the way to the police in Nerja?"

The sergeant scowled, picked up the internal phone in front of him, prodded a few numbers, waited for a reply, and then spoke for several seconds before hanging up. "Someone will be down to see you;" he said. "Take a seat over there. Next."

"My roommate refuses to share the washing up," heard Amanda as she walked toward the row of cheap plastic chairs along the wall to the left of the lobby entrance. The sergeant's response was less than polite.

Amanda dug her phone out of her purse and checked her emails. She'd hardly started when she became aware of someone sitting down next to her.

"Any ideas how we can look at this film?" said a quiet male voice.

Amanda looked up to see a well-built middle-aged man with a smiling round face topped with silver hair. "I can show you on my laptop," she said. "But who are you?"

"Detective Inspector Prado. Foreigners' Crime Department."

"Amanda Salisbury."

"I'm here because our charming sergeant assumed that you were a foreigner. Not that your accent is noticeable, but do I detect a slight drawl. American perhaps?"

"Very astute of you inspector. I'm an American citizen, but have lived in Spain for most of my life."

"That would explain it. We'll go up to my office. This way, please?"

They went over to the elevator, up to the fourth floor, along a corridor, and into the detective's office where Prado showed Amanda to a visitor chair. She took her laptop out of her backpack, put it on his desk, fired it up and set the video playing. Prado watched over her shoulder.

"The white van at the back of the picture," said Amanda pointing at the screen. "There's a blond girl on the far side. What do you think of her expression?" Amanda froze the image.

"Seems frightened," said Prado thinking, oh no, not another missing girl but at last we might have our first physical clue to finding them.

"That's why I'm here."

"Could you show me the complete clip?"

They watched the two-minute film together, ending with a shot of the van's registration plate. Prado went to sit in his chair and opened up his laptop. He tapped the number into the national vehicle registry and waited a few seconds.

"Interesting," he said, looking over the monitor at Amanda. "There's no such vehicle. Do you mind if we have another run through?"

Amanda clicked back to the video, reset it, and pressed the play button.

"I thought so. Can you freeze that, please," said

Prado moments later, as they watched the van crawl past a shaggy-haired blond man with three children. "I know that guy. Perhaps, he heard or saw something. I'll call him." Prado went round to his side of the desk, sat back in his chair and picked up his mobile. He swiped through his contacts and pressed call.

"Phillip Armitage."

"Hola, Phillip," said Prado. "Leon Prado."

"Inspector, a pleasant surprise; how can I help?"

"First, let me say thank you for emailing those translations, but that's not why I'm calling. I'm in my office with an American lady who was filming a documentary at San Isidro in Nerja yesterday. She's showing me a video of what appears to be a blond girl being forced into a white van. Seconds afterward it drives slowly past you and your three daughters."

"Can I stop you there, Inspector?" said Phillip. "Actually, they're my nieces. However, this blond girl could well be a friend of mine who's disappeared. She didn't turn up to meet me at San Isidro yesterday and hasn't arrived at work today. Even more worrying is that I've just come out of her apartment. The door was unlocked, and it has been ransacked."

"Hold on, Phillip," said Prado, holding the phone away from his mouth. "Can we email this video to him?"

"Sorry, Inspector but it's a professional video. The file is way too large for my email server," said Amanda.

"In that case, could I borrow your device? I urgently need to show the film to Phillip. The blond girl could be a friend of his."

"I'd prefer not to let my machine out of sight," said Amanda. "It has my work stuff on it."

"Would you have time to meet us in Nerja?" said

Prado.

Amanda looked at her watch. Her next appointment was after lunch.

"It would have to be quick," she said.

"Fine, let me obtain the location details. Phillip," he said, speaking into his phone again. "Can you remain outside the apartment until a local officer arrives? I'll be there in an hour or so. What's the address?"

"Diputación, Two Hundred Sixty-Six, Flat Four A," said Phillip.

Prado entered the location into Google maps and shared it with her, then called his instructions through to the Guardia-Civil in Nerja. He picked up his hat, Amanda her gear and they left the office together.

Amanda's car was parked at a meter around the corner from the comisaría. She lowered herself in, and headed through the Tunel de Alcazaba, along Málaga's eastern promenade and out onto the coastal motorway. At the Frigiliana junction, she turned down off toward Nerja where she parked her car under Plaza España and walked to Diputación. A Guardia Civil car with flashing lights stood outside an apartment block about halfway along. She presented herself to the officer standing at the entrance and was told to go up.

She turned the final stairwell corner and went out onto the landing where she recognized the man from the video talking with Prado. He was taller than he appeared in the film and had incredible blue eyes. She smiled demurely and blinked as Prado introduced them. They shook hands.

An attractive man, she thought while digging her laptop out from her shoulder bag. She booted up her device, rested it on the banister, clicked on the video, and hit the play button. Phillip stood next to her and watched as the men push the blond girl into the van. Amanda could feel his body heat as he brushed against her bare arm. She jumped at his unexpected touch.

"Sorry," he whispered, watching the video and frowning.

He nodded and said. "It's her. It's Juliet." Putting his hand to his lips.

"Juliet what?" said Prado.

"Juliet Harding," said Phillip his eyes watering. "She looks terrified, Inspector. Is this what I think it is?"

Amanda patted his arm. Phillip acknowledged her concern.

"It definitely looks like an abduction," said Prado. "Let's see what her apartment holds in store?"

They moved to the open doorway and looked inside. Amanda gasped.

In the living room, the sofa was upside down and the material underneath had been slashed several times. The kitchen cupboards were open and in the bedroom, the wardrobe had been tipped over onto the double bed. Drawers had been removed from their chests, and their contents, mainly clothing, were scattered over the prostrate wardrobe.

A dusty backpack lay on the floor by the bed. Prado picked it up and peered inside. "It's empty," he said.

"Who could have done this?" said Phillip trying his best to control his emotions.

"My question is why?" said Prado. "Did she possess anything valuable?"

"Not that I know of," said Phillip.

"How long have you known her?" said Prado picking through the clothing.

"Coming up to three years," said Phillip.

"What can you tell me about her?" said Prado.

"Not much," said Phillip. "She would never talk about her previous life in England. I assumed that she wanted to forget about it."

"Any boyfriends?"

"She split from her Moroccan boyfriend recently, but yesterday morning, when I saw her briefly, she intimated that she was meeting a new friend at the caves gardens."

"Does Juliet speak Spanish?" said Amanda.

"Enough to do her work. She's a waitress at Café-Bar Don Comer on the Balcón by the church."

"Did you see her at the café yesterday?" said Prado.

"It was closed for the Festival, but I bumped into her as she was leaving her front door."

"How was she?" said Prado.

"She was upset by something. She refused to say what but did agree to talk about it. We tentatively made a date to meet at four o'clock in the cave bar, but she never showed. To be fair, she did say that she might not make it. Apparently, it depended on her friend's timing."

"Does she have a computer?"

"Yes, a laptop and a smartphone. I have her number if you want to check her caller records."

"Can you text it to me, please?"

Phillip extracted his phone from his pocket and forwarded the number to Prado.

There was a knock on the door and a woman popped her head in.

"This is Dr. Anna Galvez, our forensics officer," said Prado. "Do you mind waiting for me at Don Comer while we attempt to make something of this mess? I'll want to talk to Juliet's boss, and have more questions for both of you.

18

Amanda followed Phillip down the stairs and out past the officer guarding the door. The pavement was busy, so they walked quickly along the middle of the street past delivery trucks unloading pallets of drinks and foodstuffs for the many bars and restaurants in the area.

"I didn't spot you filming yesterday?" said Phillip in English as they approached Plaza Cavana.

"As you can see, there's not much to me," said Amanda, grinning.

"Nice things come in small parcels," said Phillip, trying to look cheerful.

"So does arsenic. Anyway, I was sitting on top of the wall by the gate into the cave. Your nieces managed to see me. They stuck their tongues out at me, and by the way, they're gorgeous."

"Little monkeys, sorry about that."

"Their mother apologized, your sister, I assume?"

"Yes, Glenda. Are you American or Canadian?"

As they walked along the alley on the south side of the church, they shared each other's backgrounds.

When they arrived at Don Comer, they went inside, perched on the comfortable bar stools, and waited for Manolo.

"Any sign of her?" he said, rushing behind the bar, drying his hands on a cloth.

"This is Amanda Salisbury," said Phillip. "Yesterday at the caves, she filmed Juliet being abducted by two men in a white van."

"Abducted?" said Manolo with tears in his eyes. "What the fuck?"

"Her apartment has also been ransacked," said Phillip. "The police are there now. The inspector wants to ask you a few questions. He'll be here shortly."

"I better warn Pepa, she's in the office. Back in a second."

"Coffee?" said Phillip.

"Double espresso, please, and I'm starving," said Amanda. "Do they serve *molletes*?"

"With garlic, olive oil, and grated tomatoes?"

"What else is there for a Spanish breakfast?" said Amanda.

"It's my favorite as well."

Manolo returned and noted down their order. They went outside and sat down at the regulars' table.

"This might sound terrible," said Amanda, "but I'm relieved that it was your friend in the video. The more I kept looking at the film, the less sure I was that she was being abducted. I worried that I was wasting police time."

"Well, thanks for reporting it, because now we know for certain."

"Let's hope the Inspector can find her quickly?"

said Amanda, touching his arm. "Does she mean a lot to you?"

"In many ways we're close, but in others, I hardly know her at all."

"Sorry to be so personal, but I sense that she was more than just a friend."

Phillip closed his eyes, a pained expression on his face.

Amanda patted him and said, "Forget I asked. It's none of my business."

Phillip's eyes snapped open. "No," he said. "It's good to have someone to share this with."

"I know how you feel," said Amanda, blushing.

"Two lonely souls?" said Phillip, touching her arm. "Look, I don't want to bore you, but my relationship with Juliet is complicated. I've only just returned from completing the Camino de Santiago where I was trying to sort my feelings out for her."

"A tad dramatic. Did it work?"

"Actually, yes. Until this morning I was doing fine, but her disappearance has set me back."

"Let me guess," said Amanda. "By the looks of her, she can't be much more than twenty and you're what?"

"Forty-three."

"So unless she has father issues, it's unlikely that she fancies you. Is that it, unrequited love?"

"That's what I used to think, but while I was clambering over hill and down dale, I realized that I had her confused with my ex-wife. Other than their age difference, their appearances were almost identical. But I've resolved all that now, I'm moving on and was anticipating… Why am I telling you all this?"

"I'm a journalist. It gets me into trouble all the time. What were you looking forward to?"

"Just being good friends with Juliet and enjoying her company rather than torturing myself," said Phillip. "Wait. There you go again. You must be brilliant at your job."

"I'd like to think so. But… er… sorry, Phillip. You have enough of your own problems, you don't want to hear mine."

Manolo served their coffees and Amanda's *mollete.* She tucked in straight away.

"What do you do other than film San Isidro?" said Phillip, warming to this petite spunky lady.

"I make video documentaries about anything to do with Spain. What about you?"

"Have you heard of Nuestra España?"

"Of course, I often borrow stuff from it for my scriptwriting. The history articles are excellent. Wait. It's your website, right?"

"With my business partner Richard, yes. He's also an American. From Boston, Massachusetts. Maybe we can help each other?"

"I urgently need a good website. Is that something you can handle?"

"Don't see why not."

"Then we should talk about it as soon as possible."

"Why don't I call you to arrange a lunch or something?"

"Cool, then let's exchange numbers."

Prado arrived just as they were sending contact details to each other.

"That didn't take as long as I thought," said Prado, sitting down next to Amanda. "The apartment has been stripped of everything personal. No photos, computer, phone, paperwork, or passport. They left just her clothes, and Anna reckons that some of those have also been taken. I left her checking for prints and DNA. Meanwhile, Juliet's picture has been circulated to all border controls and patrol cars throughout Andalusia."

"Any news on the van?" said Phillip.

"As yet, no van has been reported stolen," said Prado.

"Fuck," said Amanda. "Sorry, Inspector, but you talking about vans reminded me."

"Of what?" said Prado.

"I think I may have seen the driver of the van."

"But in the film, his face was covered," said Prado.

"Hang on a sec," said Amanda setting her laptop on the table and putting up two images of the van.

"What are we seeing here?" said Prado.

"The image on the left is from the caves, but the one on the right is from when I filmed Maro High Street and look, the numbers and the polka dots are identical."

"But there's no driver on the Maro image," said Prado.

"No, but I saw him as I was loading my backpack," said Amanda. "He was sticking the polka dots on."

"Can you recall his features?" said Phillip.

"Swarthy, unkempt black hair, dressed in scruffy festival clothing and hadn't shaved for a few days."

"What about his face?" said Prado. "Could you remember enough to help our artist with an Identikit sketch?"

"I can certainly try," said Amanda.

"Can you do it today?" said Prado.

"I could come to your office this evening," said Amanda.

"Great, then we can circulate it alongside Juliet's

photo. Phillip, did Juliet ever mention any relatives or do you know which area she lived in before coming to Spain? Only, I've spoken with the British Consul, who needs more information and her passport details before they can do anything."

"She came from the Birmingham area, but never mentioned any family," said Phillip.

"Great thanks. It's also possible that she may have gone back to the UK, so we're checking airlines, trains, and buses. Did you mention me to Manolo?"

"Yes, he's waiting for you inside with his wife, Pepa," said Phillip. "He may well have a copy of Juliet's passport in his safe. I understand that he organized her foreigner's number and work contract."

"In that case," said Prado. "I'll go talk to them now. Can you wait? I won't be a minute, but I need to ask you both something?"

They nodded. Prado went into the café.

Phillip said nothing; he felt dreadful, his emotions in turmoil. He slumped down into his chair and hid behind his coffee cup taking an occasional sip.

Amanda sensed his pain and left him to it while finishing her *mollete* and watching the tourists stroll about the Balcón.

Several minutes later, Prado exited the café and headed toward them. He was talking on his phone and was carrying a piece of paper in his free hand. He sat down next to Amanda, finished his call, folded the paper, and said, "You were right about the passport, Phillip." He waved the paper at him and then inserted it into his jacket pocket.

"Also," said Prado. "We've found the van."

"Where?" said Amanda.

"Parked illegally around the back of Málaga railway

station. It was towed at nine twenty this morning and is now in the police pound. Anna is on her way to check it out."

"That's great news," said Phillip. "

"Before she left Juliet's apartment, Anna identified Juliet's fingerprints and has found five more sets from different people. If we can cross-reference those with any found in the van, then we'll know it was the same people who trashed the apartment or not. By the way, we'll need yours, Phillip, for elimination purposes. Can you pop into the Guardia-Civil barracks and have them done as soon as you can?"

"Fine."

"One more thing," said Prado. "Manolo tells me that Juliet and Hassan were having some heavy arguments before he left for Nador, so we're going to have to interview him. My office is in contact with the Moroccan police to obtain his address and permission to talk with him.

"Now, what I wanted to discuss with you both is this. I've only recently been appointed to this new department. It focuses on crimes involving foreigners, either as victims, witnesses, or suspects. For this, I need volunteer translators to help with languages and elucidate on cultural differences. Would you be interested in donating your services?"

"It sounds fascinating," said Amanda. "I'd love to help out, so long as it doesn't interfere with my usual duties."

"Same here," said Phillip.

"Excellent, excellent," said Prado. "In that case, the visit with Hassan would be an ideal opportunity to test how this might work. I appreciate that three of us in attendance could be called heavy-handed for interviewing one suspect, but assuming we can make the arrangements, would you both be able to accompany me to Nador tomorrow morning. We'll fly over to Melilla and then cross the border, coming back the same day."

"I'll have to reorganize some appointments," said Amanda. "But that shouldn't cause too many problems, so yes, I'd be happy to."

"Then the first thing we should do is set up a WhatsApp group. We can all post updates, assumptions, and ideas about the case as we go about our daily business. Shall we exchange numbers?"

Prado invited them both to the group, and they accepted.

"I need you to email me copies of your passports so we can book the tickets," said Prado. "And listen, thank you both for giving something back to your adopted country. Rest assured, that while we may not be able to pay you, we will reimburse any expenses you incur on our behalf. OK, that's it for now. I'll see you tomorrow."

Prado went inside to pay the bill and waved as he headed off in the direction of his car parked on Diputación.

"Another coffee?" said Phillip.

"One per day is my limit. Otherwise, I'm bouncing off the walls all night," said Amanda. "I'll take some water, though."

Phillip raised his hand, and Manolo's wife, Pepa, came to take their order. Pepa was a friendly woman with a warm smile and big heart. She was woefully thin with spindly short gray hair and a nose to beat all noses, but she was well presented and elegant in the bottle-green uniform of the café. She sat down next to Phillip and said. "Are you guys helping the cops with Juliet's abduction?"

"Yes," said Phillip. "There are likely to be several languages involved."

"Who do you think has taken Juliet?"

"Too soon to say yet," said Amanda.

"What did Prado ask you?" said Phillip.

"He wanted to know about Hassan, any relatives of Juliet and also what we were doing at the time of her abduction."

"What did you tell him?" said Amanda.

"I told him about the huge row Hassan and Juliet had just before he left for Nador."

"I hadn't heard about that," said Phillip.

"You were gallivanting up north at the time. It was here in the café. Hassan was shouting so loudly that I had to ask him to leave," said Pepa.

"What were they arguing about?" said Amanda.

"He wanted her to go with him to Nador, but she wasn't interested," said Pepa.

"I can understand that," said Amanda. "It would be difficult for her to adjust to living his way of life in Nador."

"Juliet's point exactly," said Pepa.

"Is it possible that Hassan might have taken her?" said Amanda.

"His parting words were, 'I'll be back for you'," said Pepa.

"So that's why Prado wants to talk to him," said Phillip.

"Did you want to order anything?" said Pepa.

"I'll have another coffee, Amanda will take a water sin gas."

"Coming right up," said Pepa and headed toward

the bar.

"Have you been to Melilla or Nador before?" said Amanda.

"No. You?"

"Never."

"I'm looking forward to it."

"Me too."

Pepa served their drinks, leaned on the back of a chair, and said, "There's something else that worries me about Juliet. In all the time I've known her, she's never mentioned her life in England. I've asked her about it on several occasions, but she just changes the subject. After a while, I gave up, and I think she appreciated that. However, on the eve of San Isidro, she received a call that upset her dreadfully. She was at the bar when it came, answered it curtly, turned white, and ran into the restroom. I went in to check on her and could hear her vomiting and then sobbing her heart out. When she came out, she swore viciously, and I've never heard her do that before."

"What did she say," said Phillip.

"Fucking families," said Pepa.

19

Phillip escorted Amanda back to her car under Plaza España, exchanged cheek kisses, and went their separate ways. Phillip stood and watched her reverse out and drive off. As she turned the corner toward the ticket machine she turned to him, waved and smiled tenderly.

He nodded and grinned back. Somehow, in such a brief acquaintance, this petite stranger had touched his soul and his pain over Juliet seemed more bearable. He descended to the second floor, turned the BMW's roof down, and drove up the Frigiliana Road to his villa.

After a light supper on his terrace, Phillip went into his study with a glass of Verdejo and sat down in the comfortable Eames leather soft-pad chair at his Herman Miller workstation. He'd purloined them from his office in London as a farewell present to himself.

He cast his eyes over his beloved gadget collection before turning on his Mac. He was an avid fan of anything 'techie', particularly Apple computers, and kept every machine he had ever owned on wall-mounted shelves. They represented a personal reminder to his former career, and rat-race contributions. There were also some rare models he'd picked up on eBay, including the original Apple M0001, a remarkable machine bearing in mind it only had 128K of RAM. He also had the original Sinclair Spectrum ZX eight-bit computer given to him by his father one Christmas. They used to play Pac-Man on it together; it still worked perfectly.

He sat down and did some general web searches for Nador and Melilla. He wanted to know more about where he was going tomorrow.

The Spanish enclave of Melilla covers 12.3 square kilometers of the northeastern coast of Morocco. It has a population of seventy-eight thousand people, mixed between Spanish, Berber, Jew, and Hindu. It has been an impregnable stronghold since Phoenician times when they developed it as a staging post for their trading ships.

When Spain became a nation united under the Catholic monarchs in 1492, they worried that the Moors might use Melilla as a stronghold to amass an army and invade Spain. In 1497 they dispatched troops to capture it from the Berbers and it has been in Spanish hands since.

In the mid-nineteenth century, when nation-states were defining precise borders between themselves, the Spanish negotiated with the then Berber emir who controlled the surrounding land. They came to an unusual accord on how to determine where the border should be. A cannon would be fired from the center of Melilla castle. Wherever the cannonballs landed would be the frontier—hence it's semicircular shape.

The route from Melilla to Nador is via the border town of Beni Ansar with a population of some 56,000. Nador itself is more significant with 160,000-odd inhabitants. It's a fifteen-minute drive east along a straight road from the border. On Google Earth, Phillip saw that the Nador seafront was a long elegant palm-tree-lined boulevard running along the shore of an enormous lagoon, which the Spanish refer to as La Mar Chica (mermaid). It's protected by a sandbank through which there is only one passage to the open sea. It's renowned for its natural beauty, flora, and fauna.

Now he'd visualized tomorrow's destination, Phillip was curious about his beautiful traveling companion.

He searched 'Amanda Salisbury, Spain'. The top result took him to a section of video documentaries about Spain on the CNN website. He browsed through them. The most popular was the Festival, San Fermin in Pamplona. Phillip clicked the play button.

Amanda appeared, wearing the traditional festival clothing: running shoes, a white blouse and pants, red neck scarf, and black belt. She had a chest camera fitted between her breasts. She introduced the beautiful city in northern Spain, showed the giant figures in the procession and the topless girls bathing themselves in bulls' blood before switching to an interview with an experienced bull runner.

Fernando was a man in his forties who had survived over twenty attempts at running in front of the bulls as they traversed the sand-covered streets that led to the bullring. He described his fears and the tricks that he'd learned and insisted that it was not that dangerous, provided you were relatively fit, sober, and aware of what could go wrong. He explained that most deaths happened to drunken testosterone-fueled idiots pushing the boundaries to impress their stupid friends. Occasionally, they fell and tripped over other runners, which jammed up the street and prevented the bulls from making forward progress. It terrified the poor beasts, and they lashed out with horns and feet to protect themselves. Nowadays, marshals rode along with the bulls on horseback to try and prevent these numbskulls from spoiling the run for everybody else. Fernando finished by inviting Amanda to run along with him.

Amazingly, Amanda agreed.

Phillip's heart raced at the prospect of watching her. What followed was a hair-raising film of Fernando's muscular backside as he ran in front of and alongside the bulls. The film was packed with scary moments but the most terrifying was when one mean-looking black bull swerved directly in front of Fernando, but he managed to avoid a collision, overtook the beast at the first opportunity, and settled into a more secure position some five meters in front of the leading animal. Amanda kept pace easily with Fernando. Her rapid panting on the soundtrack mixed with the deafening encouragement by the dense crowds emphasized the thrill of the chase. Phillip found himself on the edge of his seat until they reached the safety of the bullring and the animals were herded away. Amanda thanked Fernando breathlessly, and the film ended.

There were more clips of Amanda participating in classic Spanish festivals. She was covered in tomatoes at the Tomatina in Buñol in eastern Spain. She wore the chest camera again, climbing to the top of a human tower, or Casteller, in Barcelona, dressed in a red silk shirt, white pants, and a black cummerbund.

"What an extraordinary woman?" Phillip said out loud. "She might be small, but she sure packs a powerful punch."

He checked the viewing stats of her CNN films and was surprised at the low numbers. He assumed that this was down to the fact that they were buried deep in the CNN website. They would be more visible on Nuestra España. He emailed Richard the video links and then called him on Skype a few minutes later.

"Have you seen the bull running?" he said.

"Ye, gods. What a woman. Who is she?" said Richard.

"Amanda Salisbury. She filmed Juliet being abducted. I met her this morning with Inspector Prado. We're working with him on Juliet's case, and tomorrow we're off to Morocco to interview Hassan."

"Well, look at you, Mr. Gadabout. Any news on the case?"

Phillip brought him up to date.

"I'd like to meet this Amanda," he said. "She should be working with us."

"Our advertisers would love her films."

"Won't they just. Can you persuade her?"

"We've agreed to have dinner."

"Just the diversion you need."

"That's what I thought, assuming I'm not too long in the tooth."

"Nonsense, smart women go for the more mature, understanding type."

"Fingers crossed. I'm going to call her now to fix a date."

"That's my boy."

They cut the link. Phillip closed down his machine,

topped up his wine, and called Amanda.

"Hola, Phillip," she said.

"Hi, Amanda, I'm calling to make a date to discuss websites and stuff. When are you free?"

"Not until the weekend. Is that all right?"

"Of course. Hopefully, we'll have resolved this Juliet thing by then."

"As you say, hopefully. Where shall we meet?"

"How about halfway? Torre del Mar, for example, It's marvelous for seafood restaurants. I assume you like fish?"

"Are egg yolks yellow?"

"Then how about Restaurante El Yate? It's delightful."

"Good choice, I know it. See you there Saturday at nineish."

"I'll bring my tablet so we can play at websites after dessert."

"I normally prefer coffee," said Amanda, laughing, and ended the call.

Phillip went into the lounge, turned on the TV, and flicked through the news channels expecting to see an item about Juliet but there was nothing.

He turned the TV off, sat back on his sofa, sipping his wine, and examined his feelings for Juliet. While he remained desperate to find her, he realized that he was thinking more rationally about her. His heart no longer raced, and the confusion in his head was clearing. Were his post-pilgrimage rules working, or was the arrival of Amanda on the scene diluting his obsession? He put his empty wine glass in the dishwasher, set it running, and went to bed.

20

The newly formed team convened in departures just after nine-thirty the next morning at Starbucks in Málaga airport's terminal three. Prado had posted their itinerary on WhatsApp and emailed their boarding passes the previous evening. They had made their way independently through security.

Amanda was already in the queue, dressed in loose black pants and a light-gray long-sleeve blouse, her glossy locks tied up in a french plait. She wore no makeup or jewelry, but carried a shoulder bag containing her camera and the usual feminine essentials. Phillip and Prado arrived almost together. She took their requests, and they went to find a table. Phillip wore chinos, a polo shirt and carried a shoulder bag containing his laptop—and phone. Prado was in a smart beige suit, Panama hat, and carried a brown leather briefcase.

"No hijib?" said Phillip, as Amanda arrived with coffees and hot butter croissants.

"It's hijab, and no; just because my mother is a Muslim doesn't make me a believer. What about you?"

"Headscarves aren't quite my thing."

"You know what I mean," she said.

"No, I'm not religious. How about you, Inspector?"

"Only when I have to be for family events. You know, the usual Spanish obligations we have in our extended families: baptisms, first communions, weddings, etc. But otherwise, I don't have the time or the inclination. I guess it goes with the job. Not too many of my customers ask forgiveness before smashing a granny over the head for her gold teeth. Listen, before we go to the gate, I want to bring you up to date with the investigation and share our thoughts about the abductors'."

"We found strands of Juliet's hair in the van, plus prints on the steering wheel and the sliding door. They'd made no attempt to clean up after them, which I thought was terrific news until none of them matched with any known European criminals. We've extended the search globally, but that will take a few days. The prints on the van's sliding door were also found in Juliet's apartment, which leads us to suspect that the driver stayed with the vehicle while the other guy broke in.

"We also found a receipt from a stationery shop on Calle Jaen where they purchased the materials to make the polka dots. The transaction took place that morning at ten-twenty, and they paid in cash. We're making inquiries there to see if anyone remembers anything or has them on camera. Hopefully, your artist's sketch will prompt their memory. What time did you see the driver in Maro?"

"Must have been around eleven," said Amanda.

"Or just after. When do you think they ransacked the apartment?"

"Probably around one-thirty to two o'clock when the procession and crowds had dispersed."

"How did they break in?" said Phillip.

"The lock is a flimsy affair and was easily forced open. By the scratches on the bolt and the marks on the door frame, forensics thinks it was a screwdriver."

"Have you traced the van's owner?" said Phillip.

"It belongs to a plumber who lives opposite Málaga train station. He'd been off sick for three days and only discovered his loss when our officers knocked on his door yesterday morning. The original number plates were in the back of the van. The ones they'd used were taken from an abandoned vehicle near the station. They'd stuck some black tape on the F to make it look like an E."

"What about CCTV?" said Phillip.

"The only cameras were monitoring the station concourse and the man you saw matches over eighty percent of Spanish males, so we had to look closely at nearly all the men on the screen. We saw loads of guys like him, but not one that was close enough."

"Anything in the van?" said Amanda.

"The cordoba hats, red bandanas, and Juliet's dress with the rose and her black leather shoes. This suggests to me that they forced her to change into whatever clothing they'd taken from her apartment and she is now dressed entirely differently. We've had roadblocks out during the night and are watching all exit routes from Málaga Province, but so far nothing. I've released Juliet's picture to press and TV stations. They ran the story last night and again throughout today."

"Yes, I saw it," said Amanda.

"Me too," said Phillip. "What about Juliet's phone?"

"We've attempted to trace it, but they must have removed the battery and SIM card. The last signal emitted was near the abduction site. However, I do have her phone records. My office is working its way through the local calls, but there is one from England on the eve of San Isidro. Phillip, would you mind calling the number please?"

Prado dug into his case, extracted a slip of paper, and gave it to Phillip along with his phone. Phillip dialed the number on the paper. It was answered on the second ring.

"Rosemary Kitson," said a woman with a faint Birmingham accent.

"I'm sorry to disturb you," said Phillip. "I'm calling on behalf of the police in Málaga, Spain, concerning a Miss Juliet Harding."

"The Spanish police?" said Rosemary. "Has something happened to Juliet?"

"Before I tell you, I need to confirm your relationship with her."

"I'm her aunt. Her parents are deceased."

"Then I'm sorry to tell you that Juliet was abducted yesterday."

"Oh no; that was her worst nightmare."

"Why?"

"I'm sorry, Mr.?"

"Armitage, Phillip Armitage."

"Your name sounds familiar. Look, I'm sorry, but I'm not going to tell you anything over the phone," said Rosemary. "What I am prepared to do, though, is jump on the next plane to Málaga and tell Juliet's story directly to the police. Can I call you when my plane is due and could you pick me up from the airport?"

"Yes, but this a police phone, and they don't speak English. I'll text you my number after we hang up."

"Thank you, Mr. Armitage."

"Phillip, please."

Phillip ended the call and related the content to the others while texting his mobile number to Rosemary.

"Intriguing," said Prado.

"A new dimension to the case?" said Amanda.

"Let's hope we're back from Melilla by the time she lands," said Phillip.

"So, now we have two possible scenarios," said Prado. "Perhaps one of them will lead us to Juliet. Shall we go and see what Hassan has to say?"

21

The Iberia Airways propeller-powered Consorcio landed promptly in Melilla airport, which also doubles as a Spanish airforce base. The team disembarked onto the apron directly in front of the airport terminal building. The surrounding Rif Mountains were covered in haze. The heat and humidity were noticeably more uncomfortable now they were on the African continent. They walked quickly into the modern glass-and-concrete two-story building, through the arrivals hall, and out onto the front steps where a police patrol car was waiting to take them to the frontier.

"Buenos dias," said the young uniformed driver opening the doors for them. "Please get in."

They climbed aboard with Prado in the front and the driver headed out onto the main road. "Welcome to Melilla," he said. "My name is Zori. That's short for Zorion."

"Basque, right?" said Amanda.

"Impressive Señora," said Zori looking back at her

in the river's mirror. "My father moved here from Bilbao over thirty years ago to work on the ferries."

As they headed in the direction of the Moroccan frontier post, they drove past a shabby-looking building near the golf course where dozens of poorly dressed people were milling about or cooking over open fires. "It's a refugee center," said Zori. "Until we and the Moroccans reinforced the fence, it was terribly overcrowded. Now it's slowly emptying as their asylum applications are processed. Thankfully, they will all be gone soon."

"Are any of them allowed to stay?" said Amanda.

"We don't have enough space for ourselves," said Zori. "So most are deported, but actually none of them want to stay in Melilla. They treat it as a staging post on their way to Europe's big cities where they can easily blend in and work illegally."

There was a long queue on both sides of the frontier, where customs officers were opening the trunks of every vehicle. There were a few foreign tourists, but most were Moroccans driving an assortment of battered cars and vans. They crossed the border daily to purchase processed foods such as yogurt or consumer goods. On the way in, they delivered fresh meat, fruit, and vegetables. This interdependence contributed to both communities' survival. There was no space in Melilla to grow anything in volume, and in Nador, no technology for processing foods.

Zori drove alongside the queue and parked up in front of the Spanish control-post. "I'll leave you here and pick you up later to return you to the airport," said Zori. They clambered out of the car and approached the post. Prado showed his police ID to an officer who beckoned to a colleague in civilian clothes.

"Good morning, Inspector Prado," said the officer. "I'm Inspector Sanz. I'm taking you directly to the Royal Moroccan Gendarmerie office. I'll leave you in their capable hands and escort you back over the frontier on your return. Please have your passports ready for inspection."

They walked over the Spanish frontier and into the narrow stretch of land between the two countries. A uniformed Gendarme approached them as they neared the Moroccan side. He and Sanz were apparently well acquainted and exchanged friendly greetings in Arabic. The Gendarme took a cursory look at their passports and said, in Spanish, "Follow me." They crossed the frontier and dodged through the traffic queue to the Gendarmerie and stopped outside the entrance. "Wait here," said the Gendarme, disappearing through a grubby door.

Crowds of disfigured beggars and women carrying babies with extended bellies swarmed around them, holding out their hands. Prado threw a few coins further along the potholed road, and they scrambled after them squabbling among themselves. Minutes later, a short, thin, middle-aged policeman, dressed in a uniform of a white shirt, dark-blue trousers, and a peaked baseball cap, came out. A pistol was attached to his belt, along with radio and handcuffs. He carried a silver-topped cane in one hand and wore a chest camera.

"Good morning," he said in Spanish. "I am Lieutenant Dahmanias and will be your escort for the day. To avoid any misunderstandings, my camera is on and will be recording your visit. Follow me, please."

Dahmanias led them along the street at a quick pace

brushing aside any beggars with his stick. They turned down a narrow, filthy alley toward a battered, old Peugeot in Gendarmerie livery parked on the roadside at the end. The uniformed driver, sporting a broad grin of rotten teeth, climbed out, saluted, and held the door effusively for the lieutenant, who sat in the front. The team squashed into the back, and before they'd had time to fix seat belts, the Peugeot lurched off at high speed, leaving a cloud of dust behind.

The old car moved far too quickly for Beni Ansar's bumpy roads, which were teeming with Moroccans dressed in grubby white kaftans and walking in the middle of the road oblivious to the policeman's erratic driving. Phillip closed his eyes and reconsidered religion. Somehow, nobody was run over.

The differences between Beni Ansar and Melilla were notable. The sides of the road were jammed with traders and their piles of goods stacked precariously, selling everything from Heinz Ketchup to clothing, electrical products, and the ubiquitous Coca-Cola. Buyers swarmed around, hunting bargains and haggling. The buildings were dilapidated and basic. Malnourished half-dressed children stared down at them from behind barred openings with no glass. They might only be a few meters from Europe, but this was third-world stuff at its worst.

Nador wasn't much better. The white-painted three and four-story stucco buildings that lined the boulevard were well maintained. They were nicely designed with an assortment of towers and Moroccan arches, decorated with ceramic tiles bearing Islamic patterns, but the streets behind were not so attractive. Rows of unmade cluttered roads were lined with unpainted buildings many unfinished. Half-built sidewalks provided access to walled houses, apartment blocks, and a variety of businesses that obviously weren't thriving.

"Hardly any work here," said Dahmanias as they passed. "It's why more than half of our people go overseas. The money they send back keeps those who remain alive; just."

Halfway along the promenade, the driver slowed down a fraction and swerved into the car park of Hotel La Plage with a screech of tires and burning rubber. They clambered out, relieved about their survival and followed the lieutenant into the cool air-conditioned, marble-clad lobby of the hotel. It was furnished with leather sofas, chrome, and glass coffee tables, wall-mounted uplighters. Giant ferns in terracotta pots completed the modern interior design.

"The hotel belongs to the Labrat family," said Dahmanias. "They cater to the wealthy Moroccans living in northern Europe, who regularly come to visit their families. Hassan Labrat lives and works here. He's expecting us."

They went over to the reception, where Dahmanias announced their arrival. A porter dressed in a spotless white kaftan appeared and escorted them to Hassan's office. He took them over to the chrome fronted elevator, where they ascended to the fourth and top floor, along a corridor, and through a full-height wooden door. They entered a spacious square room with sliding glazed doors that opened out onto a marble-tiled terrace with panoramic views over La Mar Chica. A sofa and comfortable armchairs arranged around a glass coffee table were in the center of the room. A large rosewood desk surrounded by an assortment of office chairs stood in the far corner.

Behind the desk sat a dark-haired, olive-skinned, good-looking young man in his late twenties, dressed in a dark-charcoal-gray suit and white open-necked shirt. Phillip recognized Hassan, who stood up, came round to the front of the desk and shook hands with everyone.

Hassan indicated that they should sit around the coffee table. They took their seats and waited while the porter served mint tea. When everyone had a full cup, Hassan said assuredly in Spanish, "A warm welcome to my family's hotel. Phillip, nice to see you again. Lieutenant Dahmanias has informed me that Juliet has been abducted and you wish to eliminate me from your inquiries."

"Thank you for your friendly greetings and kind hospitality," said Prado. "Could you tell us about your relationship with Juliet, how it ended, and where you were on the fifteenth of May?"

"With pleasure, Inspector," said Hassan, still oozing confidence. "Juliet and I were together for some two years. I met her at Don Comer, on a break from my work as an assistant manager in Hotel Cavana. We hit it off, started dating, and became very fond of each other. We were two lonely people caring for and supporting each other in a foreign country. We had common gripes about low pay and not fulfilling our potential, but we were both improving our languages and learning about another culture. We were happy."

"Did she talk about her life in England?"

"She mentioned an Aunt Rosemary from Kenilworth, whom she adored. They spoke from time-to-time, but she never shared any news with me. When I pressed her for more detail, she would shake her head and change the subject. On its own, I wouldn't have read too much into it, but with that and the unusual physical side of our relationship, it led me to believe she had a painful childhood. She was terrified of intimacy, and we never went beyond kissing and hugging. She justified her condition by saying she was asexual, had no desire, and admitted to being a virgin. Consequently, I never once saw her naked and we never made love.

"Over time, though, I came to suspect that the asexuality was an excuse to conceal something much darker. I think that she'd been abused. I asked her about it once, and her reaction was horrendous. She sat on the floor for hours in a catatonic state, rocking back and forth. That was the last time I tried to encourage her to let all out, for which she seemed most grateful. It took a while for me to accept her as she was, but we enjoyed each other's company tremendously. Juliet is a lovely girl, and I miss her dreadfully."

"Why did you come back to Nador at such short notice?" said Prado.

"My father had a stroke. As the eldest son, it falls upon me to take over the family responsibilities until he recovers."

"How is he?" said Phillip.

"He's alive, but unlikely to recover enough to take back the reins," said Hassan.

"Sorry about that," said Prado. "Tell me about the argument."

"It's very simple, Inspector. I wanted her to come with me; she didn't. That enraged me, and I said some stupid things in the heat of the moment. When I arrived here, I realized that Juliet was right. She could never adjust to how we do things here. Reluctantly, I accepted that and moved on with my life."

"Thank you. I'd like to see your passport," said Prado.

"Certainly," said Hassan, standing up and going to a drawer in his desk, where he extracted a green-covered document and handed it to Prado.

Prado looked at it carefully, turning the pages and checking the date stamps.

"OK, so you haven't left the country since your return from Nerja," said Prado, irritated. "But you could still have arranged Juliet's abduction, smuggled her illegally into Morocco, and have her locked up in a garage somewhere."

"Indeed, I could, Inspector. However, if that was the case, I would need to feed her on a regular basis, which means that I would have to abandon the hotel three times a day or have it done by trusted staff. In either case, my mother, who watches me like a hawk, would know that I am up to something. Believe me when I say that you cannot lie to my mother. Nobody can.

"Furthermore, if she suspected that I was harboring any feelings for a non-Muslim girl, my life would be hell. I would lose her love and respect, be banished from my position here, and ostracized by my siblings. Inspector, I couldn't do that to my family just for a few stolen celibate moments with a beautiful English girl. I'd be stupid."

"Could we meet your mother and have her confirm this?" said Prado.

"Of course, she's waiting in the next room. She's still worried about my father, so please respect that," said Hassan, picking up the telephone on his desk, punching in a few numbers, speaking in what sounded like Arabic, and hanging up.

Prado looked at Amanda with raised eyebrows. She shook her head. She hadn't understood a word.

A few seconds later, a distinguished, senior woman, dressed in traditional Moroccan clothing and a hijab, appeared at the door.

"This my mother, Fatima," said Hassan. "Between our families, we speak in Tarifit, the Northern Moroccan version of the Berber language spoken in this region. She wishes you all peace. You may ask her anything. Lieutenant Dahmanias will translate."

It only took a few moments for Prado to satisfy himself that Hassan's mother ruled her family with an iron rod and that Hassan was telling the truth. Aside from that, common sense persuaded him that to stash a white blond girl in a nearby secure place without someone noticing would be almost impossible. The only exception would be if a wealthy sheik had hidden Juliet in his palace harem, and that seemed too fantastic in this impoverished region. However, he thought it politic to consult with Phillip and Amanda before making a final decision.

They withdrew into the corridor.

"What do you think?" said Prado.

"Not guilty," said Phillip.

"With a mother like that, he'd be roasted for even thinking of bringing Juliet here," said Amanda.

"Agreed," said Prado. "Let's say good-bye."

They reentered the room.

"For the moment, Mr. Labrat," said Prado, "we're satisfied with your explanation, so thank you and your mother for your time and the refreshments. Lieutenant, we're ready to go now."

Just as they were about to shut the door behind them, Hassan called out, "Sorry, Inspector, wait, please. There's one more thing that might help you find Juliet."

They paused and turned back to Hassan. Prado raised his eyebrows.

"In the heat of my argument with Juliet, I said that she would regret me leaving. She would be on her own, and I knew she hated the thought of that. Surprisingly, she didn't seem bothered and said not to worry, she already had a new friend lined up to replace me."

"A new friend?" said Prado, eyebrows raised.

"She told me he was an estate agent and apparently looked nothing like me—whatever that meant," said Hassan.

"Did you believe her?" said Prado.

"Juliet never lied, she just avoided the truth when it suited her. That's why I found her words, particularly painful. I felt she was being cruel to me and I didn't deserve that. They also made me insanely jealous, which is why I threatened to come back for her."

"That I can understand. Anything else?" said Prado.

"One more thing," said Hassan. "This was always her worst nightmare."

"What do you mean?" said Prado.

"She was paranoid about being taken," said Hassan. "She never said why, but I always suspected something about her past constantly haunted her. I think that's why she came to Nerja in the first place. She said she felt safe here, particularly on Playa El Salon and was always at her happiest when we were down there."

"Thanks, Hassan. That will be all."

They stood, shook hands and left Hassan being harassed by his mother.

As the police car hurtled almost on two wheels around a sharp curve on the way back to the frontier,

Phillip's phone buzzed. It was a text from Rosemary Kitson.

She hoped to be landing in Málaga midafternoon, only minutes after they did. Phillip confirmed that they would be waiting for her. She sent her photo by return.

Oh no, thought Phillip, looking at it. She's an older version of Juliet. He showed the screen to Prado, who nodded and shrugged. Then to Amanda, who smiled at him, put her hand on *his* thigh, and petted it.

"Phillip," said Prado as they settled into their seats for the return flight. "What Hassan said at the end there about Juliet's paranoia of being taken. Did she show any signs to you?"

"Not that I noticed, but he was right about El Salon, she loved it down there."

"Aha," said Prado rubbing his earlobe. "Her estate agent new friend that Hassan referred to. Could this be the same friend that she was meeting at San Isidro?"

"Could be, but I never heard her mention an estate agent," said Phillip.

"What about your regulars' table at the café. Any estate agents among them?" said Prado.

"Come to think of it, no, not a single one. I obviously know most of the Nerja agents, they're customers of ours, but they rarely come to the café; they're always too busy."

"It's a bit of a long shot," said Prado. "But could you make a list of possible agents in the area?"

"All of them?"

"No. Let's assume male," said Prado. "English speaking and under thirty-five."

"I'll work on it with Richard. It'll be a long list though, at least two hundred."

"Well, that is better than our current status of no

fucking list," said Prado.

"Good point. Any other interesting numbers in Juliet's phone?"

"No," said Prado. "Just the typical domestic assortment and a couple of girlfriends."

22

They landed in Málaga on schedule, went straight through baggage reclaim and into the arrival hall. When they checked the display board, Kitson's plane had been delayed by an hour. Amanda couldn't hang around that long as she had an urgent appointment with the director of the Picasso Museum. They exchanged cheek kisses, and she left, walking quickly toward the short-term car park.

Phillip and Prado watched her go.

"Lovely girl," said Prado.

"Mmm…" said Phillip.

"When you clear your head from this obsession with Juliet, she could be all yours," said Prado.

"That's damned astute of you."

"You wear your heart on your sleeve, any cop could see."

"Do you think Amanda spotted it as well?"

"Women have instincts for such matters."

"Oh, fuck. I'm a complete fool."

"I didn't sense any bad vibes about it on her part."

"Let's hope so."

Prado and Phillip walked over to the café in the arrival hall, ordered coffees from the counter, and sat down at a table.

"Something is puzzling me," said Phillip after taking a sip of his drink.

"Tell me."

"Abducting Juliet in broad daylight. Don't you think that smacks of desperation?"

"I agree; normally abductions happen after dark or at least in a less public location."

"Some deadline, maybe?"

"Possibly?"

"Could it be that Juliet knew those men?"

"To me, she looked frightened, not showing signs of familiarity."

"Girls don't willingly climb into vehicles with unknown men. If she was frightened, why didn't she scream or run?"

Prado chewed over Phillip's observation. "A scream would have been wasted. With all the loud music; who would hear?"

"Isn't screaming an instinctive reaction to danger, regardless of other surrounding noises?"

"Usually, yes, but Amanda's film didn't show everything that was going on. Juliet was on the far side of the van, only her head and shoulders were visible over its roof. Perhaps the men used a weapon or had threatened her in some way. Whatever the reasons for her compliance, she did climb into the van and has not been seen since. Regretfully, she's not the first."

"Are there many abductions?"

"Juliet is the tenth in the last six months and that's

just in Málaga province. Plus, there was a kidnapping."

"Why haven't I heard about these on the news?"

"Good point. I haven't told you this but my bosses are reluctant to broadcast this until we have some evidence. I'm hopeful that with Amanda's video, we can at last go public."

"Scared of damaging tourism?"

"Correct."

"What happens to these girls?"

"Fodder for our expanding sex industry."

"And you think that is why Juliet has been abducted?"

"It's unlikely to be for her ironing skills. Let me give you some background. It'll help you put things in context, and if we are to be working together, I think it's essential that you understand what's going on with one of the leading crime genres here on the Costa del Sol.

"For decades, our guaranteed weather and low-cost beach holidays have attracted millions of family holidaymakers during the peak seasons of Christmas, Easter, and summer. The rest of the year, it used to be relatively quiet. Over the last decade, we've been inventing new ways to fill the low season gaps, so that we have more efficient use of our resources all year round.

"I have to say that the marketing guys have done an excellent job. We are now the largest golf destination in the world and amazingly carry out more cosmetic-surgery operations than California. Apparently, they call them sun-and-sculpture breaks. We also offer walking holidays in the mountains, soccer training academies, athletics training, diving, yachting, culinary schools, cultural programs, I could go on. The one thing they have in common is that all these new activities have been successful. The outcome has been a massive increase in tourist numbers.

"While all this was happening and not spotted by most of us, was the massive growth of Internet pornography. Lightning download speeds may well have improved the overall browsing experience, but they have also created a considerable demand for freshly made, high-quality porn clips. Previously, these were produced in studios, but with the technological advances in recording equipment, that has changed. All filmmakers need nowadays is the latest gear, a few shapely models, and an isolated villa with a pool. With those, they can churn out new footage all year round with practically zero studio or technician costs.

"Consequently, the web is jammed with porn made in Spain, and it's had a substantial effect on sex tourism. All those naughty outdoor snippets set in our gorgeous landscapes have advertised the area to porn fans. Now they're coming here for the real thing in droves. So much so that the Costa del Sol has just overtaken Amsterdam as Europe's hottest destination. Every day, thousands of men arrive at Málaga airport, particularly from your country, looking for a good time. Some are in groups, such as stag parties, golfers, drinkers, soccer teams, tiddlywinks players, etc. But most come in ones and twos."

"I had no idea. Where do they go?"

"Mainly, Marbella and Puerto Banus, but all the west coast towns are seeing massive increases in sex tourism."

"Local businesses must be delighted."

"There are mixed feelings about it. They like the money, but not the mess and damage. As you know

Brits can be pretty disgusting when tanked up with a mix of fancy cocktails and San Miguel beer, and that's just the hen parties. The stag parties are far worse. Some of the antics bridegrooms are put through by their so-called best mates' beggars' belief. For example, only last week at the comisaría in Benalmadena we had a Scottish guy in a kilt, from Glasgow I think, complaining that he'd been raped in a gay club, but he was so drunk he couldn't remember where it was."

"I dread to think what his fiancée said to him when he arrived home."

"Oh no, you've grasped the wrong end of the stick. He didn't want to go home. He enjoyed it so much he wanted to go back for more and was seeking our help in locating the club."

"You're kidding?"

"Ojala. If only. No, there's certainly no shortage of punters of every persuasion. Consequently, the sex clubs are desperate for more, mainly girls, to keep pace with demand."

"Are these clubs licensed?"

"Most of them. Every town has at least one licensed club or wiskeria; they're appropriately controlled, have to meet minimum standards, and have their girls regularly inspected. It makes their use safer for all parties. But as business boomed, applications for more clubs increased. Typically, the buildings are located on the edge of town so as not to disturb the neighbors and cause minimum offense. They have high walls around them so that punters can drive in and drive out discretely. The idea is to prevent wives from discovering that his trip to the allotment meant somewhat more than just picking up a few vegetables. But now councils are receiving too many complaints about the number of clubs, so they have refused to issue any more permits. But that hasn't done anything to stop the demand."

"Why don't they increase the taxes? It will force prices up, which will reduce the number of punters."

"A logical British solution, but regretfully it's a tad more complicated in Spain. The hotels have become accustomed to busy bedrooms all year round. Restaurants, bars, and nightclubs prefer to be fully booked. Higher taxes on sex clubs would reduce tourist numbers and increase unemployment. Meanwhile, the sex industry has moved underground to keep pace with demand. There are now thousands of unlicensed individuals on the net offering personal services in your hotel room.

"Illegal clubs are also on the up, and they are awful, yet extremely adept at emptying wallets. They're not too difficult to find, but as fast as we close one, two more open."

"Where do the clubs, find enough women?"

"That's their main problem. They lost their best girls to porn producers, who pay more for less onerous work. The clubs have replaced them with mainly Moroccans, Eastern Europeans, and more recently African migrants. But that's still not enough.

"As you can imagine, there is a high turnover of girls. The drug addicts are disposed of, some girls escape, others crack up mentally, and the pretty ones are sold as sex-slaves. To stay in business, clubs need a continual supply of new girls. The legally constituted clubs attract the best girls and boys because they offer work contracts, health care, and pension contributions. The illegal ones, however, have to resort to ever more devious and ruthless tactics to sustain a viable number of women, and that includes abduction. Recently, they've started taking girls to order. One night last week, we stopped a boat halfway between Marbella and Tangiers. In the front cabin, we found a pair of pretty blond twins from Manchester handcuffed to the bunks. They were being smuggled out to join a harem in Tunisia. Their drinks had been spiked in a Puerto Banus nightclub. Next thing they knew, they'd woken up at sea."

"So Juliet could already be in the hands of some sweaty sheik," said Phillip, shaking his head. "How do you usually find out when girls have gone missing?"

"Sometimes their friends report them, but usually not until the next morning when they've sobered up and realized what happened. By then it's too late for us to stand any chance of finding them. The talent scouts that take these girls are extremely clever. They have a knack for selecting vulnerable women, who are easy to drug or are just happy to disappear. You'll be surprised how many come here to escape from sordid relationships and lonely lives. Sadly, when they're abducted, they have nobody to report them as missing."

"And you think Juliet may have been selected?"

"To be honest, I don't know. Juliet is more beautiful than the average sex worker and may have been targeted by a wealthy individual, who saw her at the café and wanted her for himself. Other than that, she could be working in an illegal club somewhere or on her way out of Spain. Irrespective of who has her, they have an eighteen-hour start on us."

"At least we know she's missing and have a range of clues. Surely they should help us find her?"

"They ought to, but as yet we have no real idea, just

theories. One of which is that an extremely talented person or group is behind most, even all of these abductions."

"Why do you suspect that?"

"The complete lack of evidence. Until Juliet was taken, we had not found one single scrap."

"Then fingers crossed that your team can track them down."

"Thankfully, the legal clubs are cooperative. Otherwise, they lose their licenses. It means, they too have a vested interest in helping us. Our specialist team that works undercover in these places has a photo of Juliet. Tonight they will be watching for her."

Phillip went to check the arrival board, feeling utterly depressed. Mrs. Kitson's plane was further delayed until five-thirty. He went back to the café and updated the inspector.

"Then I'll go back to my office," said Prado. "I need to go argue my case for putting out a media campaign. Would you mind waiting for Juliet's aunt?"

"Not at all. I'll bring her to you."

23

A tall, striking, svelte woman with short blond hair dressed in a figure-hugging black skirt, tailored jacket, and white silk blouse entered the arrival hall.

Phillip held up his hand as her ice-blue eyes scanned the waiting crowd. She spotted him, he nodded. She smiled sheepishly as if relieved that someone was still there to meet her. Phillip guessed she was about his age, but wasn't sure. In the flesh, her facial resemblance to his ex-wife was even closer than Juliet. Astonishingly, it didn't bother him.

"Ms. Kitson?" he said as she approached, towing a small overnight black bag and carrying a shoulder bag.

"It's Mrs., but Rosemary, please," she said. "Phillip right?"

"That's me. Welcome to Málaga. I'm taking you to the police station in the city center."

They shook hands. Phillip insisted on taking her bag.

"It's quite a distance to the visitor car-park. Would

you prefer to wait here while I fetch the car?"

"Thanks, but I'll walk," said Rosemary. "I'd appreciate stretching my legs. Forgive me for asking, but since when have the Spanish police been employing English people?"

"I don't work for them, but provide translation services on a voluntary basis."

"An Englishman with languages, that is unusual."

"If you want to be in business here, it's advisable."

Phillip led her to the back of the arrival hall and pressed the elevator button. They went up through departures and exited through the main doors. It was a warm, balmy, late afternoon.

"Rain in Birmingham," said Rosemary, sighing as they crossed the road to the parking garage.

They used the five-minute walk to exchange getting-to-know-you small-talk. Phillip paid at the machine, turned to her, and said. "My car is this way."

He escorted her to his BMW, placed her bag in the trunk and watched, puzzled as to why she opened the driver's door. She looked up, embarrassed and said, "silly me. It's been a while since I've traveled."

She walked around the front of the car to where Phillip waited, holding open the passenger door.

"Don't worry, you're not the first Brit to make that mistake," he said as he closed the door.

They headed toward the city center along the N-340 highway.

"Any news about Juliet?" said Rosemary scrutinizing him as he drove.

"Not yet, but some progress has been made. The abductors are on film, we have an Identikit sketch of one of them, and the van used has been found with prints and DNA. We're pushing for a TV campaign, every patrol-car carries Juliet's photo and border controls have her passport details."

"Sounds good," said Rosemary still observing him. "I hope you don't mind me saying, but now that I've seen you in the flesh, I can understand why Juliet was taken with you."

"In what way?" said Phillip, assuming that Rosemary had seen straight through him.

"Her father died when she was young. You're tall like him and were supportive of her when she first arrived. She told me she could trust you as a friend and trust is a difficult concept for her."

"That's good to know," said Phillip, relieved that Juliet saw him as a father figure and not an old lecher. "I didn't do much to deserve that."

"It was enough to make her feel secure."

"I concede that I've become extremely fond of your niece," he said. "And am finding her abduction hard to bear, but working on the investigation makes me feel useful and distracts me from hurting. We were in Morocco earlier today, visiting Juliet's ex-boyfriend."

"What did Hassan have to say for himself?"

"He was desperate to take Juliet with him, but she wasn't interested in adapting to that way of life. Apparently, they had a massive row about it. At the time, he threatened to come back and persuade her, but when he returned to Nador, he understood why she refused. We're satisfied that he had no connection with the abduction."

"You are fond of her?" said Rosemary, regarding Phillip's animated face as he talked.

"Who wouldn't be? She's incredibly beautiful and a lovely person. Rosemary, sorry, but I've not been completely honest with you. Until recently, my feelings for Juliet were, to say the least; confused."

"Why?"

"She reminds me of my ex-wife."

"Well done for keeping that from her. Until recently you said. Are you less muddled now?"

"Have you heard of the Camino de Santiago?"

"Of course."

"I completed the route from France earlier this week."

"That must have taken you a while."

"Over a month, but it needed that to sort myself out."

"Did it work?"

"Thankfully, yes."

"How?"

"I realized the problem emanated from my ex-wife. Even six years after our divorce, I hadn't or couldn't come to terms with it and hadn't let her go. Juliet was a constant reminder of her which was delaying my healing process. I have now resolved that Juliet is just a special friend and not a ghost haunting me. However, her abduction has temporarily messed me up and now, just to make sure I'm completely buggered; her aunt also resembles my ex."

"Would it help if I wore a dark wig and hid behind some large sunglasses?" said Rosemary grinning.

"Ha. Sorry, bit heavy there for a moment."

"No, I respect that. You'll go the extra mile to find her."

"I will, but so far have not contributed much. If only I'd informed the police when she didn't turn up to our appointment; we could have been further ahead with the investigation."

"Why didn't you?"

"She was meeting a new friend and told me that she might not make it to our drinks session, so I went home. When she didn't arrive at work the next day, it was me who went to her apartment and found the door open. It had been ransacked, and some of her personal stuff was missing."

"She wouldn't have had much," said Rosemary. "She was ever ready for a quick escape."

"They only took her passport and a few clothes."

"So you reported this to the police?"

"Not then, no. Coincidently, an American journalist had filmed the abduction, but didn't notice it until she was editing on her large screen at home later that night. She reported it to the police yesterday morning. The inspector handling the case and I have worked together previously, and he recognized me in the video near the place where she was abducted. Rosemary. The abductors drove right past me with Juliet inside the van."

"How awful. Do the police have any theories?"

"There's a booming sex industry."

"Say no more, please. I know where you're going, but believe me, there is a far worse scenario. It's why I've come here to tell you personally. Do you mind if I phone my husband?"

"Not at all, do you want me to stop, give you a bit of privacy?"

"That won't be necessary, but thank you."

Rosemary extracted her phone from her handbag, turned it on, and stabbed in the password. It took a minute for the roaming service to kick in. She confirmed her safe arrival and updated him on the investigation.

"Have you booked accommodation?" said Phillip

when she'd finished.

"There's a room for me at the Hotel Palacio. Is that near the police station?"

"Just a short walk, but I'll drop you there when we've finished with Inspector Prado."

"Is he your boss?"

"He's responsible for crimes involving foreigners and can only do his work effectively with the help of volunteer translators. I'm one of them."

Phillip pulled up at the entrance to the comisaría underground car park and announced their arrival on the intercom. The steel shutter squeaked as it rolled upwards. He parked, they clambered out, walked to the elevator door, and waited.

A couple of minutes later, the doors slid open to reveal Prado standing at the back. He waved them in, Phillip introduced Rosemary, and they went up to his office.

"Can we offer you a coffee or anything to drink?" said Phillip as they arrived at Prado's office and closed the door behind them.

"A still mineral water, please," said Rosemary.

Phillip went over to the filing cabinet, collected a plastic cup and a bottle of water and then placed them on the desk by Rosemary as Prado helped her into one of the visitor chairs. Prado retired behind his desk, Phillip took the other chair, and they both waited expectantly for Rosemary to begin.

She burst into tears.

"Sorry," Rosemary whispered moments later, after dabbing her eyes with a tissue. "I've been rehearsing what to say all the way here, but now I don't know where to start."

"Shall I ask you a couple of questions?" said Phillip.

"They might kick you off?"

Rosemary composed herself, wiped her eyes again, and nodded.

"Where do you live?"

"In… in Kenilworth," she said. "It's about forty kilometers southeast of Birmingham."

"You mentioned that Juliet's father was dead."

"Pip died of cancer about six years ago. He and Juliet were incredibly close which was just as well. Their great relationship more than compensated for her mother's maternal inadequacies. When her mother was away, working, which was often, they used to holiday in Nerja together. She had happy memories of the place and felt at peace here."

"Tell me about her mother."

"She killed herself four years ago; sat in the bath, drank a bottle of vodka, and slit her wrists. Juliet discovered her after school. She'd left a note on the dressing table. All it said was, 'Why me?'"

"Not particularly forthcoming?"

"Exactly, but hardly surprising. My sister was a successful fashion model. International catwalks, big money, the lot, but was obsessed with her looks and appearance to the exclusion of everything else. So when Juliet's father passed away, her first reaction was to complain about not having a man around to worship her. She immediately set out to replace Pip, much to Juliet's annoyance.

"Graham Ferrier was a few years younger than Rachel, but more callously, she liked that he was handsome, healthy, and wealthy. He was a brilliant photographer, she'd met on a shoot in London several years previously. They dated and married so quickly it was obscene. Juliet would have been thirteen or thereabouts, and hated Ferrier from day one.

"Juliet was a late developer. She was sixteen when she changed almost overnight from tomboy to stunningly beautiful woman. Her mother insisted that she follow her into modeling, and for that, she would need an image portfolio. During these sessions, Ferrier progressively touched her where he shouldn't. She complained to her mother, who told her to get used to it; models were groped all the time. Then on her seventeenth birthday, he tried to rape her.

"I'll never forget the night when she banged on my door, I only live a kilometer away. She was half-naked and in a terrible state. I called Rachel, who was away on a shoot. She insisted that Ferrier had assured her that nothing had happened. It was a total misunderstanding; his hand had slipped accidentally and a jagged finger-nail had cut her.

"My niece was listening in on the speaker phone and screamed at her mother. She accused her of aiding and abetting a rapist, and that she never wanted to see her again. The two started screaming obscenities at each other so I hung up and had a hard chat with Juliet. I warned her about the horrors of reporting a rape. Did she have the evidence to prove it? She stood, and exposed herself to me. What Ferrier had done to her was inhuman. He'd clawed at her like a wild animal."

Rosemary paused; breathing deeply, her head in her hands. Eventually, she looked up and reconvened.

"Sorry," she said. "It brought it all back to me. The only saving grace was that she had kicked him hard where it hurts which deterred him from completing his objective. His agony was her chance to escape.

"I called the police, who were brilliant. Their doctor was able to collect all the evidence needed to bring attempted rape charges. It was a slam-dunk case."

"I would imagine that facing her abuser across a crowded courtroom must have been more than daunting."

"She was terrified but determined that her stepfather would have his day in court. She was a sterling witness and delivered her testimony calmly and succinctly. Then handled the cross-questioning by his ruthless, uncaring barrister with a maturity beyond her years. I was extremely proud of her. One day, she could be a formidable lawyer."

"Good for her, what did the judge say?"

"Ferrier was sent down for six years. The following day, Juliet's mother killed herself."

"Juliet must have been devastated."

"She was sad that the final memory of her mother was a heated verbal exchange and at the funeral, she broke down and wept briefly, but that seemed to be it. She was withdrawn for a while, but then opened up and was able to discuss how Ferrier's abuse had damaged her. Poor thing, that bastard had put her off men for life.

"However, she declined counselling and within a couple of weeks, was back at school. Six months later, her reports were outstanding and the teachers recommended she apply to university.

"After the court case, she'd expressed an interest in studying law and seemed enthusiastic about that as we trailed around various colleges. Eventually, she was offered a place at Warwick.

"I was impressed by her determination to pass her exams and was happy that she had found her path through life. But when school finished, she had little to do and withdrew back into herself. I encouraged her to see more of her friends, play tennis which she loved, and bought her a damn horse but I knew I was losing her. Even before her results had come through, she told me that she'd changed her plans completely. All she wanted was a new life in Spain."

"That must have been a shock."

"To say the least. I could understand her wanting to move away from Kenilworth, but I objected strongly to Spain. The thought of her traveling alone terrified me, but she was insistent. I had to let her go and make her way in the world, she was eighteen after all. I gave her money and a mobile phone, then dropped her off at St. Pancras station. We've not seen each other since."

"Why did your call on the fourteenth, upset her so?"

"I told her that Ferrier had found out she was in Nerja, was on his way to her and she should run somewhere immediately."

"What did she say?"

"She was terrified."

"How did you find out that Ferrier was on his way?"

"Some four months previously he came to see me at my office."

"What on Earth for?"

"He told me that he'd been released early because of his impeccable behavior and completely reformed character. He demanded to know where Juliet was and insisted that he must apologize to her."

"What did you say?"

"I told him that Juliet didn't want to see him again; ever.

"He explained that his therapist had advised him to make amends and should write to her. It would help put those terrible events behind him and move on with his life. He even showed me a letter from the prison psychologist to that effect. Naturally, I was skeptical, so asked him to leave it with me.

"He gave me his telephone number, and I promised to call him as soon as I'd taken some advice. Then I promptly appointed a private detective to check out his story. Something I wish I'd done before he married my sister. If I had, I probably wouldn't be sitting here now."

"What did your detective discover?"

"Beyond my wildest fears."

"Juliet wasn't his first victim?" said Phillip.

"The bastard had been abusing women and getting away with it for years. There'd been a couple of complaints to the police, but they were withdrawn. The women were either indebted to him because his images had earned them lucrative assignments, or he'd paid them off. It must have been awful for those poor girls, but they weren't my primary concern. What Ferrier's probation officer revealed about his time in prison was far more disturbing."

Rosemary paused and took a deep breath.

"Let me go back to the court case," said Rosemary. "When the judge passed sentence on my brother-in-law, he went berserk. The ushers only just managed to prevent him from reaching Juliet. All we could hear echoing from the stairwell as they manhandled him down to the cells was his promise."

Rosemary raised the tissue to her eyes and sobbed deeply.

Prado raised his eyebrows at Phillip.

Phillip reached out, placed his hand gently on her shoulder and said. "Rosemary, sorry to press you, but what was his promise?"

"To kill Juliet," she whispered, put her head back in her hands and shuddered.

Phillip patted her shoulder and translated for Prado.

While he talked Rosemary sat up, her eyes stained with mascara. She took another deep breath.

"Sorry, again," she said. "But I will get through this."

"What happened to Ferrier in prison?"

"He was a pretty boy who thought he was God's gift to women. But locked up in a block full of sex offenders, he was just juicy meat. He was raped by a succession of cellmates. After the first offense, he complained to the governor and consequently, the culprits had their sentences extended. But that just made matters worse. Ferrier was sent back to the same cell where he became the sperm dump for his fellow inmates. Having realized the futility of his position, he never complained again. For over four long years, he was violated every day, occasionally several times. And every time it happened, he said nothing and showed no reaction, but mentally, the pain and humiliation accumulated in his psyche. When added to an already fragile temperament, it drove him insane. Gentlemen, we are not dealing with a rational human being here. Ferrier is a wild animal, but he is calculated and cunning, and we must find him before he kills my niece."

"I'm surprised they let him out on parole," said Phillip.

"He fooled all of them," said Rosemary. "By saying all the right things and expressing remorse for his crime. The panel's newly qualified psychologist believed him, and the others took her advice. Ferrier was let out on parole as a registered sex-offender and obliged to spend six months living in a bail hostel, wear an electronic tag and continue with therapy. The first thing he did was seek a detective to find Juliet."

"How could he afford that?"

"With Rachel's assets and the profits from his photography business, he had more than enough not to work and finance a search for Juliet."

"How did you learn about his detective?"

"My detective followed him to a park bench and recognized his detective. They used to be cops together in Birmingham."

"How did your detective uncover Ferrier's abuse in prison?"

"She had a long chat with his probation officer who showed her Ferrier's file."

"So you're saying that the probation officer spotted what the parole psychologist missed?"

"I am. He was a seasoned professional and had worked with thousands of sex-offenders on their journeys from behind bars back into society. He confirmed that most are devious liars, but Ferrier was exceptional. However, this man saw straight through him, sensed Ferrier's simmering rage and watched him like a hawk. However, after several months in the hostel, Ferrier hadn't put a foot wrong and the officer relaxed the intensity of his supervision."

"Sounds like a deliberate strategy by Ferrier."

"Exactly."

"Surely, the tag recorded all his movements."

"It did, but if he sat somewhere for half an hour, the tag couldn't tell them who was sitting nearby and instead of checking his location once an hour, they would only do it once or twice a day. So long as he stayed within his limits, he was OK."

"This sounds like a scene from a Marx Brothers movie," said Phillip. "All these people watching each other. What happened next?"

"My detective was following him and saw him meet with his detective on a park bench. She saw them exchange envelopes, and shake hands. She guessed that her former colleague was being paid off, so later that evening, gave him a call. He refused to reveal anything about Ferrier, so she could only assume that he had located Juliet. She checked the hostel. Ferrier had removed his tag an absconded that very afternoon. The police were already hunting for him. I heard about it about an hour later and contacted Juliet straightaway. That was the evening of the fourteenth of May."

"Why wasn't he arrested at either of the airports?"

"He had a ticket to Málaga from Birmingham but didn't show up."

"Let me explain all this to Prado."

"In that case, I'll pop to the restroom. Where is it?"

Phillip opened the door, directed her to the far end of the corridor, returned to his chair, and updated Prado.

"This man sounds evil," said Prado when Phillip had finished. "He has motive and opportunity, so could have arranged Juliet's abduction from England beforehand. After four years in prison, he's bound to be plugged into a criminal network, where he can purchase a wide range of illicit services. In my book, Ferrier has just been promoted to our most likely suspect."

"I agree, but we don't know where he is."

"As a sex offender living in a hostel, it's unlikely that he had the opportunity to arrange a false passport so he's probably traveling under his own name. When

Rosemary comes back, ask her if she has an up to date photo that we can circulate to all border posts. His phone number too. We need to find this man quickly before he does any serious damage to his niece."

"Fine. Any news on the media campaign?"

"Yes, they've agreed to put out later tonight and will repeat it throughout the day tomorrow."

Rosemary returned looking decidedly chirpier and handed over Ferrier's phone number, an old photo, and a wrinkled photocopy of his passport, which was due to expire at the end of the year. Prado picked them up and went out of the office to instruct his colleagues.

"What does the inspector think of my story?"

"He's convinced Ferrier abducted Juliet or arranged for it. They will put out an all-points bulletin for his arrest, but will continue with his current searches. How long do you intend to stay?"

"I have a return flight in the morning. If there are any developments, I'll be back on the next plane."

"Would you care to join me for dinner?"

"Thanks, Phillip, but you don't need to entertain me, and I have a lot of business stuff to go through. I'll grab something from room-service."

"What work do you do?"

"My husband and I build carbon-neutral housing developments. We're growing like crazy, and it's driving me bananas."

"Did I hear you right about Ferrier inheriting your sister's estate?"

"You did."

"Why not Juliet, or at least some of it?"

"Have you seen that comedy program, *Absolutely Fabulous*?"

"Many times; loved it."

"Well, Rachel was similar to Patsy, gorgeous, less lipstick but just as stupid. Kids to her were a fun accessory so long as they were decorative, seen, and not heard. Things like wills were anathema to her."

The door burst open, and Prado rushed back into the office, waving a pen drive in his hand. "I need Rosemary to look at this," he said then inserted the drive into his laptop. Prado clicked on a video and presented the screen to Phillip and Rosemary.

A smartly dressed, handsome man with dark hair and a pencil mustache was showing his passport to a border guard.

"That's Ferrier," said Rosemary.

"He arrived on a chartered jet," said Prado. "That recording was taken at Granada Airport just before midnight on the fourteenth. Now we need to trace where he went from there. His photo and passport details have been emailed to every hotel and estate agency within thirty kilometers of Nerja. Hopefully, by the morning we'll have him in custody."

"Is there anything more we can do here?" said Phillip.

"No. But may I call you if anything urgent comes up?" said Prado.

"Fine, Inspector. OK, Rosemary," said Phillip. "We can go now."

"Thank you, Rosemary," said Prado in English. "Good night."

"De nada, Inspector. Hasta lluego," said Rosemary. She shrugged as she gathered her things. "We used to go to Marbella as teenagers. That's all I can remember, other than 'vino tinto' and 'manos arriba' when amorous Spanish boy's hands wandered too close for comfort."

Prado raised his eyebrows. Phillip translated.

"Ha," said Prado grinning. "We were always suckers for blue-eyed blonds, and some of us," he added eyes twinkling at Phillip. "Still are."

24

Amanda's meeting with the director of the Picasso Museum had gone well. She wanted to make a film about Anne Pennington, a wealthy American living in Nerja, who owned several Picasso paintings. They were due to be exhibited during the coming January under the title, Picasso's Mistresses. The director had agreed to introduce Amanda to her and would organize a date for them to meet. As she walked down the steps of the historic Palacio Buenavista onto Calle San Agustin, her phone rang. It was an unknown number from Algeciras.

"Hola. Digame," she said.

"Hola, Amanda, soy Antonio Gutierrez," said a man's voice. It was the captain of the Guardia Civil patrol boat.

"Hi, Antonio, how's it going?"

"It's all arranged. I know it's short notice, but could you attend an appointment with me at the detention center in Algeciras this afternoon at two?"

"Of course. Can you email me the address?"

"On its way," said Antonio.

"In what capacity am I attending?"

"As a journalist."

"Wow, how did you manage that?"

"My boss initially declined when I suggested you come as an interpreter because you are not licensed. However, he came back to me later and said that his superiors had overruled him. Apparently, someone up high is keen that you finish your documentary but can you do voice overs in Spanish and English. They want to use it to alert Brussels to the dangers faced by the migrants, and the huge costs Spain is incurring for patrolling the channels and processing the people."

"That suits me fine," said Amanda. "See you in reception."

Amanda walked back to her apartment, worked for an hour, then popped over to the market for some early tapas.

The hundred and forty-kilometer drive took two hours, including a restroom break outside Marbella. She listened to some Spanish classical guitar music on the car's sound system and let her mind ponder over these latest developments in her life. She was intrigued by whom in the Spanish Government wanted to use her video for political gain and was enjoying working with Prado but what was at the forefront of everything, was Phillip. Is he 'The One?' she thought. He was the first man in years with whom she had been able to picture herself sharing a life. A home together, hopefully, children. He just seemed so right in all the key ingredients she was looking for. More importantly, he made her tingle inside and the anticipation of dining with him on Saturday was exquisite.

The detention center in Algeciras is a former prison.

An imposing building with bars to the ground-floor doors and windows, but condemned as uninhabitable as far back as fifteen years ago. It's just up the hill from Algeciras harbor and is the subject of much controversy both locally and nationally.

Some locals and several charities want it closed permanently. They prefer asylum seekers to be accommodated within the community while their asylum applications are being processed. They are not criminals and shouldn't be treated as such.

The government, however, plans to refurbish it. Whilst the Spanish Ministry of the Interior has externalized much of its immigration controls to the host nations concerned, for those that do make it to Spain, the authorities feel safer knowing where their migrants are. From detention centers, they can be deported easily and quickly when their application has been decided.

Amanda parked her car by several others at the front of the building, went up the steps and into the reception. Antonio was waiting for her. He sprang to his feet, came over, and shook hands.

"Here are the GPS coordinates I promised you," said Antonio, handing over a piece of folded paper. "They confirm that our position when the baby was born was outside of Spanish territorial waters."

"Thanks, but they're irrelevant now. The mother died, and the baby is due to be adopted by a Spanish family on the hospital's waiting list," said Amanda.

"That will look good in your documentary."

"Just as well, the rest is a tragedy. I wonder what we'll learn here this evening."

"Let's go and find out."

They walked over to the receptionist and asked him

to announce their arrival. Moments later, the door at the back of the reception opened, and a tall, bulky man with black hair and a severe dandruff problem, wearing the uniform of the National Police entered. He strode over to them, leering at Amanda, shook hands, and said, "I'm Sergeant Pérez, in charge of this center. The group that came in on your ship, captain, is assembled in the canteen. Regretfully, there are only fourteen remaining; the others have already been deported."

"That was quick," said the captain. "Did you not receive our instructions?"

"Sorry?" said Pérez.

"We ordered them all to be held here pending our inquiries. Some of them murdered one of their fellow travelers and we need to question them about it."

"Oh," said Pérez laughing. "We probably lost the instruction. With insufficient staff, I'm afraid it happens a lot. But anyway, why all the fuss? They're only migrants. Who gives a fuck if they want to kill each other? One less to deal with."

Antonio glared at Pérez.

Pérez looked uncomfortable.

"Perhaps the killers are still among the remainder," said Amanda. "Shall we go and see?"

Antonio nodded.

Pérez looked relieved and led them down a short corridor, unlocking and locking two barred doors on the way. They ended up in a large room laid out with tables and chairs. Amanda and the captain exchanged concerned glances. They entered and saw the people from the boat sitting around a rectangular gray laminate table in the far corner. Amanda estimated that over a hundred people could eat here at any one time. It smelled of stale cooking fat.

"Have you any particular questions?" said Amanda.

"If we can establish that the dead man was traveling on his own and why he was drowned," said the captain. "That will be enough for my report."

"Will you be bringing any charges?"

"No, we just want to close the file."

"Feel free to talk with them as long as you like," said Pérez, leading them over to the migrants' table. "But bear in mind that lunch is served promptly at one o'clock. When you're finished, please tell the canteen staff, and I will come and fetch you."

"Thank you, Sergeant," said Amanda.

They approached the migrants, pulled a couple of chairs from the next table, and sat down with them. There were twelve men and two women still dressed in the same clothes as they wore on the boat. Their body odor competed with the kitchen smells. Amanda set up her tripod, mounted the camera on top and set it recording, then turned to face the table.

"Can you all understand me?" said Amanda in French noticing that all the youngsters were gone. These were just the older passengers. Strange, she thought. Shouldn't it be the other way around?

"Oui madam," they said individually as she looked at each one.

"This," she indicated Antonio. "Is the captain of the patrol boat that rescued you the other day. He's making inquiries about the man that was drowned. I'm Amanda. My work is making a film to relate your painful stories to the world. Does anyone object to being filmed?"

They looked at each other, shrugged.

"That will be fine," said a beefy man in his early forties sitting at the end of the table acting as if he was their leader.

"Great," said Amanda. "Thanks. Can we start with the dead guy? Who was he, where did he come from, where was he going and why was he drowned?"

"He joined us at the last minute," said the same man. "He'd run all the way from the Ceuta border. Didn't give his name, though."

"He commanded us," said the man next to him. Amanda noticed that they resembled each other. "In the name of God, to go with him to France."

"He was from Algeria," said another seated at the center of the table. "Offered us lots of money, if we joined his battle against French infidels."

"We didn't want him sullying our asylum applications," said one of the women.

"He was also carrying a lot of money," said the first man who spoke. "We stole it from him. Our needs were greater than his, plus we were all enraged by his behavior toward the pregnant woman, Daraja. He was initially enamored by her, but when she told him to leave her alone, he turned nasty and was disrespectful to her. When he saw her about to jump over to the Spanish police boat, I heard him shout that she should stay, but she ignored him. He was trying to prevent her from going with the Spanish policeman. We couldn't permit that. Do you know how Daraja is?"

"I helped Daraja with the birth," said Amanda. "Sorry, but she lost a lot of blood and died quickly. Her baby is fine, though, and is in the process of being adopted by a local family."

"It is sad news about Daraja," said the same man. "Now, how may we help you?"

"Did Daraja say where she was from or anything about the child's father?"

"She was from Senegal," he said. "It took her three years to reach Ceuta traveling with various caravans. Most treated her kindly as she was just a young girl, but the last one in the south of Morocco was a mean slave trader, who raped her. When it was obvious she was pregnant, he left her for dead in the middle of the desert. Another caravan found her barely alive a day later, and brought her most of the way to Ceuta."

"Is that a typical story for most of the women?"

"Shamefully, yes," he said. The women nodded their heads in confirmation.

"Let me ask you this," said Amanda still struggling to contain her emotions. "With the benefit of hindsight, what would you say to your folks back home about taking this journey?"

The group looked at each other, eyebrows raised and deferred to the older man.

"I compare it to buying a lottery ticket," he said. "You know it is unlikely to win, but unless you participate there is no chance. We could stay at home where we know it will remain bad or," he paused. "We can chase our dreams of a new beginning somewhere nice like here in Spain. There are success stories of migrants making it big, for example, footballers, athletes, artists, and cooks. For most of us, it would probably be no worse than remaining at home. However, by taking this journey, we have seen parts of the world that offer a better way of living than we are accustomed to. We have learned new skills and seen innovative things that can help us improve matters when, or if, we return to our loved ones. So I would say yes, the more of us that take this journey and survive, in the long term our country will benefit."

"You have taken enormous personal risks," said

Amanda. "And suffered so much pain. Why do you do it?"

"We are accustomed to hardship," he said. "However, that doesn't make us stupid. We knew our journeys would be full of uncertainty, possible death or forced repatriation, but it is a price we were prepared to pay. Hopefully, our great-grandchildren will reap the benefit because our countries cannot continue as they are."

"Fair point, well made. How are they treating you here?"

"To us, it's like a luxury hotel," said the same man. "A roof over our heads, three meals a day, plenty of water and nobody abusing us. If they called us by our names, it could be better."

"How do they refer to you?"

"By numbers," he said, holding up a sign marked two hundred and three. It had been out of sight resting on his lap. "In many ways it's good, we learn some Spanish but we have observed that the staff here do not represent the sharpest of Spanish bureaucrats, or have the most retentive of memories. However, we understand that our names are difficult to pronounce and to them, we all look the same, just as they do to us. We live with it."

"Thanks, I admire your patience and tolerance. Where are you from, sir?"

"Nigeria," he said. "I'm a farmer, but drought and warring idiots drove me and my brother here from our land."

"Why not try Lagos or one of your big cities?" said Amanda.

"If you have ever been to Lagos, you would understand why we prefer Spain. The weather is more comfortable, water is clean, crossing the road isn't a life-threatening venture, and being shot for smiling at the wrong person is unheard of."

"You're right, I've never been to Lagos. I'll make a note to scratch it from my bucket list. What about the others in your group. Are they all from Nigeria and Senegal?"

"No, from all over Africa. Do you know where they are? We haven't seen them since shortly after we arrived."

"They've been deported."

"What? All of them?"

"So the man in charge says," said Amanda.

"Why so quickly?"

"Sorry, I don't know," said Amanda.

"We wondered what had happened to them. We were told that they were going to another cell as ours was overcrowded, since then we have not seen them. Let us pray they are safe and well."

"Let me explain matters to the captain," said Amanda, "and then we can talk more about your journeys."

"I have enough for my report," said the captain after Amanda had finished.

Amanda spent half an hour recording close-up individual accounts of their harrowing journeys until she had enough to finish her video. She shook hands with everyone and wished them well with their asylum applications.

Pérez returned, then escorted them back to the reception.

"Were your questions answered?" said Pérez.

"Thank you, yes," said the captain. "Although, they hadn't heard about the others in their group being deported."

Pérez glared at the captain. "We don't inform our detainees about what happens to their fellow travelers. All we tell them is that to reduce overcrowding we move them to another cell. In our experience, the less we say, the more compliant they are. They assume that while they remain here, there is a chance that their application is still being processed, and that gives them hope."

"What percentage are accepted?" said Amanda.

"Occasionally, hidden among them are highly qualified people such as doctors or nurses," said Pérez. "We keep a few of those, the others have no value and will eventually be deported."

"Surely the country needs more laborers," said the captain.

"We already have nearly a million Moroccans and eight hundred thousand Romanians," said Pérez. "How many more do you want?"

25

It was a cloudy morning with a fresh breeze and Playa El Salon was deserted. Phillip swam fast in the bracing water, thinking there was no way Didi would enter the water on such a day, even if he was in town. The Teutonic thermometer couldn't cope with such low temperatures.

He clung on to the buoy admiring the mountains and began preparing a mental list of estate agents, eliminating those who didn't meet Prado's criteria. It didn't take him long to realize that this was something he'd have to do with Richard.

He swam back, showered, and headed up the hill to Don Comer.

The café was quiet. Richard was on his own at the regulars' table. They shook hands, and Phillip sat down.

"How's it going?" said Richard, but before Phillip could respond, Manolo served Richard's breakfast then sat down with them.

"I saw the appeal about Juliet on TV last night," said Manolo. "Has that generated any new information?"

"There have been a few calls," said Phillip. "Nothing of interest though. The good news is that we've identified another suspect. It's Juliet's stepfather. Her aunt flew over yesterday evening from Birmingham, England and told us about him."

Phillip related a summary of Ferrier and his history with Juliet.

"And he's here in Spain now?" said Richard.

"The police have a video of him arriving at Granada airport on the eve of San Isidro and have circulated surrounding hotels and rental agencies to try and locate him."

"What does Juliet's stepfather look like?" said Manolo.

"Good-looking guy, aged about forty with dark hair and a pencil mustache. Has anyone resembling him been to the café, or been asking for Juliet?"

"Not while I was here," said Richard.

"Me neither but I'll ask the other staff members," said Manolo. "Personally, I don't recall anyone of that description, but an English guy did inquire after Juliet some time ago."

"When was that?" said Phillip.

"About a year past," said Manolo. "When I asked who wanted to know, he shrugged and left. I saw him again the next morning outside the church. He took a photo of Juliet while she was working and then disappeared."

"Can you remember what he looked like?" said Phillip.

"This guy was unforgettable. A giant of a man, obese, blond and ugly with a long scar on his cheek."

"And he was definitely English?" said Phillip.

"His accent was similar to yours, but he spoke with a quiet effeminate voice," said Manolo.

"Did you tell Juliet about him?" said Richard.

"No. I meant to, but we were busy."

"Thanks, Manolo," said Phillip. "I'll text that through to Prado."

Manolo went off to the kitchen. Richard and Phillip discussed the outstanding projects for their online guide. When they were done Phillip headed back up to his villa.

He was approaching his turn off when the phone rang.

He glanced at the screen. It was Prado.

"Digame," said Phillip on the hands-free.

"Drop what you are doing and head for Frigiliana," said Prado.

"I'm only about five minutes away. Why? What is so urgent?"

"Ferrier is about to check out of the Hotel Frigiliana."

"I know where it is, but where are you?"

"I'm forty minutes away and there's only one local policeman free due to a bad accident on the motorway. The officer's name is Castro, but he can't speak English. Could you go there, await his arrival and help with the arrest? If you wait for me, we might lose him."

"On my way," said Phillip putting his foot down pulse racing. "Can you inform the receptionist about me and my role in this?"

"Good idea," said Prado and ended the call.

Phillip broke all the rules of the road and more during his three kilometer sprint up to Frigiliana. He overtook on bends, narrowly missed vehicles coming down as he cut blind corners but he never blinked an eye, so focused was he on stopping Ferrier from leaving the hotel. His mood was cold and calculating. This was his chance to repay Ferrier for all the hurt and damage he'd done to the girl he adored. He gripped the wheel hard and span it back and forth as he swerved around the sharp bends on the narrow mountain road. The tires squealed and smoked as he pushed them way beyond their limits.

There were no parking spaces near the hotel, so Phillip drove straight onto the pavement, leaped out and barged through the entrance. The mild-mannered receptionist was just putting down his phone and looked up in alarm at Phillip's sudden intrusion."

"What room?" said Phillip in Spanish?

"Are you Phillip Armitage?" said the young man putting on his glasses and glancing at his laptop.

"Yes, where is Ferrier?"

"Room five-one-four, it's on the top floor, but you should know that he ordered a porter to collect his luggage some time ago. What with all these calls from the police I haven't arranged it yet."

"Good, then call the porter now, but he is to wait outside the room until further instructions. Officer Castro is due in ten minutes, send him up too. Is Ferrier's bill ready?"

"He paid in advance."

"Where's the elevator?"

"Around the corner. Turn left when you reach the top floor. The room is along to the end and on the left."

Phillip stabbed the top floor button wondering if he should wait for Castro or deal with it himself. Perhaps if he pretended to be the porter, Ferrier would let him in and he could engage him in conversation until the police arrived.

The elevator stopped on the third floor where an elderly couple was waiting to descend.

"Sorry; going up," he said in English, then closed the door with the button, his heart pumping as the machine crawled up to the top floor and creaked open.

Phillip ran along to room five-one-four and knocked. This was it, the moment of truth.

"About bloody time," shouted an English voice from within. The door was yanked open and there stood Ferrier. By the blue veins on his face, he looked as if he was about to explode. "I ordered a porter over ten minutes ago. Where the fuck have you been?"

Phillip said nothing, but stared hard at Ferrier assessing the man's stance and attitude.

"Well, pick them up man," shouted Ferrier, pointing at the one small case behind him.

Phillip said nothing, but continued to glare into Ferrier's eyes.

Ferrier was dressed elegantly in blue jeans, Harley-Davidson T-shirt, antique brown leather jacket, and expensive brown brogues. He was an incredibly handsome man except that his expression was miserable, eyes were bloodshot, complexion pallid, and his stomach bulged slightly over his belt. Whiskey drinker thought Phillip. Unfit, and relies on bluster to bully people to comply.

"Can't you understand English?" said Ferrier in a more reasonable tone.

"Perfectly," said Phillip, and I'm not the porter.

"Then get out," said Ferrier.

"No," said Phillip closing the door behind him. "We will wait here together until the police arrive in ten to fifteen minutes."

"Oh," said Ferrier crestfallen. "Who are you?"

"Phillip Armitage. I work with the Málaga police as an interpreter."

"What do they want?" said Ferrier, taking a seat at the corner table.

"Why are you here?"

"To find my stepdaughter."

"And has it been a successful visit?"

"No. She's disappeared."

"The word is abducted, Mr. Ferrier."

"So that's why I can't find her."

"Yes," said Phillip.

"When?" said Ferrier.

"On the afternoon of the fifteenth."

"By whom?"

"By two men in a white van. The abduction was filmed."

Can I see it?"

Phillip took out his phone, swiped up Amanda's video and pressed play. He went over and held it directly in front of Ferrier's face."

Ferrier watched avidly until the end, then buried his hands in his face.

"I also have an Identikit sketch of one of the abductors," said Phillip changing the image from his gallery and thrusting it in front of Ferrier.

Ferrier glanced at it and shook his head.

Have you been to Juliet's apartment?"

"Yes," said Ferrier mumbling into his hands.

"What did you find there?"

"Just a few clothes, everything else had gone."

"Was it you that wrecked her apartment?"

"I was mad at her for not being there. Where the

fuck is she?"

"You don't know?"

"Why should I?"

"So you didn't arrange for her abduction?"

Ferrier stood and glared at Phillip with a deranged expression.

"No, I did not," shouted Ferrier breathing heavily as he looked frantically around the room. He jumped up, went over to the trash basket by the far wall, bent over and began searching through it. The net curtains wafted over his shoulder in the gentle breeze from the open window."

"Then who did?" said Phillip barely controlling his anger at the pathetic man groveling through his own rubbish. What is he looking for?

"I don't know," shouted Ferrier as he threw the contents of the basket out item by item onto the rug. Finally, he found what he was looking for and picked it out. He had his back to Phillip so he couldn't see what it was.

"About a year ago," said Phillip acting on impulse. "A man came looking for Juliet at the café where she worked. According to a witness, this man was a blond, obese, giant."

"What did you say?" said Ferrier standing and turning toward Phillip.

"You heard what I said. An obese giant."

"Of course," said Ferrier shaking his head, his face a tortured expression and white with rage.

"You know this man?" said Phillip.

Ferrier stood stock still momentarily, his whole body trembling while he glared at Phillip.

Phillip heard the door open behind him, but dared not take his eyes off of Ferrier. A Spanish voice said,"

Señor Armitage?"

Phillip prayed that it was Officer Castro.

"Take care," said Phillip in Spanish as a young man in the green uniform of the Guardia Civil appeared next to him. He moved to one side to make room for him. "I suspect this man has lost all sense of reason."

Ferrier's eyes flicked from Phillip to Castro and back again and seemed to come to a decision. He thrust his arm out from behind his back. Gripped in his hand was a kitchen knife with a long sharp blade. Castro unclipped the strap on his holster. "Put the knife down on the bed," he said.

Phillip translated.

Ferrier's eyes continued to flick between the two of them.

"Put the knife down on the bed now," said Castro drawing his pistol, disengaging the safety and aiming it at Ferrier held in two hands. "Or I will shoot."

But by the wild look in his eyes, Ferrier had not comprehended.

Phillip translated again.

Ferrier charged toward Castro, his arm held out straight in front of him, the knife rock steady in his hand. There were only four meters between them and he covered the distance in a millisecond. As he neared Castro, he screamed in a drawn-out cry; "baaaaastards."

Castro shot him once.

The noise was deafening in the small room.

The bullet hit Ferrier in the nose and blew off the back of his head.

Ferrier's body was thrown backward and landed on the rug between the bed and the chest of drawers, a growing pool of blood and brain fragments pooled around his head.

Phillip moved forward, bent to his knees, lifted Ferrier's wrist and tested his pulse.

It stopped while he was holding it.

He stood, faced Castro, shook his head and said in Spanish. "He is dead."

Castro's face had turned a greenish-white as he realized what he'd done. He put his hand over his mouth and rushed into the bathroom where Phillip heard him puking violently.

26

Frigiliana is one of Spain's prettiest villages. It nestles among the foot slopes of the Sierra Almijara some seven kilometers inland from Nerja and 320 meters above sea level. Rambling, picturesque narrow streets, viewing galleries, and charming squares are linked by a labyrinth of cobbled steps and steep passageways. Quaint whitewashed townhouses garlanded with colorful plant pots complete the beautiful, tranquil setting for the population of three and a half thousand residents, including many foreigners and artists. The surrounding countryside is a patchwork of terraced allotments growing a wide variety of fruits and vegetables, including olives, mangoes, avocados, almonds, and grapes. The ancient olive mill continues to produce excellent oil.

Human activity dates back over twenty-five thousand years. Wandering nomads, Phoenicians, Romans, and Moors have all made their mark. An irrigation system built by the Moors over a thousand years ago still carries water down from the mountains. There are remains of an eleventh-century fort at the top of the village, but the existing buildings are mainly of the fifteenth century.

The Hotel Frigiliana was a more recent addition to the lower slopes of the village to accommodate the growing number of annual visitors; particularly hikers.

Phillip returned from moving his car to the parking garage opposite and joined Prado in the hotel bar.

"Forensics have arrived, they're checking Ferrier's room now," said Prado as he sat opposite. "Why didn't you wait for Castro?"

"Ferrier was seconds away from leaving the hotel. I didn't want to remonstrate with him in reception where he might have been a danger to others," said Phillip indicating to the barman that he would have the same as Prado. "I pretended to be the porter and hoped to delay him until Castro or you turned up. Then one thing led to another. Thankfully, Castro arrived when he did. He, I mean Ferrier, was completely out of his mind."

"So Castro said when he'd stopped saying hello to his breakfast."

"Was that his first?"

"Yes and hopefully, his last. Are you OK?" said Prado with a concerned expression.

"I've seen worse in Afghanistan."

"Sorry, I'd forgotten. We're putting it down as suicide by police."

"Sounds fair," said Phillip. "How did you locate him?"

"The hotel receptionist responded to our email first thing this morning. Did Ferrier tell you anything useful?"

"He admitted to trashing Juliet's apartment."

"I know that already. His file arrived from the Birmingham police last night," said Prado. "Forensics confirmed his prints are all over Juliet's door and the overturned furnishings. We're assuming that he went there after the abductors had gone, saw that everything of significance had already been taken, lost the plot and trashed the place. Did he have anything else to say?"

"Manolo mentioned that a man was inquiring after Juliet about a year ago. He described him as English, blond, enormous and obese. I asked Ferrier if he recognized such a person and that is when he went berserk."

"Does obese man have a name?"

"He never said."

Prado dug into his jacket pocket, extracted a number of items and said. "There were only clothes and travel essentials in his case, barely enough for a few days, but I found these in his man-bag."

Prado placed neatly on the table; a passport, set of car keys, wallet, notebook, gold pen, phone, a business card from a rental agency in Frigiliana and loose change. Phillip opened the wallet. It contained over €3,000 in €100 denominations, various credit and debit cards, and a photo. He winced as he turned it over and saw Juliet lying on a bed, naked. She appeared to be unconscious or asleep. Her hair was shorter, and she looked considerably younger. It had obviously been taken well before she came to Spain, yet the print was relatively new.

The phone was dead.

"Any sign of a charger in his room?" said Phillip.

"No, in the car perhaps," said Prado finishing his coffee, picking up the keys and standing. "You carry on fathoming the pocket-book, I'll check his vehicle."

Phillip flicked through the well-thumbed pages. It had the number of a local taxi company and the Nerja-Frigiliana bus timetable written in blue ink on the first couple of pages. At the back was a list of what he guessed to be pin numbers or passwords.

Prado returned and place a laptop and two chargers on the table, both were fitted with an English plug.

Phillip picked up the laptop and turned it on. The battery was flat.

Phillip explained the notebook contents and showed Prado the agency business card.

"Was he looking for a property?" said Prado.

"Perhaps he wanted to settle in the area?"

"Or looking for a place to keep Juliet," said Prado.

"We should go and see this estate agent; what's her name?"

"Maria."

"They left everything on the table under the watchful eye of Castro, whose color had almost returned to normal. He nodded curtly as they passed.

It had been a while since Phillip had been in Frigiliana village. As they ambled up the steep hill toward the agent's premises, he noticed a few new shops and a bar.

The estate agent was based on the ground floor of an old three-story townhouse. The tiny entrance was through a sky-blue-painted door. A few properties were mounted on a display board in a small window next to the door. The interior lights were on, and a well-built but smartly dressed woman could be seen sitting behind a desk and working feverishly on a laptop. Only fifty years ago, this room was where the farm animals were kept. They opened the door and went in.

The woman stood as they entered, came round to the front of the desk, and said effusively in Spanish, "Good morning, gentlemen. How may I help you?"

"Police," said Prado, showing her his ID.

"I apologize for the gushy welcome," she said. "I assumed you were customers."

"Sorry to disappoint. Are you Maria?"

"I am."

"We're inquiring about one of your possible clients," said Prado. "Mr. Graham Ferrier. He may have visited you in the last day or two. He's English, about forty, medium height, slender build, boozer's belly, dark hair, and a pencil mustache."

"Not surprised you guys are on his case," said Maria. "What a moron. He demanded to know if I had rented out a property to a giant-sized, fair-haired Englishman during the last eighteen months. I politely introduced him to the concept of client confidentiality and asked him to leave. He stormed out in a huff, shouting, what sort of fucking country did we live in?"

"When was this?" said Prado.

"Day after San Isidro."

"Did he mention the name of this mysterious fair-haired person?"

"He did. I made a note of it, just in case I came across him," she said going behind her desk and flicking through notes on her computer. "Ah, here it is. Duffy. Rick Duffy."

"And have you come across Duffy," said Prado. "Or is that still confidential?"

Maria smiled. "No inspector; to both questions."

"Thank you. Sorry to have disturbed you," said Prado.

"Glad to have helped," she said.

"Is Duffy an English name?" said Prado as they headed back down Calle Real in the direction of the hotel.

"Irish," said Phillip.

"And Manolo told you that he was seen over a year ago inquiring about Juliet?"

"Correct."

"Maybe he's a resident?" said Prado taking out his phone and calling the name through to his office and instructed them to search the relevant databases. They arrived back at the hotel and sat back down at the evidence table. Prado's phone rang, he listened for a few seconds then said, "Thanks." And ended the call shaking his head. "No trace of Duffy, but there is a European arrest warrant out for him. He failed to follow his obligations as a registered sex offender."

"Perhaps the answer lies on Ferrier's devices?" said Phillip. "I have British plug adapters at home. Why don't I take them and his book with me? See what I can find?"

"I should ask you to sign a receipt, but I forgot to bring them. I have to prepare a report with Castro on Ferrier's death. When done, shall I pop in to see what you've discovered?"

"Fine, I'll knock you up some lunch."

27

Phillip found a UK adaptor in his study drawer, plugged in Ferrier's phone, and turned it on. He was presented with a log-in screen, so he tapped in the first password from the back of the notebook. It worked. The log showed several short conversations with a Detective Agency based in Coventry, England. He checked to confirm that roaming had been activated and used Ferrier's phone to call the number.

"Mr. Ferrier," said an angry man's voice. I told you not to contact us again."

"Sorry, but my name is Armitage. I'm working with the police in Spain and this morning witnessed Mr. Ferrier's death. I'm plowing through his phone log, and you guys were his most frequently called number."

"I assumed that you were Ferrier pestering us again."

"Well, I can guarantee he won't be doing any more of that."

"Can't say that I'm disappointed. How may I help?"

"We know he was looking for his stepdaughter in Spain. Were you the people who located her?"

"Yes, although I wish we hadn't taken the case now. We didn't discover until too late that he was a sex offender and that Juliet was his victim."

"How did you find her?"

"Bit of luck really. She wasn't registered on any UK databases so we presumed she was overseas. We circulated her details to our European network and the Spaniards came back with her National Identity number, address, and place of work. One of their agents confirmed that she was still resident there."

"Juliet was abducted a couple of days ago," said Phillip.

"That's terrible," said the detective. "I hope her abduction didn't have anything to do with Ferrier?"

"No, he intimated that it was arranged by a man called Rick Duffy. Does the name mean anything to you?"

"Yes. After we'd given Ferrier Juliet's address, he requested that we search for this Rick Duffy and also a man called Malcolm Crown. But by then, we'd discovered that Ferrier was out on parole so declined and instructed him not to bother us further."

"Did he define his relationship with either of them?"

"No."

"Did Ferrier give you any idea where Duffy or Crown might be?"

"Somewhere between Nerja and Torrox."

"So specific. How did he know that?"

"Just said so."

"Anything else you can share with me concerning Ferrier or Duffy?"

"Ferrier sent us a description of Duffy and Crown."

"With photos?"

"No, but Duffy is late-twenties, giant-like, blond, and ugly with a scar on his cheek. Crown is forty-seven years old, a short, skinny, effeminate man with slender hands, blue-gray eyes and greasy dark hair."

"Any thoughts on the nature of their relationship with Ferrier?"

"Probably cellmates."

"Sounds logical."

"Good luck finding them."

"OK, thanks. Helpful stuff."

"Sorry, it's not more."

"Me too."

Phillip dialed the other numbers in Ferrier's log. One was his solicitor. Phillip informed him of Ferrier's death, but wasn't surprised when they hung up, accusing him of being a hoax caller. The other numbers were his bank, stockbroker, and a Mercedes dealership.

Phillip changed the UK adaptor over to Ferrier's laptop. The second password down on the notebook list worked. He connected it to his Wi-Fi and started browsing Ferrier's emails

His doorbell rang. He checked the security camera. It was Prado.

He went to let him in.

"Report all done?" said Phillip.

"No thanks to Castro, poor guy relapsed and is still in a real mess. HR has sent him off for counseling. Forensics confirmed that the knife was from Juliet's kitchen, her prints were all over it. Why wouldn't Ferrier have wiped it?"

"I don't think he cared about covering his tracks. I surmise that this was a last gasp mission for him. He either killed Juliet and himself, or just himself?"

"That would account for his lack of baggage. Found anything?"

"Come; see."

Phillip narrated his conversation with the Detective Agency as they walked to his study and sat down at Phillip's workstation.

"Nice chairs," said Prado after a few seconds wriggling and turning. I could do with one of these in my office. So, now we have two names, Duffy and this new one Crown. Duffy was seen in Nerja about a year ago taking a photo of Juliet. Ferrier was adamant that Duffy and Crown are living between Nerja and Torrox. What can this imply?"

"Duffy and Crown might have been Ferrier's cellmates?" said Phillip.

"Of course. Therefore, Duffy and Crown were probably Ferrier's rapists. He must have detested those two."

"And when I told Ferrier that Duffy had been seen in Nerja, he concluded that it was Duffy and Crown that had abducted Juliet."

"Indicating that his sole reason for being here had been put beyond reach. He would no longer be able to exact his revenge on Juliet for giving evidence against him," said Prado. "Leaving his final option."

"To attack Castro, knowing that he would probably be killed."

"Makes sense."

"But how did Ferrier know Duffy was somewhere between Nerja and Torrox?"

"Perhaps Ferrier overheard something in prison?"

"Could be. Anything more from his phone?"

"That's it, now for his computer. First, I want to

take you through a few emails. They may reveal some insight into Ferrier's circumstances. For example, this one is from his accountant and has a spreadsheet attachment." Phillip clicked on the file and he skimmed through it.

"What does it say?" said Prado.

"He had a net worth of slightly under £2 million."

"Good; he can pay for his own funeral," said Prado.

"The cash in his wallet should cover that," said Phillip. "This next message is from his solicitor. It itemizes recent amendments to his will, confirming everything is going to PACT, a charity helping prisoners make a fresh start."

"Nothing to Juliet. What a generous fellow."

"The next one is from his building society. It confirms the final mortgage payment for his apartment."

"Where is it located?"

Phillip looked up the address.

"Central Birmingham."

"Is that an expensive area?"

"Looks like it," said Phillip.

"And the next message?"

"It's from an online fashion website, asking for copy shots from his last session for them over five years ago."

"Are there any photos?"

"Let's have a look."

Phillip found one directory entitled 'Fashions.' It contained a range of folders, he clicked on the first.

"Impressive portfolio," said Prado as they scanned thousands of photos of attractive models in a wide variety of outfits. "He's worked with Armani, Dior, Versace, and more. He might have been a failure as a man, but he could sure wield a camera."

"That's it with emails, I'll check his favorites," Phillip switched to the default browser. "Look, his bank account is on permanent log-in. The current account shows a balance of some £17,000 and a monthly income of £8,000. There are the usual domestic payments, but his credit-card statement shows a monthly subscription to CVS (Cumulonimbus Virtual Services), totaling £900 a year plus other payments of varying amounts."

"What is CVS?" said Prado.

Phillip checked the drives and found a connection to CVS. On request, he typed in the third password from Ferrier's list. A window opened containing one directory with a single item. He clicked on it and was again invited to enter a password. He tried the fourth line of letters and symbols from Ferrier's notebook, and the file opened.

"What's the message saying?" said Prado.

"The site can only be viewed using the TOR browser. Click to proceed."

"What's TOR?"

"It's an anonymous browser for the dark web. I haven't used it since Afghanistan. Shall we look?"

Prado nodded and rubbed his earlobe furiously.

The Green Onion logo loaded and the page opened up.

It was entitled, 'Peepers.'

The splurge described it as live-streamed broadcasts for discerning voyeurs.

Underneath, was an invitation to click for a live broadcast. Phillip followed the link and was presented with a room layout similar to the TV reality show—*Big Brother*. A small rectangular room with a door in the top right-hand corner contained six beds, each with a white-painted midheight bedside cabinet between them. Three beds lined each side with low sofas back to back in the middle of the room. At the far west end was a dining table and six white chairs and an archway through to a white tiled bathroom. The beds were covered with white bottom sheets and pillows but no bedcovers. If it wasn't for six large pot plants containing bushy Ficus benjamina trees, it could have been a clinic or hospital ward.

Six gorgeous-looking young girls were sprawled on the couches, each with liter bottles of water that they sipped from regularly. They were a mix of skin colors and scantily dressed in skimpy underwear and revealing blouses. One was reading, two were chatting, two were kissing and caressing each other intimately, the other was napping.

The one reading, a young African girl, slid off the bed and headed toward the restroom. But she moved in jerky motions and then froze totally.

"Why is it doing that?" said Prado.

"My countryside internet connection is weak, and the image is buffering. Here, it's working again. Let's zoom in and have a closer look."

"It seems pretty tame," said Prado.

"It is at the moment," said Phillip but I doubt this is all there is. There's probably a schedule somewhere. Let's have a look around."

Phillip spent several minutes trying out the site navigation system.

"There appear to be cameras and microphones everywhere," he said. "I think the idea is to capture every intimate sound and movement. There's certainly no place to hide, and nothing is left to the imagination.

This menu permits viewers to switch images from a choice of eight different screens. Some closeup, others less so. Here's the schedule."

"Breakfast with the Bad Boys," said Phillip. "Followed by Lunch with Girls Only. That must be this. Then 'Evenings in Leather' and to wrap up 'Group Entertainment."

"What are they talking about?" said Prado.

"They're discussing make-up. My questions are; are they appearing willingly, receiving an income for their services, or, is this sexual imprisonment and slavery?"

"What right-minded girl would choose to do this for a living? They have to be slaves," said Prado.

"Could Ferrier have watched this for enjoyment, or was he looking for another reason?" said Phillip.

"Perhaps, Peepers belongs to Duffy and Crown?"

"If that's the case," said Prado. "Perhaps Ferrier was keeping an eye out for Juliet."

Phillip shuddered. His breakfast churned in his stomach.

"Can we have a look at his recent browsing history?" said Prado.

"There are no other searches on TOR," said Phillip. "However, on his default browser his recent searches are for 'Rick Duffy, Spain' and a Malcolm Crown, Spain but with no results."

"Try another search for those two, but without Spain."

"There's one here on Duffy," said Phillip. "It's from the Leamington Observer. He was sentenced to four years for abusing young boys at a private school near Leamington Spa, where he had worked as a janitor."

"And Crown?"

"The Warwick Courier has him down as being

sentenced to three years for sexually assaulting a young man."

Phillip guided him through the Peepers website.

"Is there a payment page on the Peepers site?" said Prado.

"Haven't seen one," said Phillip switching back. "But it would all be untraceable, that's the whole point of the dark web, total anonymity."

"To whom did Ferrier pay his monthly subscription?"

Phillip clicked back to Ferrier's bank pages and clicked on the last payment to CVS.

"I might have known," said Prado, sighing. "CVS Ltd. Hispanic-Commerce Bank. High St. in bloody Gibraltar. It'll take me months to obtain any information from that lot."

"Then why don't we prevail on Rosemary? Her bank could check them out as a potential supplier."

"Brilliant thinking, Phillip. Call her now. We owe her an update anyway."

Phillip picked up his phone and dialed.

"Don't tell me you've found her so quickly?" said Rosemary. "I've only just arrived back home."

"Sorry, no, but we are getting warmer." Phillip regurgitated the latest news on the case.

"Ferrier dead. That's wonderful news, provided it wasn't him that stashed Juliet away."

"Have some faith, Rosemary. Ferrier had nothing to do with her abduction."

"Did he know who took her?"

"Yes, but he didn't say their names. Thankfully, he'd made inquiries with a local estate agent who told us the man Ferrier was looking for was a giant obese man called Rick Duffy. Ferrier's detective also confirmed that they were asked to search for this Duffy and another man Crown. They suspected that the three of them were cellmates. We'd like to know if Ferrier's probation officer could confirm that. Could you ask your detective to find out?"

"Of course. Anything else?"

"Ferrier paid a monthly subscription to a voyeur porn website called Peepers run by a company called CVS Ltd., banking in Gibraltar. If I email you a copy of the payment advice, could you have your bank obtain a copy of their accounts and information about its shareholders and directors?"

"I'll revert to you in the morning."

"Thanks, Rosemary," he said, turning to Prado. "She'll contact us tomorrow."

"Excellent. You mentioned lunch?" said Prado. "Then we can have a close look at this Peepers thing. Try and learn a thing or two about the girls."

"We should invite Amanda," said Phillip. "Some female perspective might help."

28

"You want to cancel dinner?" said Amanda when she answered her phone.

"What makes you think that?" said Phillip.

"Happens all the time."

"You're kidding me. What is it with Málaga men, don't they know what they have in their midst? Seriously, I'm really looking forward to our business discussions and, more importantly, getting to know you better."

"Likewise, and how did it go with Rosemary?"

Phillip brought her up to date, then said. "And now we need you to look at some porn."

"What? Look, Phillip. I'm a progressive kind of girl, but that isn't my thing? Especially with two of you."

"Just teasing. We've found a voyeur's website on Ferrier's laptop and would welcome a woman's perspective. Could you meet us at the comisaría in a couple of hours?"

"Difficult, I'm on my way to a meeting in Algeciras.

What's the hurry?"

"The website could lead us to Juliet."

"Can we make it later, say around seven this evening? I should be back by six, but then have to get ready for dinner."

"Two nights in a row?"

"I'll explain when I see you. Gotta run."

Phillip opened a can of tuna and chopped up some fresh salad vegetables from his sister's garden, crumbled in some fresh goat's cheese over it then drizzled over some local olive oil.

They ate it on the terrace and chatted for a while before Prado departed for his office.

After a pleasant siesta, Phillip worked on Nuestra España projects, then followed after Prado.

The view of Málaga harbor from the elevated autovia was spectacular as Phillip sped by. Tall red and blue gantries towered over serried ranks of gray freight containers and the ferry terminal to Melilla. A long concrete wall projected out to sea. It had been built to expand Málaga's cruise ship capacity and could comfortably accommodate two massive vessels simultaneously. Today it was the turn of RMS *Queen Mary Two*, recognizable by her white superstructure, black hull, and single red funnel. Thousands of foot passengers were disgorging over her gangplanks for an evening's shopping and culture in Málaga's old town. They strode, ambled, or hobbled as best they could past the colorful cuboid glass structure at the Centre Pompidou in the direction of Calle Larios.

Phillip turned off the highway, wound his way down through densely built residential areas, and parked underneath the comisaría. Prado took him up in the elevator.

"We'll have to issue you with a permanent pass if we carry on at this rate," said Prado as the door slid open. "I'll have a word with the boss." He nodded at el jefe superior's office as they passed.

"Do you prefer to wait for Amanda?" said Phillip.

"No, no, let's crack on," said Prado watching Phillip set up Ferrier's laptop.

There was a knock on the door and a female officer showed Amanda in.

She looked stunning in a lime-green dress that hugged her figure and accentuated her silky olive skin. Her glossy raven hair cascaded over bare shoulders, and she seemed taller.

"You look special today. More elevated somehow," Phillip said, standing up and exchanging cheek kisses.

"Thank you." She blushed and flashed her high heels. "I'm meeting a producer from the BBC for dinner. Possible new client. Can we make a start? I can't stay long."

"Are you prepared to be mildly embarrassed?" said Prado. "Ferrier's voyeur services have nothing to do with playing tennis."

"I'll try and be brave."

Phillip opened up Peepers once more. The girls were all gathered around the table; eating.

"Wait," said Prado, glancing at his watch. It's just before seven o'clock, yet they are eating supper already. That's way too early for Spaniards, and look at the food, dark bread, ham, salad, Dutch-style cheese, herring, smoked salmon, boiled eggs, and coffee in a Thermos flask; that's not what we eat."

"Nor English," said Phillip. "They'd be drinking tea with milk."

"I'd say German or Scandinavian," said Amanda.

"Yet the milk carton is from Asturias," said Phillip.

"Look underneath the table," said Prado. "There's a plastic supermarket bag. Can anyone read what it says; my eyes?..."

"Aldi, Torrox-Costa," said Amanda. "And have you seen the bedside lockers. While they appear new, they are old Spanish style, made of timber, but painted white; you can see the ornate paneling on the doors. My mum has one just like it."

"So it seems Ferrier was correct," said Prado. "They are near Torrox?"

"Amanda," said Phillip. "Note that there are six girls. There are no windows, exit doors, cameramen or film directors' visible and nobody appears to be forcing them to do things against their will. Yet, the girls look obedient, happy, or at least are acting so. They're certainly not pacing about scheming or worrying. None of them bite their nails, smoke, or drink alcohol, and they appear alert and drug-free. We can see that there are two African girls, three white, and one Asian. They all speak reasonable English. There's no bitching, no complaining, and no one is crabby. It seems too good to be true. What are your thoughts?"

"Whew, where to start?" said Amanda. "My first reaction is that they are not just porn stars. There's a personal affinity between them as if they are accustomed to these circumstances."

"What do they talk about?" said Prado.

"It's limited," said Phillip. "Looks, makeup, clothes, music, and films. There's no mention of global news or their previous lives."

"Probably accounts for their domestic harmony," said Amanda, laughing.

"I suggest they've been brainwashed to behave like

this," said Phillip. "Yet I'm confused by their behavior. Why would they be so happy and compliant and not tearing the place apart?"

"I think they're prisoners," said Amanda. "That have accepted their circumstances. If you can bear to, look closely at their bodies. They are all slim. Not excessively so, but thinner than average, particularly for a career where you would expect more voluptuous figures. Perhaps food is being used as a controlling mechanism. Maybe they were starved initially, but now are fed just enough to keep them satisfied enough to comply happily with their instructions."

"I see what you mean," said Phillip. "But why do they seem so happy about being locked up?"

"Illegal migrants could enjoy this type of work. A roof over their heads, three squares a day, and no violence. That could be a considerable improvement as against their previous existence."

"Wait," said Phillip. "Looks like they're about to leave."

They watched as the girls tidied up, put on housecoats hanging from the door, waited until it was opened then disappeared through it taking their trash in the Aldi bag. The screen faded to black and the title; 'Evenings in Leather,' span in. Several seconds later, the same room setting appeared, but this time with three incredibly beautiful black girls and three pretty black boys. All six were dressed in tightly clinging shiny black leather pants and sleeveless waistcoats open at the front. Their language was English, and all had accents from various countries of the African continent, but their topic of conversation was limited, direct, and crude about what they wanted to do to each other. When two girls started undressing one of the boys, Prado said, "I think we can turn it off now."

Phillip killed the machine and started packing it up.

"The second squad was just as skinny as the first," said Amanda.

"And they all appeared to be around sixteen or seventeen," said Phillip.

"Interesting observations from both of you," said Prado. "Clearly, what we're looking at is a sexual-slavery ring based somewhere east of Málaga. My questions are, do they all live on the studio premises, or are they transported back and forth every day from elsewhere?"

"Safer to be in one place," said Phillip. "Less room for error and fewer resources to keep them confined."

"I agree, then can we discuss criteria for a potential location? For example, town, village, or countryside?"

"I noticed that the Internet transmission speed here in Málaga is amazing compared to mine at home," said Phillip. "There's not a trace of buffering. Do you have fiber optics?"

"I have no idea," said Prado. "I'll call someone." Prado picked up his phone, dialed, asked his question, and hung up. "Apparently we have the fastest available fiber optic network. The same as those who watch TV via the Internet."

"Good, because to deliver such a high-quality streaming experience, Peepers would need the maximum connection speed," said Phillip. "To date in Andalusia, fiber optics have only been installed in major towns and larger urbanizations."

"So what you're saying is that we can ignore all locations without fiber optics?" said Prado.

"Correct," said Phillip.

"Well, that should reduce our options hugely," said

Prado. "I've heard that the uptake of fiber optics has been slow as most households aren't prepared to pay the extra cost, especially for the high-speed option. We'll contact the service providers for a list of actual installations. What other search criteria should we consider?"

"I think it's in a cellar underneath a property and not in an outbuilding," said Phillip. "It's easier to soundproof, secure, and to deliver food and victims without risk of exposure. They can drive into the garage and take things directly into the house or underground out of sight. A villa with a cellar underneath located on a busy urbanization would be perfect. Whereas, a townhouse is unlikely to have a garage, and any noise would be difficult to disguise."

"I agree," said Prado. "That still means we have thousands of properties to search, but at least the list is coming down in size. Any other insights?"

"Just one," said Phillip. "Continuous streaming of high-density images to thousands of subscribers gobbles up enormous amounts of bandwidth. Most folks shut down about midnight and traffic dies off substantially. If the service providers could monitor activity for, say, three o'clock in the morning and give us a list of those areas that remain busy, it will help us refine our search zones down even further."

"There's one more refinement I can add," said Prado. "Cellars are a relatively recent feature in Spanish homes. Until the 1980s, we couldn't afford the machinery to hew them out of our predominately rocky terrain. Consequently, most speculative builders didn't bother because it was cheaper to add another floor on top. The cellars that were built tended to be commissioned by private individuals building their own properties. The clean, straight lines of the walls in the Peepers cellar indicate that it is probably under a recently built property. The lighting is modern. The taps and bathroom fittings seem new. If we check building licenses for private building projects for, say, the last twenty years and then cross-reference them with the criteria you mentioned earlier, we should be able to slash the options into a relatively short list."

"That's still a lot of information for so few people to collate and analyze," said Phillip.

"Then we'll have to find you some help," boomed a male voice behind them.

"Good evening, sir," said Prado, standing.

"Carry on, please," said el jefe superior. "Did I overhear lists that need compiling and analyzing?"

"Correct, sir. Let me introduce you to our volunteer translators," said Prado.

They all shook hands. Prado summarized the case to date.

"Good work in such a short time scale," said el jefe. "I'll allocate two officers to your team for the list production."

"Thank you, sir," said Prado.

"I'll leave you to it. Nice to meet you both," said el jefe, closing the door behind him.

Prado waited until his boss had gone, then said quietly, "Amazing, I didn't even have to ask for more resources. Something about our case must have spooked him."

"Perhaps he's worried that Juliet's abduction will hit the British Press," said Phillip.

"Of course," said Prado, grinning. "Their voracious coverage could seriously damage tourist numbers."

"You should remember that for the future," said

Phillip. "And resources will magically appear."

"Sorry to interrupt guys, but I have one more thing to tell the inspector before I have to run," said Amanda, glancing at her watch.

"Go on," said Prado.

"I was in the migrant detention center in Algeciras this afternoon to finish collecting data for my documentary. From the thirty-six-people that were actually rescued, there were only fourteen remaining. All the younger ones had been deported. They'd been there for less than three days and it would have been impossible to fully process their asylum applications in such a short period. If they have been deported, it suggests that their human rights were infringed and someone in authority might be cutting corners.

"However, that wasn't my main complaint. The man in charge there is Sergeant Pérez. A most obnoxious fellow most unsuited for such a senior and responsible position."

"Not all civil servants are as charming as I," said Prado. "And I can tell you that in this office there are several I would fire tomorrow except that they do a good job. What did you find so malodorous about him?"

"Xenophobic and racist sums him up nicely," said Amanda. "Not ideal qualities to make unbiased recommendations to the asylum panel about the future lives of these poor migrants. If you ask me, something stinks down in Algeciras."

"Mmm," said Prado, rubbing his earlobe. "I'll discuss it with el jefe, and let you know what, if anything, we will do about it."

"Thanks," said Amanda picking up her bag, slipping into a dark green wrap and heading for the door.

"Good luck with the BBC man," said Phillip.

"Woman; it's a BBC woman," said Amanda, eyes twinkling. "See you tomorrow night."

29

Phillip had just awoken from his siesta on the terrace when his phone announced Rosemary's call. He stretched, yawned, and swiped the screen.

"Good afternoon, Phillip," said Rosemary. "It's raining here again."

"Then why not build your special houses here in the sun?"

"I'm tempted, but as you said, if you can't speak Spanish, you soon go bust. Listen, I have the information you wanted. CVS Ltd. was only registered at the end of last year and so far there are no published accounts. The directors and shareholders of CVS Ltd. are Gibraltarians and almost certainly nominees. I have their names and addresses and will email them to you, but I doubt they will have any knowledge as to what the Company actually does for a living.

"Their registered address is a firm of lawyers called Martin and Bayne on Main Street. Their bank is Hispanic-Commerce a few doors down on the same street and they have a triple-A credit rating which implies a large sum of capital was invested. CVS has no associations or interests with any other company either in Gibraltar or overseas. Sorry, but that's all I have."

"It's a start."

"My lawyers can help if you need them."

"Thanks. Any news on Ferrier's cellmates?"

"They weren't in the probation officers file, but he kindly offered to obtain them for us. I'll send them as soon as I have received them, but it might take a day or two. Any more developments?"

"Yes, we've narrowed the location from where the Peepers broadcasts are being made to between Torrox and Nerja, just as Ferrier intimated. Now, it's just a tedious process of list-making and elimination."

"Do you think Juliet has been abducted specifically for this Peepers thing?"

"We don't know, but we have to eliminate the possibility from our inquiries."

Phillip returned to his study to work on the latest translations for Nuestra España.

Just after eight o'clock, he showered, changed into a black shirt and beige pants, and then drove off to Torre del Mar, where he parked on the seafront and walked the few hundred meters to the restaurant. Antonio, the headwaiter, welcomed him with his usual enthusiasm and took him to a table at the quieter end of the terrace. Amanda arrived moments later. Phillip's heart skipped a beat.

She wore a short, plain black sheath that clung to her curves. A small pair of diamond stud earrings added an alluring sparkle to her elfin face framed by her glossy hair. Her full lips carried a trace of lipstick.

Phillip stood up, placed a hand on each of her

shoulders, and kissed both of her cheeks in the traditional Spanish fashion.

"You look lovely," he whispered in her ear.

She smiled, sat in the chair being held for her by Antonio, and said, "Thank you. You too."

They were both a little shy at first, but after a glass of cava and ordering their food, the conversation began to flow.

Antonio arrived with a plate of fresh oysters, placed them in the center of the table, and left them to it. They looked at each other, then the oysters, and helped themselves to one each. They added a squeeze of lemon, a dash of Tabasco, raised the shell before their mouths, and swallowed. They nodded their satisfaction to each other and picked up another oyster.

"I saw some of your action videos," said Phillip before gulping down another.

"Been checking up on me, have you?" said Amanda, before lifting another mollusk to her mouth, and swallowing it.

Phillip watched her spellbound; it was one of the most sensual things he'd ever seen. He shook his head before replying, "I thought this special evening warranted a little research."

"You like to study your subjects beforehand, huh?"

Phillip looked directly into her eyes, smiled, and said, "I generally find that good preparation leads to a more agreeable outcome. Don't you?"

Amanda grinned and cocked her head to one side.

"Seriously, though," said Phillip, "your videos are, what you Americans say, awesome, yet the number of viewings on CNN is pathetic. Do they still have the copyright?"

"Not now, our deal was for three years only. As

from two months ago, I can show them wherever I want. It's why I need my own website."

Over the main course of fresh turbot baked in sea salt accompanied by roasted green peppers, Phillip outlined what he and Richard had discussed earlier. "We'd be happy to make a website to do what you want and sell the footage to major broadcasters, but we would also like for Nuestra España to use your videos to animate some of our historical articles. The action videos will appeal hugely to our major advertisers. They are so good they could become viral, it would mean some serious income. Is that what you are looking for?"

Amanda thought about Phillip's proposals. Then made a few false starts to reply before actually saying, "Er… wow, this really is a business discussion. My initial reaction is positive, and I promise to think seriously about what you have offered, but this is a big step for me, so I'm not going to rush into anything. Do you mind?"

"Of course not. I, sorry, Richard and I wanted to establish that we appreciate your talents and want to find a way to work with you. This offer is just one proposal."

"Listen, it's fantastic and exactly what I'm seeking. My reticence stems from being accustomed to working on my own. It would be a new experience for me to work with a team, although the thought of it is most appealing. However, before I could accept, I'd prefer to acquaint myself better with you and Richard. Not with your editing talents, which, having looked at your work on the Nuestra España site, are far better than mine, but as persons. We'll be traveling long journeys around Spain together, sharing ideas and arguing about them. Such a close working relationship means that I need to respect and trust you both. For example, I feel that you personally are sorting your emotions about Juliet. But what about your ex-wife, can you tell me about her?"

"You really want to hear this?" said Phillip, taking a deep breath. "Isn't it bad to talk about previous relationships?"

Amanda reached out, grasped his hand, gazed into his eyes and said, "Yes, it breaks all the rules. Please carry on."

"OK. Here goes," he said. "She was er… Valentina was Russian, and I loved her at first sight more than the world itself.

"But I failed miserably to match the strength of my feelings to the attention she was seeking. I was concentrating on my business and always thinking about the next deal or problem at work so I missed the, I-want-a-family hints and signals. Eventually, she gave up on me and had an affair with a Russian neighbor.

"Nobody was more shocked than I when she served me with divorce papers. I did not see that coming at all, we had even made beautiful love the night before. Like an idiot, I agreed to it, but then paid serious attention to her needs, hoping I could rescue her feelings for me. I even agreed to an onerous divorce settlement in a pathetic attempt to stay in her good books and keep her in my life. Nevertheless, she went back to Moscow with her new man.

"When my parents died, they left me their villa here in Nerja, it was just the trigger I needed. At last, I could escape the rat race and her nagging memory. Yet, as soon as I arrived here, I met Juliet, who could either have been my Valentina or our daughter. My behavior toward her has always been exemplary, but internally, I didn't know whether to ask her out or take her to the toy shop. The pilgrimage helped me put that in perspective by mentally burying Valentina once and for all. Something I should have done years before.

"Then Rosemary told me that Juliet's mother was a successful model, but a useless parent. However, Juliet had a wonderful relationship with her father, who sadly died when she was thirteen. They often came to Nerja and swam together on El Salon beach. Apparently, while I don't resemble her dad, my height and ways reminded her of him. It was why she trusted and liked having me around. It made her feel safe, especially with all these men coming onto her. I tell you Amanda, when Rosemary told me that, it shamed me. I felt like a dirty pervert. I was disgusted with myself. How dare I lust after such a loving and trusting young girl who just wanted a father figure around to turn to when she was feeling low or had a problem to share? Thankfully, my mind cleared instantly. I still love her dearly, but now I'm happy to play the role Juliet always thought I was playing."

Amanda squeezed his hand tightly.

"You shouldn't be hard on yourself," she said. "You're a man, your brains are between your legs, and Juliet is a very sexy girl. Irrespective of your confused good intentions toward her, you can't ignore natural male instincts. Any man would have felt the same, but at least you acted with decorum. Most couldn't have resisted, and you should be proud of that."

Her phone buzzed. "I'm sorry, this might be important," she said while groveling in her black purse, extracting her phone and looking at it. She shrugged. "It's an email from an unknown address, but it says for

Amanda." She clicked again. Phillip saw a video appear. Amanda looked at it. Phillip had never seen such a powerful expression of tenderness. Amanda put her hand to her mouth. Tears rolled down her cheeks.

Amanda turned the phone around and showed Phillip the video. It was a tiny baby gurgling among some cushions, wearing a pretty pink outfit and lace booties.

"It's… it's…" she couldn't speak. Her shoulders shuddered as she tried to control her distress.

Phillip was concerned. He stood up, went round to console her, and put his arm around her shoulder. She turned, buried her head in his chest, and wept. Phillip waved Antonio away as he approached.

"It's all right. I'm fine," she sniffed. "Really. It's just I never expected to see her again."

Phillip returned to his chair and nodded to Antonio that all was in order. The diners resumed their conversations. The waiters continued their tasks.

"I'm sure you remember that I was on a Guardia Civil coast guard cutter last Tuesday," said Amanda. "While on-board, I helped a migrant give birth to this baby. The mother died later in the hospital without ever seeing her child. The nurse who took the baby from me christened her Amanda. It was only meant to be a temporary name until they found adoptive parents. This video is from them. They decided to keep the name.

"It's such a pleasant surprise. I never thought that they would want to use my name let alone contact me. I'm sorry, I'm being silly, but it was the first time I've ever held a newborn baby and it drew out my repressed maternal instincts. I actually understand how Valentina felt about not having children."

"Well, aren't we both happy puppies tonight?" said Phillip.

Amanda smiled. "Do you regret not having children?"

"At the time, more than anything," said Phillip, his eyes watering. "But on reflection, I'm happy that we didn't. Long-distance parenting is extremely painful, especially for the child."

Amanda nodded, seemingly happy with the reply and said, "This is not quite how I imagined our evening."

"Me neither, but I'm not regretting a single moment."

"Knowing the baby has a proper home has lifted a heavy weight from my shoulders," said Amanda, squeezing his hand tightly and dabbing her eyes with a serviette.

"I'm happy for you, and I thought we'd be discussing BBC ladies."

Amanda looked shocked. "Shit. I forgot to tell you."

Phillip's phone rang. "Sorry, Amanda, but I set my phone so only Prado can call me. Do you mind?"

"Of course not, I'll pop to the restroom."

Phillip watched her every sensuous move as she walked into the hubbub of the restaurant interior.

"Digame, Leon," he said.

"I seem to be making a habit of disturbing you at your leisure; I'm sorry, but such is the nature of police work."

"I understand."

"Amanda's not upset then?"

"She's popped to the ladies. Has there been a development?"

"Not really, I just wanted to inform you that I have

all the lists and am cross-referencing them with my two new eager beavers. We'll be working all night, but I hope that by morning we will have some properties to visit. Any chance of a photo of Duffy or Crown?"

"Rosemary's still working on it. She'll send it as soon as it arrives."

"OK, then enjoy the rest of your evening, and we'll talk tomorrow. Buenos noches."

Amanda returned, looking refreshed and happier.

"Whew, I'm full," she said. "And a little tipsy."

"Stroll along the promenade? We could have coffee at one of the Chiringuito's."

"Great idea and I insist on going halves with the bill."

"As you wish."

Phillip caught the waiter's eye and made a writing gesture with his hand. The man nodded and tapped in the instruction to his digital order device. Minutes later, Antonio appeared with the check and offered them a liqueur on the house, which they declined. They paid half each of the ninety-odd euros in cash plus a ten percent tip and headed out toward the promenade.

As they moved away from the glow of the orange streetlights, the heavens appeared. A mass of stars twinkling in a black sky, in the center of which glowed a full moon. It carved a mesmerizing phosphorescent path over the sea from the horizon to the beach. They strolled next to each other, arms touching and exchanging tender glances. Phillip spotted several empty tables at a new Chiringuito. They walked over a canvas mat that protected their shoes from the sand, sat down next to each other, and ordered coffee. At first, they were content to soak up the romantic atmosphere.

Surf lapping gently against the shore. Couples strolled arm in arm, paddling in the wavelets, occasionally pausing to hug or embrace. Spanish guitar music thrummed at an acceptable volume.

"Can't find this in London," said Phillip, breaking the comfortable silence as the waiter served them.

"Coffee's not bad either," said Amanda, replacing her cup back down on the saucer. "Do you want to hear about the BBC offer?"

"Tell me."

"Basically, they want to use some of my videos to illustrate a documentary on Spanish culture."

"Would that prevent us from using them? You know, just in case we do agree to work with each other."

"Not at all. They are paying for non-exclusive use."

"Then that sounds like a great deal. When?"

"They will pay me in advance next week. The program won't be broadcast for another six months, though."

"Well done. I do like a one off payment, but I prefer repeat monthly income. This is what your videos would earn when working with us."

"Mmm… food for thought. What did Prado have to say?"

"Nothing really, just a progress report. The lists will be ready by morning. Then we can start knocking on doors."

"I'm sorry about the histrionics earlier."

"Amanda, it was an extremely frank exchange, and I feel privileged that you were comfortable enough with me to let rip. If you're up to it, I'd like to learn more about you."

"I guess that's only fair," Amanda confirmed.

"Well, as you probably gathered, I care enormously about children and dream of being in a loving relationship with a man who would happily contribute equally to a parental experience."

"As I said yesterday, what is it with Málaga men?"

"It's not them. I'm the problem. In the limited free time available, I've tried the online dating stuff but found that descriptions never matched expectations. I don't mind divorced, so long as there are no kids involved, as I refuse to be a stepmother or deal with ex-wives. Men have to accept me as an equal in all departments, and that includes finances and chores. Hard to find in Spain, where macho still rules and mothers do everything, especially for their sons. What about you? Do you have a girlfriend?"

"No, despite my sister's best intentions. She keeps inviting Spanish girls to dinner to tempt me, but I can't adjust to the large family thing. As Prado said, all those celebrations to attend, pretending that you enjoy the same old faces, jokes, and conversations. I prefer my own space."

"Me too, but not all the time."

"Go with that."

They finished their coffee. Phillip insisted on paying the grand sum of three euros. He then escorted Amanda back to her car.

They paused at the door as she unlocked it with the key fob.

She opened the door and made to clamber in but hesitated, turned and looked up at him gazing into his eyes. She could feel his soul burning into her and yearned for him to take her in her arms and kiss her passionately.

But he felt awkward, unsure of himself. Confused

by his anxiety for Juliet.

He put his arms on her shoulder and they exchanged lingering cheek kisses.

Amanda whispered, "Thank you for a perfect evening. I can't wait to do it again."

"Me too," he whispered back, heart thumping.

She clambered into her Prius, slipped off her heels, and drove away, waving her hand out of the window. Phillip watched her go, relishing the memory of her lips on his face and her soft breath in his ear.

"Fucking idiot," he said under his breath. "Why didn't you kiss her?"

He walked to his car and drove home, feeling more confused than ever.

30

Prado hadn't called or left a message overnight, so Phillip opted for his usual swim. The roads were quiet for Sunday morning, and the underground car park only half-full. Manolo was laying out tables at Don Comer, ready for another day's al fresco business. Phillip waved as he passed by in the direction of the beach, but Manolo was too preoccupied to notice.

As he bobbed up and down, clinging to the buoy, he pondered on the previous evening with Amanda. Half of him didn't care if she decided to work with him and Richard or not. It would be brilliant if she did, as then he'd have an excuse to see her regularly. If she didn't, he'd find another way to be with her. Tonight, he'd call to see how she was and bring her up to date with the search for Juliet.

After his swim, Phillip found himself still too early to meet Richard for coffee, so he went for a walk on the freshly washed Balcón. There weren't many people around, the cigarette butts and chewing gum had disappeared temporarily, and a few street cleaners in their high-visibility lime-green and blue uniforms were busy emptying the bins. He stopped by the statue of King Alfonso, exchanged good mornings with some keen photographers snapping away at the diminutive monarch, and looked down at the stunningly beautiful Calahonda beach.

It was less than half the size of El Salon and completely protected by limestone cliffs. Perched on top was a hotel next to an apartment block. Underneath was Puerta del Mar, Nerja's finest fresh-fish restaurant.

Short rows of sunbeds and reed-covered parasols filled the central beach area. A small cottage was built into the foot of the cliff. The ruins of a dilapidated, disused bar nestled at the bottom of the steps, awaiting a council decision on its future.

A colorful fishing vessel undulated gently as it rounded the headland of the Balcón. Two stocky, deeply tanned fishermen, presumably father and son by their close resemblances, sat abreast on the central thwart, rowing effortlessly and harmoniously thrusting their tiny craft steadily toward the shore. In the prow, a grubby white plastic container brimming with sea water was balanced precariously on top of damp folded nets. It was teeming with sardines, sea bass, and king prawns, some still wriggling. A squabble of aggressive seagulls swooped daringly close to the container, risking all for a fishy breakfast. The son stood and swung an oar at the airborne marauders in a futile attempt to protect the meager fruits of their long night's labor. Needless to say, he missed, caused the boat to rock alarmingly and almost tottered overboard. At the last minute, the father grabbed a leg and steadied him. The lad sat down, cursing. Dad laughed out loud and shook his head at such youthful folly before both resumed their metronomic rhythm. Approaching the shore, the two heaved vigorously in unison. The tiny craft surged forward and landed with a jolt in the shallows. The men shipped oars, stowed them in the bilges, scrambled out, and hauled their boat further up onto the deserted beach.

A black kitten prowled near the water's edge, monitoring the men's progress through luminous green eyes. It tiptoed back, meowing when the wavelets splashed too close. The father twisted the head of a sardine and hurled it onto the nearby rocks. The young cat scampered after it, pounced, successfully pinned it to the rock, and began nibbling.

Phillip laughed at the young cat's antics and headed for Don Comer. It wasn't busy at all, and he sat down at an empty regulars' table. Manolo served him personally, then hovered.

"If you have time, sit down a minute," said Phillip.

"I don't, but how's it going?"

"I believe we might be making some progress. We haven't found Juliet yet, but we have some real possibilities that might take us nearer to her."

"Great. I'll fetch your breakfast."

Phillip's phone rang. It was Didi.

"WhatsApp is cheaper," said Phillip.

"I can't be bothered with all that," said Didi. "A phone's a phone."

"How's Bremen?"

"Cold and gray, but I'm not calling to complain about the weather. I've just seen the Nuestra España news article about Juliet's abduction. Have you found her yet?"

"No. Why?"

"I may have been the last person to see her. She was watching the San Isidro dressage with a young man. They seemed enamored, you know, holding hands and kissing stuff."

"What time was this?" said Phillip his heart racing.

"Not long after the dressage started."

"Did you recognize the man?"

"I'm sure I've seen him before in an estate agent's office. We were looking in the window at a penthouse they had just sold. It was the sort of property we're after in town. Anyway, I saw him sitting at a sales desk inside showing brochures to someone."

"Which agency, Didi?"

"The one on Calle San Miguel, I think they're Scandinavian. I have a photo of Juliet and him if that helps."

"Are you able to send it to me?"

"I can only cope with email. Will that do?"

"Of course. Thanks, Didi."

"Auf wiedersehen."

Manolo delivered Phillip's breakfast just as the email arrived from Didi.

"Do you know this guy with Juliet?" said Phillip, holding the photo up for Manolo.

"Yeah. He's been here a few times, drinks a large latte," said Manolo. "Seemed to be hitting it off with Juliet. His first name is Lars, but that's all I know about him."

"Thanks." Phillip picked up his *mollete* and took a bite.

While he was chewing, he brought up the Swedish agency website mentioned by Didi and browsed the contacts.

He found a photo of Lars Eriksson, a brief CV, and a mobile number. He dialed it. The call was forwarded to the estate agency. A man named Steen answered.

"Lars quit on the eve of San Isidro," said Steen in response to Phillip's questions. "He wasn't doing well in Nerja and wanted to try his luck in Marbella, said nothing about a girlfriend though. Sorry, but I have no number for him."

"Thanks," said Phillip. He ended the call then forwarded the photo of Lars and Juliet with an explanation to Prado.

Prado called him back fifteen minutes later.

"They seem a happy couple," said Prado. "However, Eriksson doesn't resemble any of our abductors. We have no records about him other than he's self-employed and uses an address in Stella Maris on Calle Antonio Ferrandiz Chanquete. I've sent a local cop to check it out."

"How's it going with the lists?" said Phillip.

"We've finished cross-referencing and managed to reduce it down to some six hundred probables," he said. "These are properties that meet all the criteria; that is, with late-night Internet usage, high-grade fiber-optic connection, town or busy-urbanization location, garage access to the house, and have building licenses for a substantial cellar. Our patrol car is on its way to begin searching, but I estimate they will need at least ten days to visit them all.

"We're also building a list of possibles, whereby they meet nearly all the criteria, but I'm worried we are relying too much on honest citizens building legal cellars. Twenty years ago, many just built the damn thing without permission. I propose to contact former builders to see if we can locate a few more, but as most of them went bankrupt during respective crashes, that won't be easy. Hold on; a colleague is just handing me a note."

Phillip heard a thud, rustling paper and then Prado saying in the background, "What the fuck is this?"

31

Phillip sipped his coffee with his phone jammed to his ear, straining to hear what was going on at Prado's end. There was only a faint mumbling in the background.

"Sorry to keep you waiting," said Prado after a few minutes. "My colleagues have been monitoring the Peepers website on Ferrier's laptop. So far we've seen eighteen different participants. Seven of them are among our missing girls."

"So you were right. It is one group taking them and now we know why."

"That's not all Phillip. I'm forwarding by email a screenshot of an advert for a forthcoming event that keeps popping up on Peepers. If I've translated the headline correctly, I promise you won't think much of it. Call me back when you've read the small print."

Phillip waited, his mind running riot. It had to be something bad concerning Juliet; why else would Prado send it? His phone beeped, announcing the message from Prado.

He opened up the attached image. His heart leaped into his mouth as the pretty faces of two young blond girls appeared on his screen

One of them was Juliet. She looked terrified.

The headline reads:

'Two Reluctant Virgins—One Night Only

Starring the Danish Siren—celebrating her sixteenth birthday—and the beautiful English Rose.

On Monday at 2200 hours, CET, two beautiful, pure, young, and tender virgins will be deflowered against their will. Member's viewing fee is US$350. Warning: Adult entertainment, including scenes of sexual violence. Satisfaction not guaranteed. No refunds.

Phillip's eyes filled with tears and confusion. He was relieved that she was still alive, but despaired at her situation. He picked up a serviette from the dispenser and dabbed them away as he pondered over her destiny.

She was an actual virgin thanks to the mental and physical torture imposed on her by Ferrier. To be raped in this brutal manner was likely to destroy her psychologically and then, what would happen to her when this depraved event was over? He had to stop it.

He phoned Prado back.

"Was I right?" said Prado.

"Regretfully, yes;" said Phillip and then explained in full what was about to happen to Juliet.

"That means we only have thirty-six hours to find them," said Prado.

"Do you know anything about the Danish girl?"

"She is why I am doing this job."

"Sorry?"

"It's a case I worked on a few weeks ago. The girl's name is Angelika Jensen. She attended an international school in Rincón de la Victoria. Her father is a wealthy Danish car-hire-company owner living in the eastern Málaga district of Pedregalejo and tomorrow is actually her sixteenth birthday. On April 28, at around 1800 hours, after she finished her Spanish-dance lesson at school, she said farewell to her dance partner then disappeared.

"Next morning, her parents received a ransom note in their mailbox. It demanded €100,000 with simple drop instructions. The cash was to be placed in a knotted linen SuperSol shopping bag and left in the foyer of their branch in Avenida Principal del Candado at the busiest time of day, which was 1900 hours that evening. If the money was not there precisely as instructed, their daughter would be gang-raped and then killed slowly and painfully. No contact or negotiations would be permitted and if police interfered at the drop, the daughter would still suffer.

"I was concerned that if the money was handed over in one drop, the criminals would take it and kill the girl anyway. I persuaded the father to hold half the money back and add a note to the cash with his mobile number explaining the new terms. The abductors would then contact him to negotiate the collection of the remainder, and that would give me a better chance of locating them.

"At least, that was the plan. However, I hadn't considered the extraordinary action taken by the kidnappers. Phillip, no one could have done.

"The father delivered the money in the bag and left. I was watching the live-feed of the foyer from the supermarket security office. As soon as the father had gone, a small, slender man dressed as a tramp started rummaging through the bag. He was there for only seconds and departed almost immediately, leaving the bag and all the money behind intact. There were no further demands, no contact, and not a sign of Angelika or the tramp. Despite a massive media campaign, no additional clues were forthcoming except that Angelika's damaged phone had been handed in which hadn't yielded anything useful.

"I returned the cash to the parents, who, along with everyone was totally mystified by the kidnappers' behavior. Why send a note, then not take the money? While the parents placed no blame on me, I couldn't live with the guilt. My interference had deprived them of a loving and beautiful daughter. We assumed that she'd been killed."

"At least you know she's alive," said Phillip.

"Yes, but you must feel the same about Juliet. What happens after the event?"

"Any ideas?"

"If you recall our chat at the airport, they are sold or disposed of depending on their level of cooperation or how well they keep their looks."

"Then we just have to find them before this event. Have you started searching the properties on the list?"

"Yes, but with only one car and two officers, it is slow work."

"Inspector, we have less than thirty-six hours," shouted Phillip. "We must have more resources or we may as well give up now."

"You're right. I'll discuss it with el jefe," said Prado.

"Can you send me part of the list so I can search some of the properties?"

"Phillip, I understand how you feel, and in your position, I would want the same. However, I won't insult your intelligence by boring you with all the reasons why I cannot send the list to you. Other than to say that this is dangerous police work, I cannot risk a civilian in the front line."

"Are you joking Inspector? Need I remind you of my contribution with Ferrier?"

"Phillip, calm down. All right, I'll tell it to you straight. I received a serious bollocking for letting you anywhere near Ferrier and am forbidden to put you in the front line again."

"Well, at least let me help in some way. Surely, many of the properties will be occupied by foreigners taking umbrage at having their home searched by police. Your officers will work faster with a friendly translator around. Can't you deputize me or something?"

"I see what you mean. Again, I'll have to discuss that with el jefe. I'll go and see him now. Later."

Phillip's phone beeped again.

It was a message from Rosemary:

'Photos of Duffy and Crown attached, along with criminal records. Good luck. R.'

Phillip opened the first image. It was a full-frontal of a man's head and shoulders, holding a sign showing his prisoner details. R. Duffy was the name.

Even though prison photos aren't in the least flattering, Duffy's appearance was worse than an advert for a horror film. Cropped blond hair. Ugly face with a mean-looking expression, blue, but cold eyes, and a deep scar on the left cheek. He was huge, and although he looked as strong as a horse, he was obese with flaccid, bulbous jowls, shoulders as wide as a house, sticky-out ears, and a crooked nose.

"Not the sort you would care to bump into on the way back from the pub," mumbled Phillip out loud. "Especially knowing what he did to Ferrier."

Wait, I've seen this guy, thought Phillip, racking his brain. Where? Come on, man. Of course. Didi's photo.

He flicked through his gallery and brought up the image of Juliet and Lars at San Isidro. Standing directly behind, towering over them, and wearing a black cordoba hat that was way too small for him, was Rick Duffy. He was staring at Lars with a lecherous grin.

Phillip paid up and drove home.

He booted up his computer and took a closer look at Duffy and Crown. His pulse raced with anger as he started reading their records.

Duffy had served four years. Although it was his first offense, an early release had not been allowed due to his bad behavior in prison. Now, this was interesting, thought Phillip. Duffy's father was from Northern Ireland, but his mother was Swedish with the surname of Olsson. Duffy's first name wasn't Rick, it's Rikard. It seems likely then that Duffy has dual nationality, which would account for him slipping out of England unnoticed on a Swedish passport.

Malcolm Crown had served three years. Although born in the United Kingdom of British parents, he was actually brought up in Marbella and attended one of the international schools. He was fluent in Spanish and had been employed as an IT consultant with a major computer company based in Warwick.

He and Duffy had both been released on the same day thirteen months and twenty days previously.

He packaged up the critical elements of this new information into a Word document, added his comments, and sent it off to Prado.

32

"Come," said el jefe's voice through the door after Prado's tentative knock.

Prado entered, sat down and presented his boss with the screen on Ferrier's laptop.

"What's this," said el jefe looking disgustedly at the live 'Breakfast with the Bad Boys' gay action on the Peepers website.

"Evidence of a sexual slavery ring operating somewhere between Torrox and Nerja, but this is mild in comparison with what I'm about to show you. Hang on while I switch screens." Prado found the right page and turned it back to el jefe.

It was the event invitation.

El jefe read it once, shook his head, frowning and then read it again.

He glared at Prado, seemingly shell-shocked.

"Leon, this must be stopped," shouted el jefe banging the table repetitively with his fist.

Prado had never seen him so angry.

El jefe looked once again at the screen, shaking his head. "The English rose I understand is Juliet," he said. "But, hold on, this other girl looks familiar? Ye Gods Prado, it's her. What's her name?"

"Angelika, sir," said Prado.

"Of course. Your kidnapped Dane? She's still alive. That's fantastic, her parents will be delighted."

"That's not all, sir. All our missing girls have appeared at some time on this screen during the last twenty-four hours."

"So your suspicions were correct. It is one criminal behind all this. Dammit, Leon, you have to find these girls."

"Sir. May I suggest that we hold back on informing Angelika's parents until we have either prevented this event or know her destiny, it will only cause them unnecessary worry. Meanwhile, we only have thirty-six hours to locate them, but with more than six hundred properties to search, it's just not possible. With my current team, it'll take us twenty-four days not hours."

"Can the translators help?"

"Phillip is desperate to, but I don't know about Amanda."

"What can I do?"

"If local police forces could visit the properties on their patch, we might stand a chance of completing the lists by the deadline. They have the neighborhood knowledge and may even be acquainted with some of the owners. But that request will need to come from you, sir."

"How many towns and villages are we talking about?"

"Thankfully, only the main areas. As yet, the fiber-optic cables needed for these broadcasts have only been installed there."

"Right, give me the list. I'll start now."

"Thank you, sir," said Prado passing over the folder. "Just one more thing. I'd like to send the list to Phillip. Many of the property owners are foreigners, and some are owned by companies. The names might convey something to him and if the officers call him to help translate, he will know to which property they are referring."

"It's against protocol, but send it. We'll sign them both up later as consultants. That way we'll be covered for this and any future work; expenses only mind."

"I'll begin immediately. Will you let me know how cooperative the local police are being?"

"I will; now scoot," said el jefe, picking up his phone.

Prado went back to his desk, span his chair around and gazed out of the window seeking a miracle. Because even with enough resources it was going to be almost impossible to save the girls in the time available. They were looking for a needle in a haystack.

He spun back around to face his desk and checked his emails. He opened the one from Phillip, read the report about and Duffy and Crown then looked at their photos. Beast and the beast sprang to his mind as he picked up Angelika's case file, glanced at the neatly typed ransom note and read it through for the first time since he was fired.

The only comment he could add, after his fresh appraisal, was that the Spanish language used in the note was not quite how a Spaniard would write it. It was technically acceptable, but the word order was a little odd, some of the phrases were inconsistent with how Spaniards would describe things and the style was too personal. For the word you, the kidnappers had used 'tu' instead of the more formal 'usted'. Prado wondered what his translators would make of it.

He picked up his phone and called Phillip.

"Thanks for the photos. That Duffy is a mean-looking son of a bitch," said Prado.

"If we find him scary, imagine how Juliet will feel? How did it go with el jefe?"

"Surprisingly well. He's personally speaking with the chiefs of local police in all the areas involved, requesting that they drop everything and direct all their officers to the properties involved. I'm also going to send you the list and would appreciate your thoughts on any anomalies you may spot."

"Anomalies?"

"As you said, many of the properties are owned by foreigners or companies. The names might give you some cryptic clues."

"I hate crosswords, but I'll happily check out the lists. With regard to those properties owned by companies. Does your list include the names of directors and shareholders?"

"No, but you could search for them yourself; just pay a membership fee for one of the online directories. We'll refund it, of course."

"I'll make a start," said Phillip.

"Perhaps Amanda could help?"

"I'll call her."

"Listen, I'm going to send you Angelika's ransom note and would appreciate any comments about the language. I suspect that it may not have been written by a Spaniard. You and Amanda may be able to shed some new light on it."

"Send it over; hasta luego."

Phillip called Amanda.

"Hi," she said. "Any news?"

Phillip brought her up to date.

"Sounds like you're getting closer," she said. "But this event sounds horrific. Those poor girls must be shitting themselves."

"Look, I don't know how busy you are, but I desperately need you here to help me. Many of the properties on Prado's list are owned by companies. We need to check the names of their directors and shareholders to see if Duffy, Crown or CVS are involved. It might help us pinpoint the right property more quickly than relying on the house to house inquiries. Could you, would you?"

"Of course. I have to wrap up a few things first, but I'll be there in a couple of hours. What's your address?"

"Casa Las Rocas on Camino Viejo de Málaga. Turn left at the letter boxes just before La Molineta on the Frigiliana Road up from the motorway and follow the road that heads toward the sea. You can't miss it. There's a farm immediately before it called Los Conejos."

"Do you need me to bring anything?"

"Some pajamas and a toothbrush would be good. We could be at this all night."

33

It's incredible what ordinary people keep in their cellars, thought Prado, as he departed yet another unsuccessful cellar inspection. He'd spent the afternoon and evening flitting from one local police team to another, hoping that he'd be in the right place at the right time when they discovered Juliet and Angelika.

One family occupying three separate consecutive villas in Torre del Mar had built their own fully equipped health club. Under one dwelling was a gym fitted with all the latest machines. Under another, a luxury spa with marble tiling, whirlpool, sauna, and swimming pool. Last but not least was a fantastic children's playground full of climbing frames, ball baths, and a full-size tennis table. They were all linked together by a series of brightly illuminated passageways.

Under a townhouse in Algarrobo was a discotheque with impressive soundproofing, lighting systems, and high-end acoustic installations. Just inside the entrance was a full-size statue of the owner attired in his diamond-studded Elvis Presley gear. In Caleta de Vélez was a substantial aquarium containing a small squid and many varieties of tropical fish. He lost count of workshops and photographic studios, one with racy prints of a voluptuous wife on the wall.

"They say everyone deserves someone," he sighed to himself on the way out. "But there are some serious mismatches out there. Perhaps it's a cellar owner's thing."

Two hundred holes in the ground later, there was still no sign of Juliet or Angelika, and it was nearing midnight. The officers were hungry, grumpy, knackered, and most householders had retired for the night. Prado called it a day and drove back to Málaga, reflecting on the day's lessons to try and think of a more efficient method of searching to speed things up.

Prado pulled into the comisaría garage just before one o'clock. On the walk home, he called Phillip.

"How's it going," said Phillip between yawns. Amanda, who was working on his other computer raised her eyebrows. 'Prado,' he mouthed switching to speakerphone.

"We've stood everyone down until the morning, but it is frustratingly slow," said Prado. "We've had to return to some villas as the owners were out. Several cannabis plantations have been found, which had to be passed onto the Guardia Civil distracting the locals away from their primary task. Hopefully, it will go better tomorrow, but at the current rate of progress, I estimate that we'll still be over two hundred properties short by the deadline. How about you?"

"We're making progress but haven't spotted

anything as yet," said Phillip. "We've solved the riddle of the ransom note, though. We're both agreed that it was written by a mother-tongue English speaker with excellent knowledge of Spanish."

"Someone like Crown?"

"Exactly. Any chance of more resources?"

"There aren't any more. What we need is better intelligence. Let's hope your searches can find something, otherwise…"

"I know. It's going to be a long night. I'll wake you up if we find anything."

"OK. Good hunting. Buenos noches, Phillip y Amanda."

"Thanks, buenos noches, Leon." They said together.

"This is so frustrating," said Amanda some two hours later. "We're not finding anything. None of the property owners' names on the probable or possible list match any suspects."

"Many of the properties have names, not numbers," said Phillip stretching back in his chair. "But none hint at some hidden cryptic meaning. If I see another Dunroamin or Doghouse, I'll scream."

"It's the Company owned ones that are doing me in," said Amanda. "Each search takes ages. The ones owned by Spanish Companies I can handle, but when the Spanish Company itself is owned by a Hungarian or Finnish Company and I have to search their databases it's impossible to translate. And as for those owned by offshore trusts, I stand no chance. No wonder the world is in a mess if rich people can so easily hide their assets from taxpayers."

"We'll have to contact the Spanish Company Administrators in the morning," said Phillip.

"Meanwhile, I've found nothing owned by Crown, Duffy or their parents, so I think we should call it a night."

"I agree, my head is spinning," said Amanda.

"Need an aspirin?"

"No, just to rest."

"I'll show you where the guest room is."

They stood and she put her arm through his as they walked to her bedroom. He hugged her tight at the door and she kissed his neck briefly.

"Sleep well," she said covering a yawn with her hand. "How long to go?"

"Less than nineteen hours.

34

Four hours later, Phillip knocked on Amanda's door.

"Go away," she mumbled.

He opened the door a fraction, switched on the light and said: "Are you decent?"

"Mmm."

He went in and saw her clothes folded neatly over the end of the bed and her hair all over the pillows as she snuggled under the duvet.

"Thought this might tempt you back to the computer," he said, placing a tray on the bedside table containing a glass of orange juice, some fruit salad, and a yogurt.

Amanda struggled to a seating position, revealing a rumpled blue and white striped sleep shirt. She yawned and stretched. "Thanks," she said. "I need to shower."

"Clean towels already there. I'll see you in the study."

Phillip was sitting at the computer when she joined him twenty minutes later.

"How's it going?" said Amanda.

"I've emailed the inquiries to the company administrators and have reconvened the searches," he announced. "But, I'm worried that we're in danger of being too organized. If we carry on plodding through the properties in alphabetical order, it could take all day, and what if the actual one begins with Z? I propose that one of us works more randomly, while the other plows on alphabetically."

"OK, you start, and we'll swap over every hour or so."

"Great. It might not improve results, but it should make us feel more motivated."

The phone rang on the dot of eight.

"We've resumed searching properties," said Prado, his tired voice echoing around Phillip's office. "I'm currently in Algarrobo but I've just heard back from the Nerja police. They've been to Lars Eriksson's apartment at Stella Maris. It's a small rental unit where he lived alone.

"According to a neighbor, Lars hasn't been seen since San Isidro, neither has his red car. When the concierge let them in, they found all his things had been cleared out. However, there was a printed property information sheet hidden on top of the wardrobe, which they sent me a photo of.

"It's for a rental villa between Frigiliana and Torrox. The contact details imply that Lars was renting it out under his own name, and not the Swedish agency with which he was working. There's a website link under Lars's telephone number, and an email directing potential tenants to the Owners Abroad site. There they can see more photos, and make reservations online. Can you check Owners Abroad to see if Lars is renting out any other properties?"

"Will do," said Phillip. "Sounds a bit fishy, do you think Lars is part of Duffy and Crown's team?"

"Or he's been set up by them," said Prado. "We'll worry about that later. What I need now are the ownership details of this villa. I'll head up there now via Torrox.

"Meanwhile, with regard to checking with Hacienda for tax exemption certificates for sending money to Gibraltar. Their office opens at eight-thirty; my officers are likely to receive a more rapid response than you, so they'll call them instead of you."

"Makes sense."

"Any news at your end?"

"So far nothing, but we're soldiering on."

"Can you look to see who owns this villa while I'm driving up there? I'll send you the map shortly. If it's a problem, let me know, and I'll pop up to the Ayuntamiento in Frigiliana."

When the villa map arrived from Prado, Phillip knew instantly that it would be impossible to locate it in the land registry. He needed a plot number or a more detailed address. He called the Frigiliana town hall, but they refused to give him the information over the phone. Prado would have to go there himself. He texted Prado with the news.

"Fancy some fresh air," said Phillip just after nine.

"Great idea," said Amanda yawning.

They took a turn around the garden.

"Amazing view," said Amanda leaning on the wall and gazing toward the sparkling blue sea.

"Thanks, hopefully, we can find some time to enjoy it after all this is done."

"How long is it now?" said Amanda stretching her

arms out and twisting her neck to ease the knots.

"Thirteen hours."

"What happens if we can't find her in time?"

"I'd rather not dwell on it."

"I understand, but in the event of a negative outcome, I'm worried how you might handle it."

Phillip reached out and rested his hand on her shoulder.

"Thanks for your concern. I'll be sad, and it will take me some time to repair the damage, but I'll bounce back."

Amanda put her arms around him and hugged him hard.

Phillip hugged her back, his eyes watering.

"Come," he whispered in her ear. "We're in danger of turning all gushy again. Let's go and renew our searching. There must be some kind of clue buried among all these company names and shareholders.

They returned indoors, holding hands, and dived back into their task with a hardened resolve.

35

The name Torrox has evolved from the Arabic, Turrux, meaning tower. The small town is split into two parts. The original village, located some five kilometers inland from the coast, perches on top of the western ridge of a steep gorge overlooking the Torrox River. The more recent part of town, known as Torrox-Costa, was developed in the early 1970s as a beach tourist destination and marketed intensely to Germans. Consequently, it has one of the largest German communities outside of Germany.

Prado drove through El Morche in the direction of Torrox-Costa. He spotted the Aldi supermarket opposite the front line tower blocks. It reminded him of the girls eating together in Peepers.

"I wonder who does the shopping for all those people," he said to himself. "Eighteen or more performers, possibly some in reserve being groomed, not forgetting Crown and Duffy. That's a lot of plastic bags and a vehicle with a large trunk to accommodate them. Do they shop daily or once a week? I doubt if Duffy or Crown will do it personally so perhaps they have one, maybe two persons to deal with the catering issue. Should I initiate some surveillance to try and identify their shopper? But then I'll have to take officers away from the property searching for what is pure speculation. We might get lucky, but if they spread their purchasing around the area, I could be wasting resources. So, we'll stick with the plan."

But his decision nagged at him as he turned off at Urbanization Torrox Park and headed up to Torrox village.

Prado parked outside the town hall and admired the artistic display of colorful umbrellas suspended from a lattice of cables. They provided shade to the bustling central square.

He strolled across to one of the many tapas bars, bought a bocadillo filled with jamón serrano and a coffee to go. He chewed it on the way up to Frigiliana as he sped faster than he should around the dangerous hairpin bends on the pothole-riddled mountain road. His coffee stood firm in the cup holder, making a sloshing noise, thankfully, the tight-fitting lid did its job.

Prado found the villa two kilometers before Frigiliana and a short way down an unmade track. He parked outside the main entrance, a whitewashed archway closed by a solid white steel gate. He took his coffee with him and rang the bell. He waited a minute or so and tried again while finishing his drink. There was nobody home. He returned his empty cup to the car, clambered onto its roof, and heaved himself over the high wall next to the arch. He sat astride it, planning his descent, and then eased himself down onto a green trash container and onto the ground.

He peered through the glazed kitchen door and tried the handle, it was locked. He smashed the glass with his elbow, reached through carefully avoiding the glass shards, unbolted the door, turned the handle, and pushed it open. There were no signs of occupation. The fridge was turned off, ajar and empty. Prado assumed that he would, therefore, not be disturbed by current tenants returning unexpectedly. He scouted all the rooms quickly without noticing anything out of the ordinary and then checked the garage.

Inside was a chili-pepper-red Nissan Qashqai. It was unlocked. In the glove compartment, Prado found a phone and a laptop. Both batteries were flat. In the trunk were several suitcases. One of them was labeled Lars Eriksson. Prado opened the cases and established that they contained only clothing and personal items. Prado assumed that Lars must have been heading somewhere that wasn't Marbella, as he'd told his former boss. Had he come here to hook up with Juliet? Was this where they would stay hidden together while Ferrier was found and sent home? If so, it hadn't happened. There wasn't a sign of anyone, and the place was spotless as if it had been cleaned recently. Perhaps Duffy has taken Lars to wherever he had stashed Juliet. Maybe Lars is also due to participate in the event this evening?

Prado pondered over these options, trying to make sense of them, as he opened the french windows and went out onto the spacious terrace. At the far end, steps led down into a ten-meter swimming pool full of gleaming blue water. The garden was lovingly maintained. The view was of a beautiful inland valley dotted with olive and almond trees and a few isolated properties. Prado concluded that this was a perfect location for the Peepers' broadcasts, except that there was no cellar or fiber optics, and it wasn't on his probable or possible list.

Then he panicked as a thought flashed through his mind. Are Peepers using satellite instead of fiber optics? Because if they are, the telephone service providers won't know their location, and our lists would be wrong. We could be wasting our time. Phillip would know.

Prado went back inside and locked the french windows behind him. This place is fabulous and well cared for, thought Prado as he headed into the hallway. I wonder if Phillip has traced the owner yet.

He went through all the rooms, looking in drawers and cupboards for any utility bills, rental contracts, and emergency contact numbers, but found nothing. He let himself out the front door, closing it behind him, went out through the gate in the low wall that fronted the villa, and headed back to his car. He called for forensics to come and see what they could find at the villa and then sat in his car and thought about anything else he should look for.

There hadn't been a letterbox.

Back at the front door, he saw no sign of anything to receive post and then realized that as this was a rental villa, the owners would have mail sent or forwarded directly to them. Otherwise, how might bills be paid? The village post office will have that address, he thought.

He returned to his car, drove into the more modern quarter of Frigiliana, parked on Avenida de Andalusia, and walked across the road to the post office. It was open mornings only. Prado cursed under his breath.

Now, he would have to make a fuss to locate someone to answer his question. This was all biting into their deadline. It was already two-thirty, and they had just over seven hours to find Juliet.

He walked along the avenue, past Las Chinas hotel then El Boquetilla restaurant to the local police kiosk opposite the old Guardia Civil building. As he approached the circular booth, which was also the tourist information center, he glanced across at the former barracks. They were now a pharmacy and a bank. He wondered how many more cuts to law-and-order services the province could sustain before anarchy prevailed. Thankfully, the local police knew the woman responsible for the post, called her and arranged to open up for him.

Half an hour later, he had what he needed.

All mail addressed to the villa was collated in a Post Office Box registered in the name of a property-management company.

Prado called Phillip.

"We're not having much luck here," said Phillip, "and I'm conscious that it's approaching three o'clock. Anything back from Hacienda?"

"Not yet."

"Have you been to the Town Hall?"

"I didn't need to. The owners have a Post Office box. Can you make a note of the name? It's Inmobiliaria Rustical Andaluza SL based at Abogados Sanchez and Sanchez, a firm of lawyers based in Calle Larios, in Málaga center. Take a look at the land registry for a complete list of properties owned by the Company. One of them has to be where they are holding Juliet.

"Also, Lars Eriksson's car is in the villa garage with

his phone and laptop. I'm going back to the villa now to meet up with forensics, and then I'll bring his devices down to you. Perhaps you'll have something for me by then."

"Let's hope so. By the way," said Phillip, "Lars has two other properties advertised on Owners Abroad, but neither of them is on any of our lists nor matches any of our search criteria."

"Fine, so we can forget him for the moment. One more question. What if Peepers are using satellite to broadcast their signals?"

"They won't be. Satellite only streams up to thirty megabytes a second. For buffer-free streaming of TV-quality images like Peepers, they need five hundred, and that is only achievable using fiber optics."

"I was beginning to fear that our lists might all be wrong."

"No, the lists are good," said Phillip.

"Then why aren't we finding Juliet and Angelika?"

36

Amanda wheeled her chair around next to Phillip and watched carefully as he logged back into the Málaga property registry and typed in Inmobiliaria Rustical Andaluza SL.

A list of results appeared instantly.

"Bingo," they said together exchanging excited glances.

Phillip scrolled through the entries.

"Let's compare it with the probables," he said going to collect a printed copy of yet another list.

"And the possibles," said Amanda.

They browsed through them together with heads touching. Amanda noted down those that coincided while Phillip switched to the commercial register to check the ownership of the company.

He called Prado and said. "They own thirty-five properties scattered from Málaga to Nerja. There are six matches and four more among the possibles."

"Now we are getting somewhere. What about the

shareholders?"

"Ignacio Mereno Sanchez is the administrator, and the other director and single shareholder is Sergio Mereno Sanchez. Probably brothers."

"Then we'll need to organize a search of their offices but we'll hold off until we've checked all the properties. Email me the list highlighting those that match ours. I'll direct our search teams to those first. I'll call you with any developments."

Phillip ended the call and turned to Amanda.

"Shall we carry on searching?" he said.

"Best if we do and I can't just sit here waiting for Prado to call back."

"At least, let me make you a coffee."

"Instant?"

"Amanda please, no blasphemy in this house. I have a machine and even know how it works."

"Unusual for a man to be so domesticated. Mine's a double espresso."

Phillip checked his watch and went to make the coffee.

Twenty minutes later he came back with a tray loaded with steaming coffee cups and some chocolate biscuits.

"Sorry for the delay," he said. "Had to wait for the machine to warm up. Found anything?"

Amanda looked up and shook her head.

"Then let's go and sit in the garden and enjoy our refreshments. I can't face another second looking at the damn monitor and no results."

"You must feel frustrated not being with the search team," said Amanda following him out to the terrace.

"Prado refused to put me at risk. Especially after the Ferrier fracas."

"I can understand that."

"So can I, but not being there is like waiting for a Terrorist bomb to be defused. Will all hell be let loose or not? My mind is spinning around all the potential outcomes. In this case, finding Juliet, but not knowing what condition she is going to be in. Or worse, finding the Peepers location, but with no Juliet. Even more horrendous, not finding anything and being left up in the air for the rest of my life."

They sat down and Phillip served them coffee. She declined a biscuit. He gobbled down three in quick succession.

An hour and forty minutes later, Prado called back.

"Hola, Leon," said Phillip his gut churning.

Amanda reached out and stroked his arm, a concerned look on her face.

"I'm in the Comisaría in Torre del Mar. We've just had the result in from the last of thirty-four properties that we've searched," said Prado. "The cellars were there just as the list described along with fiber optics and everything but Phillip. I'm so sorry. Juliet wasn't in any of them."

Phillip put his head in his hands, breathing heavily.

Amanda jumped up and put her arms around his shoulders

Then Phillip snapped out of his misery and said "Thirty-four properties?"

"The thirty-fifth property is located in Baviera Golf. I'm confident that our discovery there will lead us to her."

"Leon. Please stop messing with me. What discovery?"

"Phillip, we've found Juliet's abductors."

37

"Are you sure?" said Phillip standing up and hugging Amanda to him.

"Absolutely. The man that answered the door resembled Amanda's Identikit sketch of the man she saw sticking on the polka dots in Maro. He and his younger brother were arrested pending fingerprint checks. Both their fingerprints match those found in the stolen van used to abduct Juliet and one set was in her apartment. Parked outside the house was an identical white Renault Kangoo registered to Inmobiliaria Rustical Andaluza S.L. The van's keys were hanging on a hook inside the front door. In the back, we discovered a faint fingerprint from Angelika."

"Who are they?"

"Neither speaks much Spanish, but can manage some English. Between the two, my officers established that they are from Syria. They came via Morocco over a year ago on a smuggler's boat, but were picked up by the Guardia Civil cutter just off

Algeciras. They were locked up in the detention center for about a week until two English-speaking foreigners came to collect them. One was a giant, ugly, blond man, and the other smaller and more elegant. They offered them a free home and a little money in return for maintaining their properties and any other business they wanted without asking any questions."

"And they presumably accepted the offer."

"The alternative threatened was instant deportation for them and their wives and children."

"Do they know where Juliet is?"

"That is a translation too far. Can you and Amanda meet me at the property and we'll see what we can persuade them to tell us?"

"Where in Baviera Golf?"

"It's a townhouse that overlooks the fifth fairway. As you turn in off the main road, it's along on the left. You'll see our vehicle there. They'll be expecting you. I'll join you as soon as I can."

"Best if you buckle up and shut your eyes," said Phillip as he and Amanda departed the villa in his BMW.

"On the contrary," said Amanda. "Four eyes are better than two. And I enjoy an element of danger."

"Sorry, I forgot I was traveling with an action-girl. In that case, my driving will seem a little tame compared with bull-running."

"Just get us there safely. Juliet needs us in one piece. How long now?"

"Two hours."

Twenty minutes later, Phillip was directed where to park by a Local Police Officer outside the house in Baviera Golf. Prado was standing outside the door, peering anxiously at his watch. They followed him indoors.

Two men, their wives, and four children huddled together sitting around the kitchen table. Their exasperated expressions were painful to see. They'd come so far from the horrors of war back home, only to find themselves in the clutches of the Spanish police.

Phillip leaned against the kitchen worktop, feeling sorry for them, but they were his only route to Juliet. Amanda stood next to him. Prado was by the door. Another officer, with a holstered weapon, stood in the narrow hallway.

"Is this the man you saw in Maro?" said Prado.

"Definitely," said Amanda.

"Do they have passports?" said Prado.

Phillip asked in English.

"No," said the elder man. "We have no papers." He could have been a Spaniard from his Mediterranean coloring, which is probably why they had survived unmolested to date. He was below average height, with unkempt black hair, bushy mustache, wild eyebrows, brown eyes, and a couple of days' stubble. He was dressed in jeans and a T-shirt as was his similar-looking accomplice. The children, aged between four and eight, clung to their respective mothers, not daring to look at the intruders.

"We'll talk about your identities, paperwork and how you come to be here later," said Phillip. "At the moment we only have one question that needs answering and urgently. Several weeks ago you kidnapped a blond girl from outside her school. Five days ago you abducted another slightly older blond girl from the San Isidro Festival in Nerja. We need to know where you took them and now."

"Our employers will kill us all if we tell you

anything," said the elder.

"Would they be Rick Duffy and Malcolm Crown?"

The elder man shrugged, then exchanged concerned glances with the other man, but he said nothing.

"Silence is not helping your case," said Phillip. "You either tell me where you took these girls within the next two minutes, otherwise both of you will be taken to the police station in Vélez-Málaga where you will be charged with kidnapping, theft of a vehicle, and obstructing the police. That means at least eight years in jail each and instant deportation for your families. Your choice."

"I understand," said the elder looking petrified. "We need to talk about this among ourselves in Arabic, so everyone is clear on our position."

"Fine, go ahead, but we remain here," said Phillip, glancing at his watch.

It was just before nine o'clock.

They listened to a heated exchange between the two men.

"Can you understand?" whispered Phillip to Amanda in Spanish.

"The odd word or phrase, but their Arab dialect is different from Moroccan, particularly in pronunciation. I think they are comparing options."

Prado edged over toward them and said, "If they don't respond, offer them an olive branch."

"Such as what?" said Phillip.

"If they help us find the girls and tell us about their work for Crown, we'll look favorably on a fast track to Spanish Citizenship. They could have passports, health care and school for their kids in weeks."

"Time's up," said Phillip moving toward the table.

The women shrank back from him.

He tried a reassuring look, but it didn't help.

"Will you tell us where these girls are?" said Phillip.

"No," said the elder man shaking his head vehemently.

"Let me try Prado's offer in Arabic," said Amanda moving forward to stand by Phillip. "I'll address it directly to the wives. Then we should see some sparks fly."

Amanda repeated Prado's offer a few words at a time making sure they understood her dialect before moving onto the next sentence.

When Phillip was speaking, only the men had reacted, but now the women nodded. Their enthusiasm grew with each of Amanda's explanations. Now they were looking directly at her, their eyes shining with hope. The children slowly raised their heads and looked at Amanda.

Their appealing little faces and big, round brown eyes tugged at Phillip's heartstrings.

One of the women addressed her husband; the younger man.

A short guttural instruction.

The man glared at her, but he knew when he was beaten.

"OK, OK," said the elder man. "Torrox Park. They are in a cellar under a villa."

Phillip translated for Prado, who swiped his phone and brought up a map of the urbanization.

"Show me," he said, passing the device to Phillip.

The elder man took the phone and enlarged the screen.

"There," he said, pointing to a corner villa just over the bridge that provided access to Torrox Park over the Rio Torrox.

"Where is the main access?" said Prado.

Phillip translated and spent five minutes extracting the details of the villa, its security systems and the people running the show.

Phillip checked his watch. The event was due to start in forty minutes.

"We should leave now," he said.

Prado beckoned for them to join him outside where Phillip explained what he'd learned.

"That's a lot of people to secure with three escape routes," said Prado. "Garage door, front and back doors. I have to leave two officers here so we won't have enough resources to cover them all. We're going to have to wait for back up."

"Leon, the event is due to start anytime," said Phillip. "And we have to prevent it from happening, whatever the cost. That should be our priority, not preventing escapes."

"Phillip, we must bring these men to justice," said Prado.

"Of course," said Phillip. "We have enough evidence to do that, I just want to stop them from raping my friend. Now. I am getting in my car to do just that. Are you coming or not?"

38

"You can't save Juliet on your own," said Amanda as Phillip turned onto the coastal motorway.

"I know," said Phillip with a grim, determined expression. "But I didn't want to hang around procrastinating about justice with Prado when we need to be at the scene to prevent a heinous crime from happening. Hopefully, if my tactic has worked, Prado has two things to worry about. Stopping the event and deterring me from doing anything foolhardy. It should help him to raise resources from somewhere."

Phillip's phone rang.

"I know I can't say anything to stop you barging into the villa," said Prado's voice on the speakerphone. "But I'm right behind you and a Guardia Civil traffic car will be there by the time we arrive. They have layout drawings being sent to them by the builder and the necessary equipment to force entry. We will enter the property precisely at three minutes to ten and make a hell of a lot of noise. Between us, we should be able to stop the rape and hold everyone there until reinforcements can be diverted from other incidents."

"Great, thanks, Leon. What do you want me to do?"

"The officers and I will go in through the front. If you could station yourself at the back door and prevent anyone from coming out that way, you should be at minimum risk. But please don't take up position until we are ready at the front. As soon as everything is under control, we'll let you and Amanda in to translate and calm the victims. Agreed?"

"Fine. Where should I park?"

"It's a corner property surrounded by a low wall on three sides. The main entrance and garage are on the north wall so park by the south."

"Will do."

"If anything changes, I'll call you but change your phones to silent until this is over."

They turned off the motorway at the Torrox junction, drove down to the roundabout and across the bridge into Torrox Park. There was another roundabout at the top of the hill illuminated by the soft glow of halogen street lights.

There was the white stucco bungalow in front of them with its low white wall.

The garden was basic but the grass lawn was short and tidy with three stubby palm trees planted equidistantly between the wall and window. A small timber shed had been added adjacent to the back door. A semicircular bay window opened out onto a paved terrace and black security bars protected the side windows. The external plastic roller blinds were closed and no lights were visible. It was eerily quiet and hard to conceive that such cruel depravity was about to happen right under their feet.

They turned right, stopped as instructed behind a sleek black Porsche Cayenne and clambered out, shutting the doors as quietly as they could.

Phillip checked his watch.

The green LED glowed briefly, brightening his face.

Five minutes to go.

Phillip grabbed a tire lever from the trunk. Amanda closed it with a dull thud.

"I suppose it's pointless to ask you to stay in the car?" whispered Phillip.

"Completely," said Amanda as two cars, one a Guardia Civil patrol SUV stopped outside the front blocking the gated driveway. The occupants dressed in protective clothing climbed out, leaving the doors open and hopped over the wall, one officer carrying a battering ram. Prado gave Phillip the thumbs up and joined the officers by the front door. One drew his pistol.

Amanda and Phillip stepped carefully over the wall and stood by the timber shed watching the solid timber back door.

The time dragged by.

Not a sound came from the neighborhood and there wasn't a person to be seen.

Then all hell let loose.

A massive crash was followed by loud shouts in Spanish. Then the noise stopped and all went silent.

Phillip had his ear to the back door, but could hear nothing. He assumed that they must all be underground and was itching to go in to find out if Juliet was there or not.

Then there was a noise behind him.

He turned as a massive shape appeared out of the timber shed wearing a full-length white silk robe.

Phillip threw himself at what must be Duffy only to be brushed aside and smashed back against the door. His head spun and his legs refused to respond as the giant plucked Amanda off the ground with one hand as if she was a rag doll. He lumbered to the Porsche, opened the rear door, heaved Amanda onto the back seat, and slammed the door. He squeezed into the front and took off with a squeal of burning rubber.

Phillip's head cleared, his legs regained some control and he limped to his car and raced after them.

The Porsche headed out of Torrox Park at phenomenal speed. Phillip was a hundred meters behind. He could see Duffy reach back to thump Amanda as she fought to open her door. She fell back out of sight. Duffy turned to concentrate on his driving as he raced over the bridge crossing the Torrox River and up toward Torrox Town.

Duffy was driving way too quickly in the dark and narrow road.

Somehow, he safely negotiated the speed humps and hairpin bends, drove through the town, and out onto the Competa Road, renowned for its dangerous curves bordering on almost vertical ravines.

Momentarily, Phillip lost sight of the Porsche as it disappeared around a bend. Duffy was leaving him behind, but then he spotted the bright glow from the headlights of the big SUV. He wasn't that far ahead.

Phillip pressed his accelerator to the floor. The powerful BMW surged forward. He looked across a ravine and observed the Porsche slowing almost to a stop to negotiate an exceptionally sharp hairpin.

Phillip had to concentrate on his driving, so he saw nothing more. He sped along a short straight. His lighter, more nimble vehicle slowly gaining on the

Porsche.

He was only fifty meters behind. He slowed because he knew the road well, and there was a terrible hairpin coming imminently. The Porsche failed to notice in time, jammed on its brakes too late, smashed through the crash bar and sailed out into the darkness, headlights illuminating the olive trees and grapevines as it descended into the valley.

Phillip stopped his car by the damaged railing, leaped out and looked down just in time to see an enormous explosion some two hundred meters below.

His heart sank as the flames set fire to the surrounding bushes and spread incredibly quickly.

Nobody could survive that.

He called Prado.

The signal was pathetic, but he managed to hear Prado's voicemail message. He spoke quickly, then hung up.

Phillip opened his trunk. Put on his high-visibility vest and placed his luminous warning triangles on both approaches to the crash site.

Then he leaned against the barrier, put his head in his hands and wept for the life of the new woman in his life.

39

Twenty minutes later, a vehicle stopped behind Phillip's car, but he was too distressed to notice. The vehicle door clunked shut and someone approached, footsteps crunching on the gravel verge. "The fire brigade and a patrol car will be here shortly," said Prado. "I suggest you go and sit in my car until they arrive, then we can go and sort out the mess from the villa."

Phillip looked up and shook his head. "What's the point?" he said. "I've lost them both now."

"Phillip, go and sit in the fucking car," said Prado grabbing his arm firmly and marching him over. He opened the back door and shoved him inside.

Phillip was too distraught to care.

He leaned back in the seat and closed his eyes.

Then a hand stroked his cheek.

A familiar fragrance wafted up his nose. Surely not.

He sat bolt upright, grasped the hand and looked at the tiny figure crumpled in the other corner of the back seat.

"Yes," said Amanda. "It is me."

"But how?"

"The big hairpin, as he slowed, I rolled out and landed on the verge."

"Are you OK?"

"Badly bruised and shaken but no bones were broken. Prado spotted me. He explained that you thought I was still in the Porsche. That must have been…."

"Words can't describe. What about Juliet?"

"He never mentioned anything."

The front door opened and Prado slid into the front seat. "Recovered?" he said.

Phillip leaned forward and gripped Prado's shoulder. "Thank you," he said.

"The patrol car is here so we can go. Ready to talk to some victims?"

"Yes. Is Juliet there?"

"I don't know. I left to come here before I had a chance to look. Amanda, an ambulance will be waiting for you at Torrox Park."

"I don't need…"

"Amanda, my boss insists that you have a full checkup. The emergency department is awaiting your arrival. Phillip, are you good to drive your car?"

"Fine."

"Then I'll see you back down at the villa.

Phillip kissed Amanda's hand and said. "I'll find you wherever you are."

"You better," she whispered.

Entry to Torrox Park was now blocked by a patrol car and two officers from the Local Police. Prado and then Phillip were waved through and sped up to the villa where four more police cars and a forensics van were parked where they could. Spotlights had been placed around the villa and a group of twenty-odd people wrapped in foil robes were sitting on the grass in neat rows.

Phillip left his car where he had earlier and walked around to the front door.

"I want you to talk with the victims," said Prado. "Find out what you can about each."

"Are they all here on the grass?"

"No, two were injured, one slightly the other badly. They are still in the cellar awaiting the medics."

"Were we in time to stop the event?"

"Yes; well, more or less."

"Am I allowed in the cellar?"

"Anna is there, so report to her."

"I'll start there, then," said Phillip heading toward the front door.

Inside the house was a mass of activity.

"Where's the cellar?" he asked an officer standing outside the living room door.

"Into the garage and down the steps," said the officer.

Phillip glanced into the living room and saw a row of two desks loaded with computers and several monitors showing black screens. A small, slender man with greasy hair was seated in an office chair and handcuffed to one of them. Must be Crown. Thought Phillip. A scruffy middle-aged woman with unkempt gray hair was seated on the other chair and handcuffed to the other desk. She looked Spanish. Both of them looked miserable.

He headed into the garage, spotted the stairs and trotted down.

At the bottom to the left of the stairwell was an open, thick steel door, soundproofing lining its inner side. It led to a passageway. To the left was a single door. To the right were three more. Phillip peeped into each room as he passed. The first was a small kitchen. The second a dormitory containing eight, three-high bunk-beds. A small bathroom led off one end, which had no door, only a curtain. The third room contained another passage with three small rooms off to the left. A serving hatch was cut into each door and each room was furnished with a three-high bunk bed, a sink and WC. The light switches were outside each room. Like prison cells. He thought, heading back to the main passage.

"Hi Phillip," said Anna as he approached the single door now on his right.

"Hola Anna. Is it safe to have a look?" he said.

"Yes, we're all done here."

"How are the casualties?"

"The boy is still unconscious. Apparently, he was thrown across the room by Duffy and banged his forehead against the corner of a cupboard; possibly a cracked skull. The girl is conscious, but won't or can't respond to questions. She has a broken arm. I've strapped it up as best I can and she seems comfortable. Could you have a word with her in English? Might help."

"Fine, how did Duffy escape?"

"There's a sliding panel by the shower. Take a look."

Phillip went into the room. It was The Peepers studio.

Two bodies lay on two of the couches covered in red blankets. The first was Lars. He looked pale and haggard but despite lying motionless, he was breathing regularly. The second lay facing away from him tucked completely under the blanket. A scrap of blonde hair peeking out the top. He went around the other side and saw her face. Pale, eyes tightly shut. It was Angelika.

"Angelika," he said, bending on his knees.

Her eyes snapped open at hearing her name.

"How are you?" he said in English.

She gazed blankly at him.

"I'm Phillip. Juliet's friend."

She struggled to sit upright. Phillip reached out to help her, but she cowered away from him.

"It's OK. You are safe now," he said in English. "The monster man is dead. Crown and the lady have been arrested. The ambulance will be here soon and then you can see your parents."

"Parents?" she said English. "Are you sure?"

"The Inspector is calling them now. They will meet you at the hospital. In a few days' time, the police will need to ask you questions about your kidnapping and your ordeal here, but after that you can return to school, dancing lessons and your normal life. How does that sound?"

She burst into tears and fell into his chest sobbing.

He stroked her hair and murmured soothing sounds into her ear until the ambulance crew arrived and took her and Lars away.

Phillip was impressed by the thought and ingenious engineering put into the escape panel, but he didn't linger for long before trotting back up the stairs and out onto the lawn. He was just in time to see an ambulance leaving. He assumed Amanda was also on board and crossed his fingers for a positive health check.

He walked up and down each rank stopping and regarding each of them. Many wept, some were lost in another world, but the last person on the middle row with head buried under the thermal blanket was rocking back and forth like a metronome. The foil rustling with each movement.

Phillip recalled Hassan's description of Juliet's behavior when she was upset or depressed.

This had to be her.

He took it real slow and lowered himself gently to the grass wondering what he should say.

"Juliet," he said clearly. "It's Phillip and I'm here to take you home."

The rocking stopped instantly. She ripped the foil from her face. Phillip was shocked how gaunt she was and when she gazed up into his eyes, they were wild, searching and penetrating. Slowly, her twisted expression softened and she fell toward him, head on his chest. He held her in his arms and rocked her gently.

He waited for ten minutes before talking again.

"Your stepfather is dead. You have nothing to fear from him ever again."

"Dead?" she whispered.

"Yes. I saw it myself. Now I'm going to take out my phone and call your Aunt Rosemary to tell her we've found you. Are you OK with that?"

She nodded.

"Is that you Phillip?" said Rosemary.

"I'm with Juliet now," he said. "She's in shock, but OK. Here, say a few words."

Phillip held his device to Juliet's ear and watched her expression as she listened to her aunt talking. Slowly, her shoulders relaxed and she said, Yes, and

No, a few times, then Bye, and handed the phone back to Phillip.

"Hi, again," he said.

"My husband and I will be on the next available plane. Please don't let her out of your sight until we arrive."

"Of course. Call me with your timings."

"OK, see you."

"Can you stand?" said Phillip.

"I don't know," said Juliet moving her legs and trying to squat. The foil fell aside, revealing a white silk robe, but underneath that she was naked. He slipped off his sweater, wrapped it around her shoulders, and then helped her up. With each shuffle, she grew stronger as they went in search of Prado.

They found him by the gate talking on the phone. He made his excuses and hung up when he saw them.

"Is this Juliet?"

"Yes. I'm going to take her to the hospital. Is that OK?"

"It'll be fine. Report to our officer in emergencies and log Juliet's details with her. None of the others are in a fit state to be interviewed yet and we have to find them some clothes, so I won't need you again tonight."

"What will you do with so many?" said Phillip.

"We're taking them to the Convento Santa Claras in Vélez-Málaga. A bus will be here shortly."

"I thought Las Claras was an old ruin."

"It is, but a brand new but smaller convent was built out on the Arenas Road over ten years ago. The remaining nuns relocated there and have agreed to help us try and ease them back into some sort of normality."

"What will happen to them?"

"That will be up to the asylum panel. Hopefully,

they will be sympathetic. May I call on your services sometime tomorrow, also to speak with Crown?"

"Fine, Rosemary is arriving tomorrow. I'll be free after that."

All the time Prado was speaking, Juliet was gazing at him intently.

"This is Inspector Prado," said Phillip. "He's the man that spearheaded the operation to find you."

"Nonsense," said Prado. "Without Phillip's contribution, we'd still be chasing rainbows. How are you feeling?"

Juliet said nothing, but she moved toward Prado, put her arm around his neck, pecked him on the cheek and said in Spanish, "Thank you, my knight."

Prado blushed and half made to pat her shoulder, but stopped his hand before it touched her. "I will need to talk with you at some stage," he said. "Do you think you can manage that?"

"Oh yes, I want to make sure those animals are locked up forever. Especially that big brute."

"Thankfully, you won't have to worry about him. He's been killed in a car crash trying to escape, but we will need to hear your evidence against the other one."

"You can rely on me, Inspector. I have some prior experience in court."

"Your aunt told me about your bravery," said Prado. "Rest assured that this time it won't be such a harrowing experience. It will take a while, but Crown will be not be allowed out on bail, and will serve well over twenty years for his crimes. It should allow you to move on with your life."

Juliet nodded and looked at Phillip expectantly.

He guided her to his car, settled her in the front seat and drove off in the direction of Torre del Mar.

40

"Are you up to talking?" said Phillip as they headed toward the coastal motorway. "It could make it easier when you have to make your statement."

"Yes, I'd like to tell you what happened," said Juliet shakily. "Where should I start?"

"The night Rosemary called to tell you that your stepfather had been released and been to see her."

"Has my aunt told you everything?"

"Yes."

"Thank God. I've been on the verge of discussing this with you so many times."

"Why didn't you?"

"Shit, Phillip. I was so ashamed about it all and was frightened that if I told you, it would scare you away because you'd think me unclean." Juliet reached out and grabbed his hand as he changed gear and filtered into the motorway traffic. "I couldn't bear it if I lost the only real friend that I had in Nerja."

"I understand, but your fears were groundless."

"I know that now," she said between sniffs. She cried for a few seconds, then began. "That call from my aunt was the lowest point since the bastard tried to rape me. After his trial, I've shit myself about what he might do when released, so much so that it has totally dominated my consciousness. To try and counter the angst, wherever I was, even in a hotel, I developed an escape plan. At work, I would run out the back door, with Hassan it wasn't necessary to say anything to him, because I knew he would protect me, even take me to Morocco if I asked. So, when he had to return home prematurely because of his father's illness, it killed my plan. That was why I was so angry with him. It was selfish of me, I know, but fear drives one to strange places. Thankfully, I met Lars before Hassan left and devised a new plan with him."

"You'd have been safe with me."

"I know that and believe me, I had a hard time deciding not to involve you. However, you had your business, and weren't in a position to drop everything and vanish. I needed someone with whom I could snap my fingers and go. I couldn't do that with you."

"I agree, it would have been difficult, but you know I've always been there for you."

"I know. In the beginning, I was severely tempted to make something more of our friendship, but sorry, you reminded me too much of my Dad. Anyway, thank you for your gentlemanly control. It made it easier for me. I hope it wasn't too painful for you."

"It was for a while, but the pilgrimage helped me work it out."

"I thought so. You seemed more relaxed around me afterward. What was all that about?"

"You're the spitting image of my ex-wife. Much

younger of course, but my real problem was that I hadn't let go of her and you were a constant reminder."

"Now I understand."

"I hope you didn't think I was a dirty old man lusting after you?"

"Of course," said Juliet half crying and laughing. "But it never bothered me."

"That's a relief. Why Lars?"

"He was sweet and caring, but more importantly accepted my weird rules about sex. You know about those, right?"

"Hassan explained."

"You went to see him?"

"We did. He was most helpful and concerned for you."

"Bless him. I'll call in a day or two. Anyway, Lars rented out various properties and said he had some contacts that would pretend to abduct me from San Isidro. The plan was that we would hide in one of his villas near Frigiliana until Ferrier had been arrested or gone back to the UK, but it all went wrong."

"Did you know that Duffy was standing behind the two of you at the dressage?"

"Really? So that explains it?"

"Explains what?"

"Lars and I were to be watching the dressage. The abductors would come and fetch me and drive me to the villa. Lars would drive up later to join me. The abductors arrived on time and just as I was about to climb into the van, one of them said that they had new instructions for me. I asked if they were from Lars and he said yes, but I didn't believe him and we had an altercation at the van door. So if Duffy was there supervising, it must have been him that changed the plan."

"What were the new instructions?"

"I had to take all my clothes off. I told them that was not part of the arrangement so he drew a knife on me and forced me into the van. He then informed me that the van was stolen and was to be abandoned near Málaga train station with my things in it to give the impression that I'd been taken. I understood that, wasn't happy, but stripped and put on my own jeans and blouse. I asked how he had come by them. He told me that they broke into my apartment and took a few items with my passport etc. That was also a new part of the plan."

"Ferrier also went to your apartment, but it was after the robbery. Sorry, but he wrecked the place."

"Doesn't surprise me, but it matters not. I won't be going back there."

"What will you do?"

"No idea, but with Ferrier dead, my mind has been released from its darkness and I'm free to do something."

"Good for you. I presume that the abductors delivered you to the cellar instead of Lar's villa?"

"That's right."

"I saw the tiny rooms."

"I shared one with Angelika."

"I noticed that you'd lost some weight."

"Not through choice. They starved us to force our cooperation."

"What did they want from you?" said Phillip dreading he answer.

"Duffy came in twice a day to taunt us with a plate of food. If we complied, we could eat and drink."

"What did he want?"

"To remove our clothes."

"And did you?"

"Not for three days."

"Did he harm you?"

"Physically, he never touched us, but mentally he was vicious. Dangling the food under our noses and gulping down water in front of us. That effeminate whining voice of his will go with me to my grave."

Phillip shook his head, anger burning through his veins. "What a beast?" he said. "What prompted you to concede?"

"He threatened to split us up. Remember, Angelika had been kidnapped three weeks previously. She'd been totally on her own for all that time. The only human interaction being when a little food and water was placed in the serving hatch three times a day. She was tearing her hair out with boredom and fear. When I arrived, she was so grateful for my Company and became paranoid about losing my companionship. When Duffy opened that door and yanked me toward it, she stripped on the spot. Duffy then turned to me leering and drooling knowing that he had defeated one of us, but it was the look of despair on Angelika's face that tipped me. I couldn't leave her on her own, so I nodded. Duffy closed the door and turned his attention on me. I was so angry, I didn't bat an eyelid and threw my clothes at him. He took them away and returned with a loaded tray, but he wouldn't let us touch it until.... Shit, this is difficult." Juliet paused, breathing deeply and gripped Phillip's arm even harder.

"We had to do things to each other while Duffy watched and played with himself."

"Juliet, I'm so sorry."

"Actually, I'm going I tell you a secret, but you must

swear never to tell my aunt."

"Are you sure?"

"I have to tell someone before I scream. Phillip, I liked what Angelika did to me. For the first time in my life, I felt like a complete woman."

"With Duffy watching?"

"No, after he'd gone, we finished what we'd started while he was there."

"Does this mean you've turned?"

"Lesbian? No, well, I don't think so. At least I now know that I've unblocked whatever was holding me back and can look forward to some kind of sex life, whatever gender orientated that turns out to be."

"That must be a relief, but I'm surprised that you could function in such dire circumstances. You're imprisoned by monsters, have no idea what will happen to you, yet still, you can get it on with Angelika."

"I admit, it does sound weird and don't get me wrong, I was petrified. Especially when Duffy announced that he was going to deflower us both. However, I'm not exactly the sanest of people. Thanks to my fucked up mother and perverse stepfather, my values were totally screwed. I was just happy to glean some benefit that was powerful enough to override the nightmare."

"Then let's hope the experience hasn't damaged you mentally."

"Me too, but I will organize some counseling when I've resolved what to do with my future."

"Good luck with that. Did you see any other jailors?"

"Just an old Spanish lady. She was the one that fed us and took the dishes away."

"Can you remember the event at all?"

"Every second. It reminded me of a satanic ritual I saw in an old movie. When we were taken into the room by the Spanish lady. I was surprised at how many people were in there. Abba music was playing real loud, half a dozen skimpily dressed girls were dancing to the music. Six muscular black boys in tight leather pants dressed us in white silk robes, lifted us onto separate couches with our backsides in the air and held us down. Then Duffy brought in Lars who struggled, but was helpless and was soon restrained as we were.

"The music switched to 'The Final Countdown.' Duffy stood behind Lars and raised his robe and then the lights went out. I heard a thunderous crash, screams and then the next thing I knew was sitting on the grass wondering where I was. Then I heard your voice and dearest Phillip," she said, trying hard not to cry. "You… you'll never know how sweet a sound… that was." Then she cried her heart out, hanging on tightly to his arm until they arrived at the hospital.

41

Phillip and Prado sat opposite Crown in the interview room at the Comisaría in Málaga. You could cut the atmosphere with a knife as they glared at each other. The wiry Crown appeared tiny compared with the burly Inspector and tall Englishman.

"Twenty-first May, seventeen hundred hours, "said Phillip after Prado pushed the button on the recording device "Interview with Malcolm John Crown. Also present are Inspector Leon Prado and translator Phillip Armitage. Mr. Crown can you confirm your full name please."

Crown nodded.

"You are obliged to speak out loud," said Phillip.

"I confirm that I am Malcolm John Crown, forty-seven years old and a British Citizen," said Crown clearly irritated.

Prado whispered something to Phillip.

Phillip nodded and looked at Crown.

He stared back arrogantly.

"For the record, no charges have been made and Mr. Crown has elected not to be represented by a solicitor. Mr. Crown, our investigations into kidnapping, abducting persons against their will, imprisoning people against their will and operating a sexual slavery ring are still ongoing concerning you and Rick Duffy," said Phillip. "However, as Duffy is now deceased, full responsibility for these criminal activities will fall upon you."

"Duffy is dead?" said Crown. "How?"

"He drove through a crash barrier and landed in a ravine. The local farmers will also be seeking recompense from you for the extensive fire damage caused by the accident."

"They'll be lucky," said Crown.

"The thirty-five thousand Euros we found in cash at the villa along with the proceeds of sale of the villa plus the insurance for the vehicle should more than reimburse them for their loss."

Crown's expression turned sour and he combed his greasy hair with his fingers.

"The evidence we collected from Torrox Park and the statements made by your victims are already strong enough to put you away for well over twenty years. However, there are a number of outstanding issues for which we need further details. If you are prepared to be cooperative, we might consider lighter charges."

"How can I help?" said Crown.

"Many of the statements from the African migrants confirm that you or Duffy collected them from the detention center in Algeciras. They all mentioned that it was a Sergeant Pérez who handed them over in exchange for a thick envelope. What that implies is that the Spanish civil servants who run the place are selling migrants and not just to you. We want to establish who was involved in the center and who else is purchasing them. Was Pérez your only contact there?"

"He was."

"How much did you pay per person?"

"Three thousand Euros."

"How many people did you purchase?"

"Sixteen. I only took the young pretty ones."

"What happened to the others?"

"No idea. You'll have to ask Pérez."

"How did it work?"

"Pérez would email me pictures of new arrivals. We would select our preferences, then go and collect them subject to language skills and physical examination."

"How many trips did you make to Algeciras?"

"Maybe seven or eight."

"What dates?"

"Duffy picked up the last two about ten days ago, but I'd have to check my files for the remainder."

"Are they on the two computers we found at Torrox Park?"

"Yes."

"Are they your only devices?"

"Other than my phone, yes."

"The emergency switch you used to cut the power also disabled your computers. I'm sure our experts will find their way in sooner or later, but it would help your case substantially if you gave us the password?"

"It's *torroxparkvilla*."

"Thank you. Moving on to the other victims. Other than Lars, they were a mix of local and foreign girls. Between Duffy, the Syrians and yourself a dozen victims were yanked off our streets from normal lives to use as sex slaves for your subscription service. Not only were their family members distraught; one mother actually committed suicide. It will be difficult to gauge how well they recover from your depravity. Unfortunately for you, all their statements are crystal clear. When did you start broadcasting with Peepers?"

"Not long. About five months ago."

"So it took you about seven months to set it up."

"We thought about it for several years in prison. It was why we were able to move quickly after our release."

"As registered UK sex offenders, how did you avoid border controls on your way to Spain?"

"No comment."

"Buying the property, the vehicles, website design, setting up the business with the lawyers, etc. must have cost a fortune. Where did you obtain the money?"

"No comment."

"How many subscribers do you have?"

"About six thousand, but it's expanding fast. It's the special events that attract them."

"Such as 'The Reluctant Virgins' that we just managed to prevent."

"Correct."

"All paying nine hundred pounds a year?"

"Yes, plus the event income."

"That's good business."

"Ain't it just?"

"How do subscribers find you?"

"Word of mouth."

"Do you vet them to make sure they are not the police?"

"No, we accept everybody's application."

"Would it surprise you that one of your former cellmates was also a customer?"

"Whom?" said Crown.

"Graham Ferrier. Juliet's stepfather."

"Fuck," said Crown, a red blush covering his face. "So that's how you found us?"

"Correct."

"Wait until I see him inside," spat Crown.

"Unlikely; he's no longer with us. In fact, he died only a short distance from here trying to find Duffy and yourself."

Crown shrugged, then said. "One less problem."

"Tell me about CVS Ltd."

Crown turned pale and started chewing his already depleted nails. Phillip turned to Prado, who urged him on.

"We will be applying to the Gibraltar Courts to see the Company files and gain access to its Bank Accounts. Those are bound to lead us to your investors whom, I assume, will be extremely ungrateful that they have been uncovered. If that happens, I reckon your chances of surviving will be zero or lower, no matter where we lock you up. If you reveal their identities now, we may be able to offer you witness protection. Who are they, Malcolm?"

"No comment."

"Mr. Crown. What are the investors' names?"

"No comment."

Phillip turned to Prado and translated a summary of Crown's answers.

"OK. Let me have a go. I want to test his Spanish."

"Thank you for the help so far, Mr. Crown," said Prado. "Where were you born?"

"In Bournemouth, England," said Crown in excellent Spanish. "My family relocated to Spain when I was four."

"I understand that you went to school in Marbella? Can you remember when?"

"Until I was fourteen when we returned to England."

"Thank you. We are not ready to press charges just yet, but will continue to collect evidence. An officer will escort you back to your cell here in the Comisaría and we will talk again."

42

Two days later, Ingrid and Richard arrived with their usual Teutonic promptness for the grill luncheon at Phillip's villa. Richard handed over his entry fee of two bottles of Arzuaga Crianza, their favorite *vino tinto* from Ribera del Duero. Rosemary Kitson, her husband Martin, and a pale, but happy Juliet arrived marginally behind them. Their contribution was Belgian chocolates.

Prado came next with a bottle of Málaga wine, followed by Manolo and Pepa with platters of recently cut jamón ibérico/pata negra with sliced Manchego goat and sheep's cheese. Amanda was last carrying a wine bag stuffed with half a dozen chilled bottles of Reserva de la Familia by Juves y Camps; Spain's prestigious cava. She limped slightly and the graze on her cheek was covered with make-up but she smiled warmly at everyone. Glenda, José, and Phillip's three nieces had been there most of the morning, helping prepare.

Phillip loved cooking on the BBQ. His father had taught him the basics years ago. Since he'd lived in Spain, he'd experimented further and developed his own recipes and spicy marinades. He'd simmered the ribs in water. When cooled, he marinated them in olive oil, crushed garlic, a touch of chili, molasses, and tomato paste. For the fish, he melted brown sugar with butter, added soy sauce, freshly grated ginger, Dijon mustard, and olive oil. He smeared the mixture over the salmon fillets and left them in the fridge on dampened cedar planks while he cleaned his Weber charcoal grills. One was for fish, the other for meat and vegetables.

The wine flowed, the conversation volume grew louder, the delicious, grilled food devoured, and the kids released with an ice-cream each to run around the garden. Leaving the adults sitting around the table nibbling cheese.

Rosemary cleared her throat. Everyone went quiet.

"I just wanted to say thanks to all of you for your contributions in rescuing Juliet."

"Auntie, please," said Juliet. Don't embarrass…,"

"Sorry, Juliet" interrupted Rosemary. "It's not every day that your niece is brought back to you from the clutches of the grim reaper. I know it was bad for you, Juliet, but it was pretty dreadful for us too, not knowing where you were and imagining the worst. And poor Amanda, thank god that your injuries were only minor. Anyway, I propose a toast to say thanks."

"Salud," said everyone, clinking glasses.

"Inspector," said Amanda in Spanish. "I've been out of sorts since my sudden desire to be stunt woman of the year. How's it going with the investigation?"

"First, I want to thank Phillip and yourself for your

bravery with Ferrier and Duffy and your input to this puzzling case. Without your language skills and insight, we would still be thrashing around Andalusia like headless chickens. My boss is more than happy, and believe me, that is a rare condition. Phillip and I have been interviewing all those involved, and I believe that we have now reached an understanding of what Crown and Duffy were up to and the activities of Pérez and his cohorts in Algeciras.

"Crown reluctantly explained about the abductions and kidnapping saga. They targeted pretty girls they spotted as they traveled around with specific criteria in mind. Young, beautiful and with a working knowledge of English. As for Angelika, one weekend, he and Duffy happened to hire a vehicle from her father. They overheard her working in his airport office and decided that she would be perfect for one of their depraved events. They tracked her for a week, and made their plans for the Syrians to take her. The difference was, that because she came from a wealthy family, they decided to try and earn some cash at the same time, but only if it was ultra-safe. It was Crown dressed in a wig and tramp's old coat who had checked the bag outside the supermarket, discovered that they'd been short-changed, and left the cash where it was, assuming that it had been marked in some way."

"Is she OK?" said Juliet

"A broken arm, but happy to be home," said Prado.

"What about the Syrians?" said Juliet. "To me, they were also victims."

"To some extent, I agree," said Prado. "They were between a rock and a hard place, but that was a choice they made when they ventured forth on their voyage of illegal migration. They were fully aware of the risks.

However, all they did was follow orders. In mitigation, the men had never been inside the villa or the cellar. Their job was purely collecting or delivering which they did professionally, but without harming any of the girls. Once they were in the villa's garage with the doors shut behind them, Crown and Duffy took over. The only variation was that sometimes they had to steal a vehicle or use Crown's. Crown insisted that all stolen vans were to be the same color and model as his. This should avoid raising suspicions among the neighbors when arriving or departing the villa's garage. Anyway, as a thank you for their cooperation, they've been accepted by the asylum panel."

Phillip translated.

"What will happen to the other victims?" said Martin when he'd finished.

"It will vary," said Prado. "Like Juliet and Angelika, the girls taken have all returned to their homes after making condemning statements that will ensure Crown spends many years in prison. Some will bounce back and return to their former lives. Others were so seriously damaged mentally, I fear they will need therapy for a long time."

Juliet stood up suddenly, tears dripping down her cheek. She went over and hugged Amanda then sat on Phillip's lap, and laid her head on his chest.

"Thank you," she said between sobs. "You saved my life."

"And you mine," said Phillip, stroking her hair, his eyes watering. "But, we can't sit around here bawling all day, life goes on. What are your plans?"

Juliet sat up, Amanda passed her a tissue. "I'm going back to England to study law," she said dabbing at her eyes. "I'm determined to make up for my stolen life and begin my journey back to boring old normal."

Amanda translated for Prado. He nodded approvingly.

"What have you done with Crown?" said Amanda.

"He's languishing in our guest quarters underneath the comisaría, pending the outcome of our inquiries," said Prado. "I have to say he is an unusual criminal. Most of the time, I feel that he's playing with me. For example, he kindly told me the password to access the computers we found in Torrox Park. When we typed it in, a comic character popped up saying nice to have known you and goodbye. Then the whole system imploded and wiped itself clean. On the other hand, he's been most cooperative on issues such as the abductions and people trafficking in Algeciras. However, when it comes to the Company behind it all, he remains completely silent. I can only conclude that the mastermind running CVS uses fear extremely effectively. No matter what dire threats I throw at Crown, he reveals absolutely nothing."

"What about these lawyers in Málaga?" said Phillip. "Surely they've been helpful."

"We're still talking to them," said Prado. "However, they are saying nothing and I fear that their high up contacts are likely to grant them bail. I've delayed charging them, but that deadline is about to run out."

"Did they use another company for the villa in Torrox Park?" said Phillip.

"Yes," said Prado. "They didn't want to confuse rental properties with those for their own use."

"What's happening in Algeciras?" said Amanda.

"That is a lot easier than the CVS investigation," said Prado. "We've arrested Sergeant Pérez and three senior civil servants from the Ministry of the Interior in Madrid. They've been charged with human trafficking and corruption and face up to twenty years each behind bars.

"They'd built an impressive operation. When new migrants were delivered from the coast guard, they filtered out the unsuitable ones and processed their asylum applications diligently. We uncovered a special room in the basement where they cleaned up the pretty ones, dressed them smartly, and filmed them. Pérez uploaded the clips to his own website, where they were auctioned to the highest bidder. Crown and Duffy bought the majority of their sex slaves through this network."

"Pérez told me that most of the group on the boat I was on, had been deported," said Amanda. "Was that the case?"

"Whenever Pérez used the 'deported' word," said Prado. "It usually meant that he had sold the migrants to people such as Crown and Duffy or for slave labor. According to the highly detailed records Pérez stored on his laptop, your particular group was sold to a farmer in Castilla La Mancha for two thousand euros per person. Plus an optional thousand each should the buyers want work permits and Spanish passports for them."

"Have you been to the farm," said Amanda.

"No, but I have read the report from our colleagues in Valdepeñas. The farmer provides them with accommodation and food in return for free labor. If you consider that one legal worker would cost him at least fifteen thousand euros annually, the farmer is making substantial long-term savings on his labor costs. At first, I couldn't understand why the migrants all needed Spanish passports, but then I realized that farmworkers were highly visible. Passersby can see them working in the fields. It wouldn't take long for someone in authority to notice that a farmer who previously employed wandering Rumanians or light-skinned Moroccans suddenly had fields full of Africans. The Ministry of Labor would crack down on them and put them out of business.

"This is where the civil servants in the Ministry of the Interior earned their thousand euros, by making sure the farmer had legal paperwork for all his migrant workers. By the way, Pérez had over a million euros in a Gibraltar bank account."

"Can you trace previous migrants who were auctioned off?" said Amanda.

"We found detailed records of transactions going back four years. Now we have to trace them, which won't be easy as they are spread all over Spain. We've handed everything over to the National Crime Squad in Madrid. It's way beyond our resources."

Amanda summarized for the English speakers.

"What did Lars have to say?" said Juliet in Spanish.

"He's still in a coma, but is expected to recover. Crown explained that he needed Lars as a plausible front man for their property rentals. They'd also bought him his car and paid for the rental of his apartment in Stella Maris. It was why they were most supportive when Lars asked to borrow a villa to hide himself and his girlfriend from her stalker.

"However, when Lars told Duffy that his girlfriend was Juliet, they recognized her as Ferrier's stepdaughter. It prompted their warped minds to dream up the event with Angelika as a form of revenge against Ferrier because he'd reported Duffy to the prison governor for raping him. As a result, Duffy had to serve his full sentence."

Glenda served coffee. Rosemary passed the Belgian chocolates around. They chatted a while longer and watched the beginnings of another stunning sunset. Then Ingrid and Richard said their thanks and farewells, which prompted a mass exodus. Juliet was reluctant to leave. She clung to Phillip, weeping and thanking him repeatedly for saving her. Eventually, after more hugs, cheek kisses, and tears she departed holding her uncle's hand. Phillip heaved a sigh of relief. He was sad to see her go, but relieved that, finally, he was free from the daily torment of her pretty face and the ghost of Valentina.

Prado shook hands with everyone and departed, promising to keep them up to date with the ongoing investigations into CVS.

Glenda and José took their daughters home to bed.

Manolo and Pepa were the last to leave.

Phillip and Amanda stood together, arms touching, waving good-bye.

When the gate had closed, and the final set of car taillights disappeared into the darkness, they turned face-to-face and gazed lovingly into each other's eyes. They wrapped their arms around each other and kissed deeply.

The Author

Paul S Bradley, originally from London, England, has lived in Nerja, Spain since 1992, where he established a marketing agency to help Spanish businesses sharpen their communications to the rapidly growing number of foreign visitors. He's traveled extensively around the Iberian Peninsula visiting most of the ancient cities and hundreds of wine bodegas. In the early years, he published lifestyle and property magazines, guidebooks and travelogues in English, German and Spanish. More recently, groups of discerning Alumni of Americans and Canadians have enjoyed his tour director services. He's lectured about Living in Spain and bullfighting and has appeared on local radio and TV. The Andalusian Mystery Series draws on his own experiences as a volunteer translator in hospitals and police stations.

What did you think?

Reviews, good or bad fuel this independent author's continuous effort to improve.

If you enjoyed this book, please leave a comment on my blog, Amazon or Goodreads, or follow me on Facebook or Twitter.

See the website for more details.
Thank you

www.paulbradley.eu

Printed in the USA
CPSIA information can be obtained
at www.ICGtesting.com
LVHW021410170923
758448LV00011B/454